LOVE LIES
A LOSS

An Autobiography
1946–1959

THEODORA FITZGIBBON

CENTURY PUBLISHING

LONDON

PA- 200827

FiT

Photoset by Parker Typesetting Service, Leicester
Printed in Great Britain in 1985 by
Redwood Burn Limited, Trowbridge, Wiltshire

*To all my dear friends
in this book, especially
George, with love.*

ILLUSTRATIONS

Riding at Annesgrove, County Clare

Georgette in Bermuda

At Tranquillity House

With the two dogs, 1947, Graysbank

Throck and Constantine on Somerset Beach

Graysbank from the sea

Father Tom and Constantine at Graysbank

Constantine at Graysbank

Casa Solatia, Capri

Baron Schack (photograph by Islay de Courcy Lyons)

Constantine and Norman Douglas at Giorgio's
(photograph by D'Elia)

In rehearsal for *Her Favourite Husband*

Gerald Kersh (photograph by Carl Perutz)

With Constantine and Flotow, Piazza di Spagna
(photograph by Carl Perutz)

Sacomb's Ash, 1950

Giles Playfair and Constantine on board MV *Grebe*

Constantine, Diana Graves and Minka

Mimi in London

Along the 'engine path' in Allen's Green, Hertfordshire

Arland Ussher

George Morrison (photograph by Patrick Sarsfield)

LOVE LIES A LOSS

Born in London of Irish parents, Theodora FitzGibbon is currently living near Dublin with her husband George Morrison, the film-maker and photographic archivist. Cookery editor of *Image* magazine and the *Irish Times*, she has contributed to many other periodicals including *Homes and Gardens*, *Cosmopolitan* and *Harper's Bazaar*. Her novel, *Flight of the Kingfisher*, was made into a successful BBC TV play. Theodora FitzGibbon has written thirty books, three of which were awarded bronze medals at the Frankfurt International Food Fair and one of which won a special Glenfiddich award. This book, covering the period 1946–59, is a sequel to *With Love*, the author's autobiography of the years 1938–46.

Also by Theodora FitzGibbon

With Love An Autobiography 1938–46

CONTENTS

Now their love lies a loss
And Love and his patients roar on a chain.

Dylan Thomas, 1944

PROLOGUE

There had been many sea voyages right from the beginning, for I had started to be born on a ship coming from France to England. Maybe it was preordained that my life would be lived in many countries. Each time there was not only the excitement of travelling, but the thought of the pleasures of discovering new countries and people. A time was when the cabin trunks seemed so large I could stand in them, then later I could only sit down on one side waiting for unfamiliar clothes to be arranged on hangers in the space. Each boat had a distinctive smell: the French steamer taking me to school had a rich, smoky odour like cigars; the English one smelled of fish, and the boat going to Ireland always reminded me of frying bacon and beer. It was a warm smell which made me feel I was almost home again. When I thought of my family in County Clare it was always the summer holidays, the ponies to ride, the companionship of cousins my own age, my father, who had influenced my life so much, and of the love they had all given me.

As I sat in the luxurious but impersonal hotel room in New York, where no traumas lingered to ruffle the *toile de jouy* curtains, and the silk-covered beds seemed as undefiled as a unicorn's virgin, my mind was filled with pictures from the past. The images were clear, the ships of my scattered childhood anchored in a harbour of my own memory.

Attempting to visualize what sort of new life I would live, in New York, I recalled all the anticipation in my journey on the P&O liner to India when I was sixteen. I had refused to go back to any school. My father was returning to India, and at the last minute he had said:

'Do you want to come out? You'll have to make your own arrangements. I'll leave money in the bank. You'll have to work too, running my house and seeing the horses are looked after properly. White women with nothing to do get ruined in India; too many servants, so they gossip all day to amuse themselves.'

When he had left I asked my mother what she thought, and she replied it was a long way if I didn't like it. But first, knowing my father, she suggested that I go to the bank and see whether the money was actually there. It was and I decided to go.

At first it was very exhilarating; the ship to be discovered thoroughly, as well as the passengers. The brief stops and shore excursions at various ports absorbed me. North Africa was like something out of the *Arabian Nights* and equally compelling. It was magical. I wished I could have stayed longer. The stultifying heat of the Red Sea; the joyous shoals of dolphin or flying fish. There were young officers to be flirted with, constant entertainment and nobody in charge of me. However, as the weeks went by I realized it was in fact a monotonous routine, that I was being treated more and more as a pretty child and not as a wayward young woman – to me, much more attractive. Families tended to encourage me into their tight middle-class circles, but this I avoided deftly. I was not allowed in the bars, not that I drank, but all the gay young people were there. I read most of the books in the ship's library, especially those about India and I longed to get off the boat and explore this strange new country.

Always a recalcitrant child at school, I had refused to continue with geography once it reached the stage of isotherms and isobars.

'How are you going to know about other parts of the world if you don't learn geography?' they demanded.

'When I grow up,' I replied, 'I'm going to travel a lot and find out for myself.'

So it came about that, after reading and listening to travellers' tales of India, I determinedly disembarked when we reached the large, strange-looking port of Bombay. My destination was Calcutta.

It was very terrifying; I had never even contemplated such crowds of people, such confusion, such a babel of strange tongues, such a mixture of machines, vendors, porters, powerful smells. I was rescued by one of the young officers from the ship.

'Someone meeting you, then? Or are you travelling on?'

'I'm going on, but I don't know how to get to the station. Can I get a taxi?'

'Hold on, you stay there with your baggage. I'll fix something.'

I was very thankful when after some time I saw his spotless white uniform appear again and he arrived with two very thin but muscley Indians.

'I've got two cars; we'll go in one and the baggage in another. I'll come with you if you like.'

There was something to being a pretty child still, for he treated me like an enlightened ten-year-old. When we reached the big, dusty old station, he said he'd buy my ticket.

'Where are you going?'

'Calcutta.'

'Calcutta!' he almost shouted it. 'But that's the other side of India. You'll be in the train for days. Why didn't you stay on the boat?'

I begged him just to get my ticket and take me to the train. I was almost in tears and bitterly regretting having so precipitously left the safety of the floating hotel. I was astonished to see the size of the compartment; it was like a sitting room, something you could imagine Queen Victoria travelling in, heavy furnishings and comfortable chairs like an English gentleman's club.

'How many others will be in here?' I asked.

'Oh, it's all yours, it's a bogie-car for long distances; you'll need it, I think. It's a long way, you know. Sure you'll be all right?'

I assured him I would be fine and we exchanged addresses in Calcutta. I was sad to see him go, and I waved from the window until the last glimpse of white uniform had disappeared into the homogeneous crowds.

Exploring the bogie-car was fun; the bed was covered with heavy, Indian material, I found a little wash-place and a tiny galley-like kitchen. I wondered what it was for, as surely there was a restaurant car on a great train like this. However, at that time, as I soon discovered, there weren't communicating carriages. I was beginning to feel very hungry, and wondered how to get some food.

I had to wonder for nearly two days; frightened to leave my carriage lest the train started off again, or worse, in case I lost it to someone else, for there were people on the roof and hanging on the sides. I bought foods standing on the steps by the door – samosas, chappattis, nuts, fruit and some awful, over-sweet gummy things which gave me a dreadful thirst. I didn't know what to make of the countryside, but then I didn't know what I had expected. Some places were very arid: red, dusty earth with an occasional tired-looking shrub; then it would be greener with sheep, and vivid red flowering trees amongst others which looked quite dead. Later I was to know them well, *gol mohurs*, 'the flame of the forest', which blossom profusely from the dead-looking trees around April or May. One day, emboldened, I walked on the platform towards a military looking man, and his wife and young daughter. They seemed astonished to hear I was on my own and invited me to their carriage for a meal, which I readily accepted. I was to go back at the next halt. My healthy young appetite did full justice to the large meal, which had been prepared by their bearer.

When I got back to my bogie, I found the most beautiful young

Indian boy sitting on the steps, very poorly dressed. He got up as I approached.

'Missy Sahib need looking after?' he enquired tentatively.

I certainly did, and Hari, for that was his name, seemed agreeable to work for a very low salary. Hari was a most diligent and attentive servant. He tidied my compartment and gave me delicious meals with rice, chicken, Indian spices and vegetables. Sometimes he would find some eggs and some beer. When the train stopped he would run off like an eel and come back in a very little while, his arms full of food. He showed me how to open the heavy windows, for the heat was sometimes overpowering, and got the fan working. At night he slept on a mat in the hall.

We would talk together in the evenings, Hari squatting on the floor by the door. He came from the south, and wanted to find work in Calcutta. Sometimes I found his quick, rhythmic, light voice difficult to follow, then he would speak more slowly. His uncle had been in England, he told me, and when he was a little boy had taught him some English so that he could get a good position later on. The train rolled on, through villages and small towns, every station crowded with people all carrying bundles. It was as though the train and the passengers were a travelling theatre. At the smaller stops everyone, it seemed, came to look at us.

One day Hari came back with a bunch of very sweet-smelling flowers, probably picked from the stationmaster's cottage. He said it was frangipani but it didn't sound like that when he said it first. The scent permeated the whole car, disguising the dusty, slightly frowsty smell it had before. He was about my age, I think, and was already affianced, but needed money before he could marry. The journey had an air of enchantment with Hari there; I was glad I had left the ship, and it was certainly a far cry and better than going back to that convent. He would tell me tales of India in his singsong voice and, by the time we were approaching Calcutta, I felt I was returning, rather than just arriving.

As we were nearing our destination, he carefully repacked my cases and enquired where I was going to meet my father. I showed him the address. He said he knew where it was and would take me there. He did everything he could to make it as easy for me, getting porters and an enormous but very old taxi cab which groaned loudly when the luggage was put in. The springs of the seats had long since broken; sitting almost on the floor we set off at a breakneck pace to the address I had. When we arrived he said he would go in first to enquire, and was soon back, the huge, black, liquid eyes looking sad:

'No Sahib, missy, we go on to next place. We will try the clubs.'

This was repeated several times, each time his face getting more and more sad. The traffic was appalling, people weaving in and out all over. We were bewildered and didn't know what to do. We sat, taxi driver as well, staring at each other wondering what on earth to do. Suddenly Hari looked up, face brightening.

'One more place, naughty place,' he said, and we set off again.

In fact it wasn't at all naughty but allowed women in, a great departure in those days. He came down the steps, smiling, those expressive eyes dancing.

'Sahib here, missy. Will you come in?'

So in I went, hot, dusty, but with a rising excitement. I was ushered into a large room with a verandah along one side covered by a creeper. There weren't many tables filled, but coming from the verandah side I heard that unmistakable laugh. Looking over I saw my father, another man and two rather pretty women. He was sitting with his side towards me as I walked to within about ten feet of the table.

'Hullo, Daddy,' I said.

He turned round, stared as if at a ghost, and said:

'What the bloody hell are you doing here?' Then he laughed, put out his arms and kissed me.

My arrival was, of course, quite unexpected. If I'd stayed on the ship and gone round Ceylon, I wouldn't have arrived for some time. He thought it was all rather splendid; the only thing was, he hadn't moved into his house yet. Oh, well! I could help with it. I told him about Hari, who was engaged on the spot to be a special bearer.

What had transported me back so naturally to India, I wondered? That voyage seemed closer and more real than the one I had taken a few days ago, with my strange G.I. bride travelling companions from England to the United States, in very over-crowded conditions. That journey was still stored in my memory, waiting to be re-examined, before it became part of my life.

The insistent ring of the telephone startled me back into the present, for I was still contemplating the magic spell that Ireland and India had cast over me. Who could be telephoning me in this strange country which I had not explored? Where, as yet, I had no friends?

MANHATTAN
AND BERMUDA

CHAPTER ONE

In 1946, New York was an extraordinary experience, for it was quite unlike any city I had ever visited. It is now a cliché to speak of speed in connection with New York, but after the almost car-less, depopulated and still-rationed city of London, it was very noticeable. Not only were there crowds of people and automobiles, but they all seemed to be travelling very fast. They even spoke fast; asking a simple direction produced a few rapid sentences containing several numbers. Everyone said I couldn't get lost in New York, and, having wandered about Budapest, Belgrade, Rome and several other cities, I believed them. But somehow I did. In fact the only place I could find my way about was Greenwich Village, which had only street names.

This well-dressed motley crew never mooched along the streets chattering to each other; they walked purposefully, seemingly knowing exactly where they were going and why. This went on day and night. A friend assured me that thousands of New Yorkers preferred to live through the night and sleep all day. Restaurants, cafés, small grocery stores and drug stores were open all night to look after them. Sometimes it seemed to me the streets were brighter at night, with all the blazing neon lights outside cinemas, theatres, clubs and on advertisements, than on some days when the skyscrapers cast their long shadows. So, to me, there was always the noise of traffic and the smell of petrol, something I had never noticed about Chelsea or Paris once it was nighttime.

However, we were fortunate to be staying at the Plaza Hotel which overlooked Central Park on one side and always had a line of horse carriages parked outside should you wish to take a discreet drive. The horses were well looked after, my favourite being Geraldine, whom the cabby assured me couldn't find her way around the West Side. My husband Constantine FitzGibbon had met me when as a GI Bride I had arrived in New York on the SS *James Parker*, on March 30th, about ten days earlier. Having no idea where we would live, he had cleverly found that all New York hotels with empty rooms had to take veterans of the forces for around $5 a night. We had been installed in a splendid suite with positively no prospect of finding anywhere else. Still, I don't think we tried very hard, for the few friends we had in New York were determined to show us their city.

The Plaza Hotel was built early in this century with all the comfort and sumptuousness that its wealthy clients demanded. If they were to venture outside their large, lush houses, then they must feel at home. There was a Palm Lounge where a small orchestra softly played pieces like 'Tea for Two' as a background to the conversations of the hatted, befurred and jewelled ladies. There was the wood-panelled Oak Room, for gentlemen, a grill room and a charming dining room where in the evening the best, and also the most appropriate, cabaret was performed. When we were there it was Paul Draper, the magical dancer, a nephew of Ruth Draper the great impersonator.

Our friends, mostly brother officers of Constantine's, included our wedding night guest Ferdinand Helm, and our best man Teddy Rose. Teddy was big and bluff in manner, an Old Etonian who had lived in Paris for years. Without doubt he was the best raconteur I knew. My go-ahead grandmother also gave me the names of two actor friends of hers. All were anxious for us to leave the placid delights of the Plaza and join them. Whatever you feel like eating you can have, they said. The best bortsch is in 3rd Avenue; the best Italian restaurant is on 2nd Avenue; fine French food at La Grenouille in the 60s, where the frogs' legs were as good as any in France. Or maybe Chinatown where our host insisted we drank only tea, yet on the way out we saw Chinese dining with a bottle of Scotch on the table! My favourite was a tiny Basque place in Greenwich Village called I think Jai Alai where we had been taken by Peter Boyne my grandmother's actor friend; I was able to indulge my quite unreasonable passion for kidneys. Swordfish steaks, snapper, fillet mignon, asparagus, we had them all. Teddy Rose entertained us in his Park Avenue apartment to a Lucullan feast of Maine lobsters. Constantine's colonel, Bill Jackson, took us to the theatre and I wore the purple velvet dress Caitlin Thomas had given me, which she had bought secondhand in London. I must have looked like something from a B-movie costume drama, but at least nobody else had anything like it. We went to the Metropolitan Museum and were drunk with looking, then drunk with dizziness at the top of Radio City. Ferdie Helm introduced us to editors and writers including the beautiful Jean Stafford, who was experiencing great unhappiness with her husband, the brilliant, outrageous and sometimes brutal Robert Lowell.

As I looked out of the hotel window overlooking Central Park, the scene was like a Willard Metcalf painting, and I thought of many things, few of them connected with New York. What on earth were we doing here? How long could this interlude go on? Opening the windows brought in the noise of traffic and the smell of fumes. I closed it quickly and picked up Prosper Merimée's *Le Soulier Satin* which I had borrowed from Peter Rose Pulham in Paris so many lifetimes ago. Constantine had that morning had a letter from his mother who was staying with one of her sisters at her house in Bermuda. It had enclosed a letter for Constantine from a down-town bank which requested him to call. He had left when I was having my bath, saying I was to meet him for lunch at the Russian restaurant on 3rd Avenue.

I moved moodily from the chair by the window and looked through the few wartime clothes I had brought with me. Was it cold out? How could you tell in these hot hotels? If it was, I definitely wasn't going to wear again that old mohair coat which smelt of goat when it got wet. I counted my money and decided to go out shopping. The prices all seemed amazingly high until I realized you had to divide everything by four (the dollar was around five shillings), then they all seemed amazingly cheap, so I left the shop positively purring in a soft, pale green suit and a top-coat. It was known as a three-piece. I had just about two dollars left as I went to join Constantine for lunch.

At first we didn't recognize each other. He was standing at the bar in an extremely handsome tweed suit, sipping a large vodka. He beamed when his very short-sighted eyes focused on me.

'You look very smart,' we both said together, 'I almost didn't rec—' Then we both laughed.

'Have a drink and I'll tell you what's happened.'

It appeared that when Constantine was born in 1919 his godfather, Hamilton Benjamin, a rich man on the Stock Exchange, had given his godson $10,000. Ten years later the crash came and the money was almost worthless. However, a small sum had survived, been forgotten by everyone and had been collecting interest over the intervening quarter of a century, to make the very handy lump sum of about $1,000 in 1946.

'So, I went to Abercrombie and Fitch and got this. It's the first ready made I've ever had. Good isn't it?'

It was.

'I hope you've got some left because I bought this and I've only got $2,' I answered.

'Of course I have,' he replied rather scathingly. 'And I've been to a travel agent. We're going to Bermuda and I can write my novel.'

'But how? Where?'

'It's Mummy's letter this morning. Aunt Maud's got this big place in Bermuda with two cottages on it, and we're going to have one. We'll go down there in a few days when we've made the arrangements.'

'Sounds wonderful,' I said. 'Is it free? How do we get there?'

'We'll find all that out. Aunt Maud can't charge us much, if anything. Come on, let's order some of that good beef stroganoff.'

We met Ferdie Helm that night and he thought the news great. Could he come and stay? He wanted to work on his Alexander Pope thesis. Of course he could.

Constantine concentrated on getting us there and I was to pack our things. This sounds simple but the luggage was extremely battered by this time, and as usual we had acquired more secondhand books, which were decidedly heavy. This problem was soon solved in an army surplus store where we bought canvas bags and a very ugly but strong expanding suitcase, which I think still survives stuffed with old galley proofs. The boat was obviously a cheaper but slower method of getting to Bermuda, so we decided to take a flying boat from Baltimore; the only snag was that most of the luggage would have to go by ordinary boat. We had quite persuaded ourselves that hanging about in New York would eventually cost more than the difference between the fares. Perhaps we were right. Nevertheless we had to have some clothes for hot weather, and so rushed off to Orhbach's where for about $100 we bought what seemed like half the shop. The days of the Palm Lounge, the Oak Room and the Plaza Suite had ended as suddenly as they had begun.

Once more we bundled our things into taxis, some for the boat and the rest for the station to Baltimore. I remember crossing the immensely wide Delaware River, and finding Baltimore a most attractive city, with its tall brick houses with delicate iron railings either side of the steps leading to the highly polished and painted front doors. There was an impression of regularity and order which the bombings and blastings had destroyed in London. The streets were clean, quiet and peaceful as we made our way to the immigration office before embarking on the huge flying boat.

Inside the flying boat it was very spacious – much more like a liner than any modern aeroplane. There were small tables to eat from and large windows in the cabin, which was about twice the height of our aeroplanes. Stewards were dressed like ship stewards in short white coats. When the engines started the sea churned up alarmingly and made a lot of noise. Then, slowly, we were airborne, feeling not a little excited at going to a new place, and not a little relieved at having got off the merry-go-round of New York. Our hopes were as high as the flying boat coursing about the clouds. We ate a leisurely meal chosen from a menu, and it was some hours before we started to lose height, followed by the thundering splash and shudder of the landing at Perrott's Isle in Bermuda. On the dock the sun was strong and hot as we looked around, across water the colour of viridian green, to the white houses on the nearby mainland; then into a motor boat and a swift journey across the bay to the capital of this coral reef, Hamilton. It was quite an experience.

Constantine said we must telephone his mother to find out how to get to Somerset, so we took the light luggage we had and went to the nearest place which had a telephone, a waterfront bar. The streets seemed very empty, no cars anywhere and but few people. Soon he was back with the news that we were to take the train which went close by the house. The bar-owner called a carriage which seemed very small for us and the luggage, so I got in with the bags and Constantine said he would follow – for the horse couldn't go very fast. It was the smallest railway station imaginable, like something out of Toytown. The train, too, was very curious and very uncomfortable. The wooden-slatted seats were high and narrow. It looked and felt like some old relic of a distant and backward country. We found out later that it had been bought secondhand from the Belgian Congo, and it felt like it. It rattled and shook alarmingly like an old-fashioned tram, particularly so when crossing what seemed a very rickety bridge high up on stilts over the sea, which the single passenger told us was Somerset Sound.

'We must be near, then,' I said.

'I hope so; this is terrifying isn't it? There must be another way of getting to Aunt Maud's. Why couldn't we have come by boat?'

The passenger told us the last ferry for Somerset had left just before we had taken the train. The place at which he told us to alight turned out to be a halt with hardly a house in sight. Dusk, which falls quickly in these parts, would soon be down; and there we were, luggage dumped around us on the roadside, hot, thirsty and tired.

'Oh, Mummy's so hopelessly impractical – what are we supposed to do now?' Constantine stalked off in the direction of the nearest house while I waited with the bags. He came back looking very frustrated and cross.

'She said to take a carriage, though where she thinks we'll find one on the roadside I don't know. Anyway I told her, with the luggage we were too heavy for a horse, so she said she would ring the only taxi here. Apparently no cars are allowed in Bermuda, and taxis are few and far between. How in the name of God did people get all the furniture in their houses in the past?'

When it was quite dark and our spirits were very low, the taxi came, picked us up, whizzed round a few corners and we were there, but he couldn't take us up to the house because the drive was too steep. So we had to carry the bags, stumbling about for several minutes in the dark amongst bushes which appeared to have arms to grab you. The large, low whitewashed house, named Tranquillity, with its welcoming steps up to the door, was ablaze with light, and through the wire screen door we saw the two dear welcoming faces.

'Come in, have a whisky. You must be exhausted. Sit down.' It was all said at once.

'Mummy, why did you send us on that ghastly train? Why couldn't we have had a taxi from the beginning?'

'Oh, Connie, it's the best way. Much cheaper than a taxi, which is about five pounds.'

Like many elderly people who have a certain amount of money, Georgette would always practise funny little economies at the most awkward times, and then be wildly extravagant – or so it seemed to me – at other times.

Aunt Maud said we must be hungry; and yes, we were, very. Two trays were instantly produced with a plate on each, a few slices of spam (which we had thought never to see again), a little square of mousetrap cheese, two slices of bread and a little butter. Lavishly we spread the butter on the bread.

'I say, be careful with that butter. It's our ration for the week.'

Such was our introduction to Bermuda; a very different island from Manhattan.

The cottage was across a courtyard from the big house. It was small but adequate, since there were about three acres of grass lawns to sit, read and eat in. The unaccustomed April heat and sun woke us early and we walked around, thankful for the thin clothes we'd bought.

Glorious bushes of multi-coloured hibiscus, poinsettias, olean-der and lilies set in clumps on the lawns were sometimes over-shadowed by trees of tropical fruits from which flew vivid blue birds, the scarlet red cardinal bird, and the black cat-bird which made a noise like a mewing cat. High up in the sky, the long-tailed white tropic bird flew effortlessly. Through the trees we could glimpse the opalescent sea which graduated from a pale green to a deep, deep blue.

'It's like a paradise and everything's so green,' we said to each other as we wandered through a hedge into a small plantation of sweetcorn and crisp green lettuce.

Quite far away from the house was another whitewashed cottage of one large room with a bathroom and kitchen. This had been the studio of Clark Voorhees, Aunt Maud's husband, an American landscape painter who had died some years ago. As we neared the house we saw a small building with steps up to what must have been one room.

'I wonder what that is. Maybe a servant's room?' I said. Constantine's mother, Georgette, told us it had been the buttery but wasn't used any more. We went up to look at it and Constantine said it would make a perfect writing room, so that is what it became. Aunt Maud suggested we go down to Mangrove Bay to see about our ration cards and also to hire some bicycles.

We wandered downhill along the sandy lanes, past round-moon gates and a few houses, many cedar trees, some festooned with spagnum moss, hanging like a water nymph's hair, until we came to a small settlement overlooking the bay. It consisted of some little cottages, shops, a bar called the Loyalty Inn and the Mangrove Bay grocery stores.

'Let's get something good to eat,' said Constantine. 'You know Mummy can only just boil an egg and, if last night's supper is anything to go by, Aunt Maud's cooking is not much better.'

Alas the Mangrove Bay grocery store did not live up to its exotic name. It was rather depressing, with shelves full of American cereals with names like Cheerios or Brekkos, and rows of cans of clams, cans of tuna fish, Campbells soup and, of course, Spam.

'Aren't there any fresh foods?' we asked.

We were shown some fish, which raised our hopes, but that was either tagged or stamped with purple ink in large letters 'CHICAGO', a curious place to find fresh sea fish. We bought some bananas and cans of beer.

Further down we found a sad-looking black butcher who really didn't want to sell us anything, but finally parted with some pork chops and a few pigs' tongues. On the counter he had large bowls of intestines called chitterlings, which he said were good with mustard greens, but as I didn't know how to cook them and had never heard of mustard greens, I left them alone. The meagre rations of butter and cheese were a bit daunting after the plenty of

New York, but maybe the rationing wouldn't last very long. We decided to buy two secondhand old-fashioned, high bicycles, on the grounds that we were going to live here. When I saw them I was sorry I couldn't have brought my brand-new Raleigh with me.

Then a drink at the Loyalty Inn before going home: they weren't a bit keen to serve us either, as it was a bar for coloured people, though we didn't realize that at the time. I think they felt that if they weren't allowed into white bars, why should we be served in theirs? However, they brought us a cold beer and Constantine told me about the novel he was going to write. Our life together, unimpeded by war, was just beginning. We had just enough money, with army back pay, to survive for several months, and we were starting out in a paradise of our own choice.

It is hard to describe Bermuda in 1946 without making every word a superlative. This tiny coral island set alone about eight hundred miles out in the Atlantic was so very beautiful to look at; it was just as Andrew Marvell's words:

> Where the remote Bermudas ride
> In th' ocean's bosom unespied.

Some of the beaches were quite pink, made by the seas pounding up the fresh coral. If you owned any land there, house-building was simple. You dug a hole the size of the house you wanted, and the coral blocks were used to make the walls, the hole at the side being used for your water tank, as there were no fresh springs in Bermuda. There were no squalid settlements, for many of the islanders built their own houses this way. The climate all the year round was warm; at Christmas you could go on picnics and swim, and when rain and wind came occasionally, we were only delighted that the water tank (in which was housed a toad to catch the flies) was full again. There was only one kind of poisonous animal on the island, a large scorpion, and during our time there I saw only one. There were huge toads, which gathered round the street lights at nighttime, like Italians, as Con said, but they were quite harmless to people, although if attacked by a dog they could spurt a poison into the dog's mouth. There were masses of a certain cockroach-like animal which didn't bite, but in summer took to flight and could fly into you. There were huge spiders, quite harmless, which I found could be channelled into one place if you played some music. This they seemed to love and about two at a time would gather on the walls to listen. I grew rather fond of them.

The exotic-looking trees in time bore such fruit as pawpaw, loquats, guavas and tamarinds; these grew almost wild. Almost every garden had a banana plant where great bunches clustered. At night, the tree-frogs chuckled until dawn. The waters were so clear that large and brightly coloured fish could be seen close up to the shore, and there were sea-gardens of anenomes and corals. Fish with glorious names like yellowtail, angel fish, parrot fish and bonito seemed sometimes too beautiful to eat. We had sweet potatoes, Bermuda potatoes and the sweet Bermuda onion, as well as home-grown pale gold corn called Country Gentleman. We almost forgot what red meat tasted like and didn't mind a bit. Eggs from chickens fed on corn had orange yolks, and the birds themselves tasted almost like young pheasants. If we wanted something special we took the leisurely steamer to Hamilton, which had big hotels, cafés, bars, big stores and shops which sold almost everything. It also had the island's only indoor cinema.

Constantine had fixed up the buttery with a table, chair and bookshelf. Most mornings, starting quite early, he would go there and write. Then we would perhaps take a picnic to nearby Long Beach, or a longer expedition to King's Point Islands where we would swim sometimes without our suits for it was deserted, and afterwards make love on the warm sands. When the tide was out, little pools held tiny brightly striped fish called sergeant majors, and we would catch them in our glasses to look at them more closely before putting them back. In the evenings, sitting on the lawn with long cool drinks, Constantine would read aloud to us what he had written that day, and then we would have another long glass of the pale gold Martinique rum which was a guinea a gallon, with some fresh lime juice in it.

In May, Aunt Maud said she would be soon going back to her house in New England and why didn't we move into her house and let Georgette have the cottage which was more suitable for one person? Before she left she gave a party for us to meet all the old families of Bermudians who lived in Somerset, such as the Gilberts, the Onions, the Misicks, as well as David Huxley, then attorney-general, with his wife Nancy, a childhood friend of Constantine's, and some American friends who had lived there for many years.

Two large tables laid with white damask cloths were set out on the front lawn, and on them were put bowls of deceptively innocent-tasting rum punch. Hibiscus blossoms were strewn around. Myrtle, the Negro maid, cooked all afternoon with her pretty little daughter; nobody else was allowed in the kitchen. It was all delightfully gracious and old-fashioned, as were the guests. Much later that evening Constantine, who never ate anything much more than a few peanuts at parties, told me he was feeling decidedly odd. His head felt quite clear, but his legs felt as if they would buckle under him. I told Georgette that the punch must have been stronger than we thought, and she mentioned it to Aunt Maud, who replied:

'Ah, well, with some it goes to their heads and with others it goes to their legs.' She had served that punch before.

CHAPTER TWO

Laughter and literature typified most of the next few months. In the larger house, which wasn't in fact so large but had big, airy rooms, we had friends from America to stay, notably Ferdinand Helm, who was there for some months. As well as working on his Alexander Pope thesis he was doing a key to Joyce's *Finnegan's Wake* for his own pleasure. Quite rightly, he said the only way to understand it was to read it aloud, which he did very well. For some time after, phrases from the book were applied to various people in Bermuda: 'a woman of no appearance' was one, and 'Jerk the Beanstalk' fitted many a visitor. Sometimes we toyed with the idea that, instead of Marvell's 'remote Bermudas', it might have been more like 'Tristan da Cunha, isle of man-overboard'.

Ferdinand was a strange person, for he could be so charming and amusing, then without warning, sentences vitriolic with venom and hatred would tumble out, many times without apparent reason. He seemed to have a museum of hatreds from which he would produce one piece every so often. I think he was very fond of Georgette, who was always kind and understanding even during his outbursts. He had a sort of cameraderie with Constantine, but I was the person he trusted with his fears. He told me he was bisexual, mainly because he was frightened of being rejected by women. Unprepossessing in appearance, he won both my affection and sympathy, although the latter was the last emotion I would have shown him openly. What *did* attract me was the brilliance of his thought, rapier sharp and full of originality. In many ways I think he associated himself with Pope, and would have wished to be as Pope wrote:

> Happy the man, whose wish and care
> A few paternal acres bound . . .

Alas, he never was.

Constantine was busily writing his novel, his day's work always being read to all of us. We thought it extremely good and looked forward eagerly to the evening drinks and the readings. I was very contented, for Aunt Maud had an excellent, although not large, library of American writers. Sitting in the shade of the lucky nut tree I would enjoy the books of Willa Cather, John Dos Passos, Thomas Wolfe's *Look Homeward Angel*, William Faulkner's *Sanctuary*, and several works of Edith Wharton. Georgette told us Edith had been a friend of her father and mother in Lenox, Massachusetts, but the seven little girls (Georgette and her sisters) didn't approve of her at all, for she bitted her horses too tightly in the carriage for the sake of a smart equipage. The girls would run out to give the horses sugar, but the coachman told them they wouldn't be able to eat it. Ring Lardner was a favourite of mine, especially his superb *How to Write A Short Story*, and Ferdie had brought down some critical essays of Edmund Wilson's and also a book of Sherwood Anderson's. It was during this period of reading that I found an apt title for Constantine's book, a quotation from the Earl of Rochester's poems of the seventeenth century:

'Tis the Arabian bird alone
Lives chaste, because there is but one.

That evening we christened *The Arabian Bird*.

We still had our picnics although it was getting too hot for prolonged sitting in the sun. There were convenient rocks nearby where we always swam before lunch and sometimes later in the day as well. As the novel neared completion, Georgette and I took turns at typing it. Neither of us could type very fast, but somehow after endless hours it was finished, then we punched holes in the side and made it into a very handsome manuscript. And so with pride, pleasure and relief it was despatched to a literary agent in London.

There were a great many cocktail parties, of which we enjoyed those of our friends the Misicks best. They had a pretty house near Somerset Bridge and were interested in writers and writing. There were several American bestseller writers in Bermuda then, Munro Leaf, the creator of *Ferdinand the Bull*, and James Ramsay Ullman and his pretty wife Elaine. Jimmie and Elaine became great friends, also their tiny monkey. Jimmy, although he looked like a genial businessman, was an adventurer at heart. He had a passion for mountains and mountain climbing which is no doubt why his first great success *The White Tower* had such veracity. Every book he wrote was a bestseller, book of the month, film and everything that goes with that kind of success. Yet withal he remained unassuming, kindly and determined to get as near the top of Mount Everest as he could.

In July my aunt wrote to say that our large poodle Mouche,

whom I had left with my grandmother, was coming out on a
Royal Mail Line ship. Con and I hired a carriage to meet the boat
and we waited under the shade of some trees for it to dock. We
could see Mouche, running around the decks, putting her paws on
the rail and looking over.

'She's not kennelled,' I said.

'You know how clever she is, darling. Mouche could get round
anyone.'

As soon as the gangplank was lowered she ran down, no lead,
the captain behind her. She stopped at the bottom, obviously
waiting for a friend. Right at the end came a small man in shirt
sleeves and Mouche bounded up to him. Yes, she was very
pleased to see us, but taking her friend by the wrist she brought
him forward. It was the ship's carpenter, or 'Chippie', and he had
had her in his cabin all through the journey.

'She liked the Azores,' he said. 'I thought a bit of *terra firma*
would be good for her.'

She was very fat, but it might have been overgrown coat.

'How many meals a day did you give her?' I asked.

'It's difficult to say, you know. I'd always bring her a bit of
what was going. She didn't like my mate being in the cabin,
though.'

That evening we had the whole crew up to dinner. Not the
captain, though. When he heard I had asked Chippie he refused,
having accepted earlier on. He missed a fantastic evening, fresh
corn from the garden, a roasted ham and many exotic fruits.
Nobody got back to the ship until early morning. Mouche had
certainly arrived, and had behaved like the dowager she was. It
was a very happy time.

The small Catholic church was about a twenty-minute walk
away over fields with just a few houses here and there. Mouche
would walk with me to church, then sit outside, except when
communion was given and she heard the shuffling of people
walking. Then she would come in, walk down the aisle to find
me, and sit in the pew with me. After that I always sat at the back.
Father McPherson, the priest, had been a friend of Aunt Maud's
and often called. I didn't catch his name at first; when I queried it
he said:

'McPherson, son of a parson!'

He was a good jazz musician and loved to play on Aunt Maud's
piano. The only Somerset taxi driver was expert on the guitar, so
sometimes we had impromptu concerts. It was through Father
McPherson we met Father Grace, our dear friend for many years.

The book finished, we had more time to explore the island on our bicycles – going out to Beebe's museum in St George's, or Prospero's Cave (it was generally held that Shakespeare had set *The Tempest* on the newly found island) with its stalactites and stalagmites; or perhaps to the sea gardens, where in glass-bottomed boats you could see the busy but clear underwater world. At Harrington Sound you could hire an old-fashioned diving helmet and be lowered down about twenty feet in your bathing suit to walk amongst the ever-moving inhabitants with their brilliant colours. Or there was Cambridge Beaches, a charming hotel development of small cottages, with a central building for meals or drinks if wanted. It was quite the nicest place to stay in Bermuda. However, as the idyllic summer ended, our money dwindled to an alarming degree. We waited eagerly for the English mail to hear about *The Arabian Bird*. At last a letter came from the agent saying, cursorilory, that he couldn't handle it as it had no 'reader identity'! We were all stunned; for once I was without words and we all went about the house as though a dear friend had died. I wonder if anyone not connected with creative people ever realizes the shock that a rejection of their work means to them. The book, painting, sculpture or piece of music has been as much a part of them for months or even years as is an unborn child to a woman. It *is* them, for ultimately what has any artist to express but their own thoughts and personality?

Unusually, Constantine was very quiet. He put the manuscript into a drawer and went for a long walk with Mouche. He came back in quite a different mood and said, why didn't we spend our remaining money on a party? Then maybe he could find a job. Georgette, knowing the delicate coil on which her son's emotions balanced, was delighted, and as it happened it was a most fortunate decision. Constantine never again mentioned the unpublished novel to anyone. At the party I talked to a studious man, whom a friend had brought, and mentioned the need for Constantine to get a job if we were to stay in Bermuda.

'Oh, he'll soon find one,' he said, and paused: 'I'll give him a letter to Booker of the Saltus Grammar School. He's always looking for teachers.'

School? Teacher? Neither sounded like Con, still I did get the letter, which surprisingly delighted him.

'Let's go into Hamilton and see about it,' he said; 'though I didn't hang around at Oxford to get my degree. What on earth would I teach?'

'French?' I replied hesitantly. 'Or English maybe?'

Both the Saltus Grammar School and Bobbie Booker were like something from the pages of Evelyn Waugh. Perhaps Bobbie thought we had come to pay a social call, for a tray of delicious drinks was brought in, and then we were asked to lunch. Bobbie was a man of medium height with a very lined but humourous face. He spoke almost entirely in 1920s slang and kept calling me 'old thing'. As we got jollier, the asking for a job receded, and the diaquiries took over. Constantine, always a splendid raconteur, was at his best. Bobbie, probably homesick for England, was delighted. I was getting alarmed that nothing would be mentioned, and was trying hard to frame a sentence which wouldn't look as if I was taking over. Then unexpectedly at the end of a splendid meal, over coffee and brandy, Constantine asked:

'I suppose you haven't got a job going here, have you, sir?'

Bobbie thumped the table hard, so that the silver cream jug slopped over.

'Old chap, you wouldn't, would you? The last fella Gabitas Thring sent out I had to return (like a parcel?). He was a raving lunatic.'

Nothing was asked about credentials and Constantine was to start at the beginning of the September term in a few weeks' time. As we were leaving we were asked to a party the following week and Bobbie whispered to me:

'You wouldn't like to be Matron, would you old thing?' I declined, but I did say I would help out with prizegiving at speech day.

The next morning the buttery was in use again. Georgette, delighted, led me into the huge old-fashioned larder and shut the door.

'Let's have a snifter to celebrate,' she said, handing me a glass of whisky, 'and not a word to Connie about writing again.'

That evening he read us part of an article he had started.

'I'll send it to the *Atlantic Monthly* when it's finished. It's the sort of thing they like.'

When term started he would cycle to the ferry each morning with sandwiches for lunch and in the late afternoon I would walk down to meet him on his return. The pupils were mixed Bermudian, American and Portuguese children, yet every morning they had to salute the Union Jack and sing 'Land of Hope and Glory'. They seemed to enjoy it in a puzzled sort of way. Constantine taught all subjects to eight- and nine-year-olds, but French and English to older boys. He even got them to learn a short Molière play, at

which the Portuguese were so brilliant that the promised performance never came off, as the others were too slow at learning the
French. He seemed to enjoy the school very much. It wasn't
arduous work, there were weekends, quite long evenings and long
holidays to look forward to. Writing was done in the buttery from
time to time, but he never discussed it as before.

The school brought many new friendships, mainly parents of
boys there. Amongst them was Frederic Wakeman, who had just
published a bestselling novel *The Hucksters*, and was negotiating the
film rights. He lived near us with his wife Margaret and their two
children, the little boy, Freddie, being one of Con's pupils. Fred
was to play a prominent part in our lives. He was an interesting man
with a lineless slightly Asiatic face, his brown hair worn in a
crewcut. His Asiatic features were emphasized by his hairless chest
and loose-limbed walk which reminded me of the movements of
one of the larger members of the cat family. His first book, *Shore
Leave*, was excellent, about his experiences in the navy during the
war. After that he had gone into advertising, and *The Hucksters* was
a vivid exposé of this. Overnight he was a celebrity; James Thurber
referred to him as 'the millionaire novelist'; film companies vied
with each other for the rights, but his Midwest astuteness took it all
very calmly. The family lived very simply, Margaret's mother
taking care of the two children. Margaret had been Fred's college
sweetheart and I got the feeling that whereas he had read a great deal
and missed nothing, Margaret had remained as she was when she
left Missouri. However, she had a lively sense of humour. Fred was
then working on a new novel, which was already sold, film rights
as well. He had put a lot of his money into the New York
publishing house of Rinehart, of which he was a director.

When Ferdie went back to New York, Fred and Margaret
became our closest friends, and we were introduced to many of the
people he knew. One evening we were asked to dinner at the Coral
Beach Club, and when we arrived it was exciting to see that James
Thurber was one of the party. By this time his sight was very bad,
hardly noticeable, but since I was sitting next to him I saw he cut his
food up quite small before starting to eat. I had just been reading
and re-reading some of his books, and we talked mainly of large
poodles, to which he was devoted. He told me the story of the
strange dog at the front door of a house he was visiting, which
followed him in, jumped with muddy paws all over the sofas and
beds, then turned out not to belong to the house owner, who had
thought it was his. That was the end of that friendship!

Then he turned to converse with the woman on his left. I don't

know what they talked about to begin with, but in a silence that
sometimes occurs at dinner parties I heard him say:

'What is the thing you have done in your life which you are
most ashamed of?'

The woman was silent for too long. Not a word or a splutter
did she make.

'Do you mean to tell me that you are so self-satisfied that it
doesn't immediately occur to you?'

More silence, then a blather of talk. Ever since then I have had
something ready for that question, but no one has ever asked me.

We used to meet Thurber fairly often on the ferry from
Somerset; Mouche, who knew a poodle-lover when she saw one,
was always going to greet him.

One hot afternoon when Constantine was at Saltus, a telegram
came saying that my father was dead. I read it through as though I
were studying the lines of a play. It was so very impersonal, the
printed letters on strips of paper which said nothing except that he
was dead: not where, or how or even when. I went into the
bedroom and closed the louvres of the shutters to keep out the hot
sun. I lay down on the heavy wooden half-tester bed and shivered
slightly despite the heat, drawing a coverlet over me. I didn't sleep
and no tears came, for it seemed impossible that the vital Jupiter
man I had seen so little of had gone from my life.

I have no memory as to how long I was lying there, but the heat
became very oppressive and a heavy sweet smell hung like a solid
cloud above me. I was back in the hill station in Kashmir, India, in
bed early in the morning. The previous day my father and I had
been to a race-meeting in Rawalpindi and had come on for the
night. This was long before the formation of Pakistan, in the days
of the British Raj when the Afghans were fighting a bitter guerrilla
war with the British. Around Peshawar was the North West
Frontier, and driving through the Kyber Pass it was often necessary to lie flat on the floor of the car to avoid snipers' bullets. As a
sixteen-year-old I found it exciting.

The drive had been long, hot and dusty in the open car; conversation had dwindled as we contemplated a bath, then dinner. At
race meetings when it was very hot we often took a change of
clothes with us, wringing out the sweat of the worn ones before
packing them up. But high up with the cold air from the Zasker
Mountains the evenings were pleasant and the nights cool. I
wandered around the compound enjoying the air, then went in to
sit on the verandah, the punka-wallah still working the fan with
his foot. Dinner took a long time with many courses; my father,

in the best of form, told outrageous stories which were no doubt a relief in this remote place. When the port came I excused myself and went to bed. The heavy smell of the Indian night, bursts of laughter, strange outside noises, all were soon forgotten as I went into a deep, youthful sleep.

When I arrived in the breakfast room my father was already there looking very cross, yet making a hearty meal. Maybe the night had gone on too long, and too much port had been drunk. No pleasantries were ever allowed at breakfast other than the simplest enquiry.

'Was your bed comfortable?' I asked.

'No, it wasn't,' he snapped at me with unaccustomed testiness, 'and I don't like people coming in to take my money in the middle of the night.'

'Who was it? One of the men at dinner last night?'

He relaxed slightly and told me he had woken up to see a tall, fair, thin young man with a high collar bending over his dressing table. Then the man had turned and my father saw his face quite clearly through the mosquito net. As he was about to lift the net and get out of bed, the figure receded into the shadows.

While my father was talking, the commanding officer came in, then asked my father to meet him in the library after breakfast. I could come too, if I liked. I joined them when I had finished; they were looking at old photograph albums, heavy and ornate with brass corners. My father was talking, his voice as light and clear as ever. The colonel shut down the album with a snap and, taking up another, said:

'Look through this one and see if you recognize anyone.'

Turning the pages slowly, still looking annoyed, my father stopped suddenly.

'That's the fellow, but no, it can't be. He's got the wrong uniform on, must be his father.'

'No, that's the same man. It's a long story but, briefly, he gambled very heavily and got into very deep water, even regimental funds too, I think. It was about twenty-five years ago that he shot himself in the room you occupied. Very occasionally he does appear. I saw him myself once, always goes to that dressing table, looking for money, I suppose. Strange story, there's no telling when he will turn up. Feel sorry for the chap myself.'

Slowly and thoughtfully we left the room, the bearer put our luggage in the newly cleaned car and we went down the long hill.

It was not a dream for my eyes were wide open all the time. I knew for that brief period I had somehow been with my father again, and heard his voice quite clearly. I was content.

CHAPTER THREE

After a time the lack of mental stimulus in an island Eden is noticeable. Used as we were to the richly tapestried conversations of Dylan Thomas, Norman Douglas, John Davenport and many others, it was similar to being on an ocean liner stopping at ports to pick up people who are merely pleasure-bent. Although it had been without peer for a holiday, the mood unavoidably followed that we should be getting home now.

In 1946 there was a library set in the beautiful Par-la-Ville Gardens, Hamilton, riotous with tropical flowers. The small building had dark rooms and a very mixed selection of books. The gardens also housed a little open-air theatre (where Constantine would have staged the Molière) but in the two and a half years we were there a play was never performed. The only indoor cinema was also in Hamilton, which meant only a matinée for us as the last ferry and train left early. Outdoor cinemas showed rubbishy films which competed with aeroplane noise, flying beetles and cigarette smoke. There was no local radio, only crackles on Aunt Maud's old set. No transistors and, perhaps mercifully, no television. Local newspapers were just that, foreign ones always a day late and generally only available in Hamilton.

Therefore when one's own imagination and thought wanted a rest or a new injection it was to people one turned. We valued those few friends who wrote books, painted pictures, played music or had interests other than in sunbathing, swimming and cocktail parties at which conversation was at the level of, 'Aren't the tray ceilings charming?' 'Yes, we just love the hibiscus too.'

As Eugene O'Neill had written twenty years earlier:

Here in Bermuda one rarely gets the chance, especially now in the slack season, to say a word to a human being above the intellectual and spiritual level of a land crab, and this solitude gets damned oppressive at times. But it's a fine place to get work done . . . and that's why I'm here.

This reflection of O'Neill's was vividly emphasized for me once when a prominent businessman there asked where Constantine was one evening. I replied he was working on his book and didn't like social engagements at such times.

'Oh, I know just how he feels. Eugene O'Neill was just the

same when he was here. On Fridays when I have to write the notes for the yacht club, I don't set foot out of the house either.'

After the war in Europe it had been unbelievably wonderful, but nearly six months of living in Bermuda, with very little money, made us realize we were not perhaps good candidates for paradise. The cast of Prospero's island had long since departed; only the beauty of the sets remained.

Cleon and Juliet Throckmorton were the most stimulating pair I have ever met. Being with them (and they were seldom apart) was like enjoying a marvellous surrealist exhibition, and then going on to the finest revue you had seen for years. Throck, as he was called, was in his late forties then, Juliet a few years younger. His round face under ruffled dark brown hair always looked good-humoured, his eyes twinkling, his generous mouth appearing to have a quip or a witty remark waiting to be said; yet behind the gentle eyes lurked the mask of tragedy. Although of medium height, he was broad-shouldered, inclined to fat, but he walked very lightly. The surprise was his high, rather squeaky voice which somehow added to the fun and made him an original. When I knew him better I asked him if he had always had that voice, for Throck was a man of many parts.

'I come from Snicker's Gap, Virginia,' he carolled. 'Everyone speaks like me in Snicker's Gap.'

Then he went to the telephone.

'Who are you ringing?' asked Juliet.

'I'm ringing the Snicker's Gap operator, so Theo can hear for herself.'

I did, and he was right.

Juliet was a very pretty woman with dark hair and laughing brown eyes. Her maiden name had been St John Brenon, her father having been Irish. She had met Throck in the late 1920s and her uninhibited manner was characteristic of those days. Even her simple clothes on a very slim body would not have been out of place in 1928 or so. Although I was in my twenties, there were days when the two of them made me feel old. Their fun was enchanting and we had another bond in common, the theatre.

When *Emperor Jones* opened at New York's Macdougal Street Theater on November 1st, 1920, it unveiled the work not only of a major new American playwright, Eugene O'Neill, but also of a new and important stage designer, Cleon Throckmorton.

That is what was printed in the *New York Times*, which also wrote:

In the nineteen-twenties Mr Throckmorton became so busy and so prominent that his name, it was said, appeared on Broadway playbills with a frequency exceeded chiefly by the Fire Commissioner.

Juliet told me that Throck had worked with O'Neill for many years at the Provincetown Players set – designing for all of O'Neill's well-known plays. With Christopher Morley, the playwright and author, they had started the Hoboken Theatrical Company in New Jersey, which brought society and celebrities across the Hudson to see the plays. That was only at the beginning, for he designed sets for over six hundred plays some of which were on exhibition at the Museum of Modern Art.

Never was anyone endowed with as much gaiety as Throck, startling you with his imagination and his sometimes slapstick behaviour. His impersonation of Queen Victoria delighted us as much as it had Noel Coward. He also loved to play practical jokes, but I didn't know that to begin with. While Constantine talked to Fred Wakeman about books I would spend hours talking to Throck and Juliet about the theatre. Sometimes, late at night, he made it seem as if the theatre was nearby and we had just left it.

There were some very rich Bermudians, who called themselves 'the forty thieves'. Eldon Trimingham owned the large store, Gosling and Gilbert were liquor merchants, and there was also Sir Howard Trott, who did all sorts of things. They brought Throck to Bermuda to start a theatre company there, similar to the Provincetown Players. When I met him it seemed it would all take place and I would be in the company. Alas, well after a year later everything was to fall through. I don't think 'the forty thieves' saw much financial return in a theatre, and as the income tax in this Crown Colony was remarkably low they had no need to undertake any venture to make a tax loss. Failure, however, was in the future. At this time it was an exciting project to be discussed, enlarged and dreamed about. I would act, Con would write plays and Throck would design sets. Maybe this paradise would have its angels.

After some months of our idyllic life we, too, were to have an upheaval. Aunt Maud died, so Georgette went back to Massachusetts to stay with her younger sister, Constance. Aunt Maud's son, Clark Voorhees, and his wife and young daughter came down to stay. He was a sculptor and it was obvious they had very little money, young sculptors seldom making a very handsome living. With reluctance they said they must raise our very modest rent, an impossibility for us, as the school didn't pay very much. So unhappily we looked for somewhere else – but winter, the high season in Bermuda, was approaching and rents were at their highest. In the end we heard of a newly built cottage miles away, the other side of Hamilton, near Spanish Point. For lack of any-thing in our price range we took it. It was called The Small House, Cheriton, which made all the Bermudians smile, as 'the small house' was their euphemism for lavatory. I could have been more Anglo-Saxon about it.

The complete property, both a large, elegant house and the three-roomed cramped small house, was owned by a painter called Verpilleux and his wife. Despite his name he was English, quite genial and with large brown eyes. The paintings which he turned out very regularly were larger-than-life portraits, painted in bright colours, as the sitters wanted to look. He had painted most of the rich Bermudians and people who owned property and came for the winter. I don't think he ever painted anything or anybody unless he had a good fat commission. He was always friendly, and he dressed, when working, in a spotless smock with a floppy bow. It was a theatrical sort of garb and far from any of the good modern painters I had known in Paris or London. Possibly his wife, rather a bossy little woman, thought cleanliness gave a good impression to his sitters, and no doubt it did. We were politely asked to drinks when we first arrived, and for devilment I mentioned names like Picasso, Max Ernest, Graham Sutherland and Victor Pasmore, at which he evinced no interest except to say he hadn't been in Europe for some time.

The house was kept impeccably; before one had even left the room cushions were plumped up. Once, when we went to lunch, Constantine dropped a lettuce leaf on the table when helping himself to salad, which caused consternation, and cleaning materials to be brought in.

Our cottage still smelt of new concrete floors, on to which rush mats had been laid. When Mouche had eleven poodle puppies I had a wired-in enclave with a kennel built for them in the garden. Nothing as natural as puppies in the house, yet later on, when the rush mats frayed and rotted on the damp concrete, it was thought I'd let them pee on them.

It was difficult to have more than four or five people in the small rooms, but there was quite a lot of rough ground in front of the cottage where we could at least have tea or drinks. The sea was nearly a mile away along a lane, but when you got there Spanish

Point was quite attractive for picnics and swimming. It was certainly nearer for Saltus Grammar School, but the desk where Con
could write was in the bedroom, and the atmosphere just wasn't
right for us.

 Our friends Gay Coulter and Lorna Temple lived fairly near and
Constantine would often stop off there after school for drinks or
tennis. Their house, Quickswood, was so much more attractive
than ours. Their two small boys who were at the school would
cycle up to us sometimes to play with the puppies. However, after
we had sold the puppies ('Once more I'm living on a dog,' said
Constantine) we had enough to entertain occasionally in a simple
way. Father Tom Grace would often arrive with some steaks from
the American base, always enough for at least two meals or a small
dinner party. We lived very simply and were often strapped for
money. There seemed to be no way of making any more, apart
from Christmas time when I made Christmas cards to order,
painstaking work which brought in very little and was very
tedious.

Most of our friends lived near or in Somerset, yet we were
several miles on the other side of this narrow, curved island
twenty-eight miles long. To get out to see them was a day's
excursion and, unless we came back early, very expensive as the
boat and train didn't run very late in the evening, so that meant a
taxi home. Therefore, as drink was cheap, we asked friends to our
house.

It was one such evening, when Fred, Margaret, the Quickswood girls and a dull man called Murdoch were there, that I was
talking to Fred about books.

'Why doesn't Connie write a book?' he asked. 'I'm sure it
would be good.'

'But he has.' And I told him the story about what the London
agent had said, which he said was meaningless crap.

'Let me read it, I'm going to New York in a few days' time and
if it's any good I'll show it around.'

Knowing Constantine's reluctance even to talk about it, when I
took it from the drawer I wrapped it in brown paper and put it
under his jacket in the hall.

'Don't tell him I gave it to you,' I begged conspiratorially. 'If
you like it, well that's different.'

The next afternoon he rang me and said he thought it was swell
and was taking it to New York. He would be back on Saturday.

Still I said nothing.

On Sunday morning, as we were making up a picnic, the

crunch of tyres stopping on the rough avenue alerted us.

'Why, it's Fred, he's up early. I wonder what he wants,' said Constantine.

Fred came in, his usually placid face alive with excitement. He cleared his throat, as was his habit before speaking:

'Well, Connie, I sold your book for you. They went overboard for it at Rineharts.'

'What book? How?'

Unable to keep quiet any longer, I blurted out the whole story; Fred, nearby, looked like a cat that had eaten *all* the canaries. He added that he had sat up all night reading the typescript, becoming convinced it was a seller. He'd be hearing from Rinehart in a few days and they were rushing through the printing. So *The Arabian Bird* was christened again, and toasted many times that day.

The change in Constantine was extraordinary, almost magical. His voice became lighter and the generous mouth couldn't stop smiling. That week when he came home he sat for hours in the small, dark bedroom, hunched over the desk writing, until I suggested moving it out to the small sitting room. After all, it was a writer's house now, what did we want a sitting room for? New novels were planned, discarded, then new ideas developed to be worked on. It would have done any publisher good to see the change wrought overnight. The letter came, giving very good terms and followed by the contract. That same week a letter also arrived from Edward Weekes of the *Atlantic Monthly* accepting the article, and offering what was to us the gigantic sum of $500. We were rich again, and life was sweet.

Constantine grew a small beard, which gave him a scholarly appearance. It might intimidate some of those little blighters at school, he mused, but I don't think it did. Now that all the puppies were sold, except one we were keeping called Flotow, we decided that the house had become too small and unpleasant. There were constant complaints from Mrs Verpilleux, who would dash in at odd hours and find something wrong. I think she wanted us to go, so she could find more compliant tenants. Penniless writers were not really her style. So many weekends we went over to Somerset, asked friends to look out for something and visited some of Aunt Maud's old acquaintances. Finally, a charming New England lady, Mrs Dodge (the same family as the motorcars), said that she had a cottage at present inhabited by a painter called Staempli and his wife who would soon be leaving.

The moment I saw Graysbank Cottage at Somerset Bridge it won my heart. It was situated right on the sea, in a sandy lane which led only to a jetty, at the end of which the ferry took up passengers. It was small, but the rooms were large and beautifully furnished. There was a large sitting room with a bay window overlooking Somerset Sound, and underneath, an equally large bedroom; there was a medium kitchen and bathroom, where salt water was piped for the loo, which meant it could always be pulled. Fresh water was often scarce. Adjoining the house was a well-built structure which had originally been a boat house, but was now another bedroom. The dining room was on the terrace which ran the length of the sea wall and there was a small changing room.

On the terrace was a little rock garden with very exotic plants; even an orchid *rothschildiana* flowered prolifically. Leading down from the terrace was a captive fish pond about fifteen feet square, fed by the tide, in which swam brightly coloured fish amidst huge conches. Across the sandy lane in the front was a wild overgrown garden full of loquat, guava, the fast-growing pawpaw trees, prickly pears and a passion fruit vine, as well as vivid flowering shrubs.

A pathway led to an old square stone building, originally Somerset Bridge Schoolhouse. It was partially furnished with a large bed, chest, wardrobe, table and chairs. The schoolhouse was where Constantine worked on his second novel when school closed for the summer holidays in June 1947 and we moved in.

Before that was prizegiving and speech day at Saltus, which I had promised to help out with. Con said I should buy a hat to make myself look more the part. Gay Coulter gave me a pretty pink straw with a flower which she said made me look like a Manet painting. I loved it, although it was totally unsuitable for the occasion. I had no idea what my duties would be; most of the masters were unmarried so there was no one to ask.

Bobbie placed me on the stage next to him, other masters on the sides. The large hall was full with shining little boys and their parents. Their names were called out, and they would come up to receive their book prizes. While they were walking up Bobbie would hiss in my ear:

'Damn pretty woman, his mother, wouldn't mind a fling with her,' or 'Face only a mother could love, that one, don't know how she got a husband.'

Each female parent was described according to Bobbie's feelings. Sometimes I feared the other masters would hear, so I would cough or shuffle to mask his comments.

'Now, look at this, fetching little bum isn't it?'

About halfway through I felt the urge to giggle uncontrollably, it was like a Ben Travers farce acted to perfection. Bobbie's lined, happy-hound face was perfectly in character. I wasn't in the least surprised when some time later I heard he had eloped with one of the prettier mothers.

We had never lived anywhere as pleasant as Graysbank Cottage; it was even nicer than Tranquillity, for we were quite alone, and we pretended it was ours. The sea was our front garden, the water so clear that perforce we became amateur piscologists. We swam several times a day, the hot sun making it unnecessary to towel afterwards; we ate in the little dining room out of doors, lit at night by wall lamps, eating inside only if it rained or a wind was blowing. Then we might light a cedarwood fire which smelt like 10,000 lead pencils burning, in the Bermudian fireplace which was situated waist-high in the wall, as were all fireplaces there. We had a vast tray ceiling in the sitting room painted cerulean blue with a few rafters across, relics of an earlier age when the house was built.

The kitchen, I must admit, was a bit of a let-down. A two-burner electric stove which gave out massive shocks, and, separate on the other side of the room, the oddest oven, which you opened like a large box – I believe it is called a Dutch oven and I didn't think much of it, often preferring to cook on a grid over the wood fire.

At the road end of the lane was a grocery store run by a very jolly black man called Mr Gilbert, and on the other end of the bridge crossing the Sound was Mrs Skeffington, who ran the post office. Bermudian friends were fairly near, Throck and Julie not too far at Angel Steps, the Wakemans a bicycle ride away, although often Fred and sometimes little Freddie too would sail over in their large boat, often insisting we return with them. One day we did, got a little way out and saw, swimming feverishly, the two little brown heads of Mouche and Flotow who thought we had left them behind. It was quite a business lifting them into the boat. After that they usually came too.

Flotow had some endearing habits. He was perhaps the most amusing dog I have ever owned. He loved collecting; old tins and pretty stones were picked up and arranged in separate piles. If you disarranged them, with the best of goodwill he would set about rearranging them to his liking. He also loved classical music, Mozart and Bach being his favourites; if the wireless was left on, he would sit and listen for hours.

Home-made soup, cold or hot, and cheese with a little free fruit was always our staple lunch. (As yet there were no avocados or melons on Bermuda, although they would have grown profusely.) It was cheap and didn't make us too sleepy afterwards. I must admit that the steaks Father Tom brought were very good for a change.

Everybody loved Graysbank Cottage. The terrace was full of people most evenings and we shared what we had: Throck and Juliet, Father Tom, the Ullmanns, the Wakemans, also friends they might bring. On a very hot night we would swim, then resume our drinking and talking. We had a wonderful climbing plant called a night-blooming cereus. This huge white waxy flower with a yellow centre was about twelve inches across, and opened slowly during the night, when it was almost luminous. But it was closed and finished in the morning.

Father Tom arrived one day in a high state of excitement. His face looked more Irish than usual. 'Like, a map of Ireland,' Con used to say, 'if you look hard you'll see Bantry Bay.'

'I can get you a couple of fruit machines from the US base,' he said.

'What on earth would we do with them?'

'Theo, you know you can't afford to entertain all these people. If you had these on the terrace you'd make up the cost.'

I felt it would rather spoil the atmosphere, so, to his disappointment, refused them.

'Why don't you fish, then?' he asked, and the next time he came armed with tackle. We all sat on the precarious edge of the fishpond and felt foolish with no catch when a Portuguese fisherman came by in his boat.

'Hey there, I bring you feesh if you want.'

Jimmy, for that was his name, stopped his boat and threw over several large fish, the like of which I had never seen before.

'Good to cook in oven. See you tomorrow,' he said as he chugged away, waving his hand.

I took them up to Mr Gilbert at the grocery shop to ask what they were: one bonito, one yellowtail and several small red snappers.

'What you want is a fish-pot,' Mr Gilbert said, laughing. I didn't know what it was, but agreed. The next day he turned up with a large wire cage with a small round entrance on the side.

'You put some fish-heads in that, then tie string on it and throw it in the sea.'

We did as he told us, and the next morning hauled it up, to find two good-sized crawfish in it. The waters were too hot for lobsters.

'How on earth do you get them out?' There was a small door at the side which opened and Con said:

'*You* put your hand in; you're more used to animals than I am.'

A new world was opened up to us so far as free food went. We hardly needed to buy anything except basics. We had found the ground amazingly fertile. If you put fifty lettuce seeds in, fifty lettuce plants came up in an astonishingly short time, yet vegetables in the market were poor and there were no herbs except those grown privately. I found a deserted house with banana-trees in it, and struggled over walls with a huge, heavy stalkful of them. I think I learned more ways to serve bananas than anyone around.

Traditional Bermuda food was restricted to a few rather strange dishes such as cassava pie, an elaborate dish made from cassava root grated, washed, squeezed and then dried in the sun. A mixture of butter, eggs, nutmeg, sugar, salt, salt pork and a whole chicken was put into a huge dish lined with the dried cassava and baked for about eight hours. It took two or three days to make and I must admit although I tasted it I never made it. I don't know what the Dutch oven would have done to it. I did however bake a Bermuda sweet potato pudding, which was traditionally served with cedar berry beer on Guy Fawkes's Day. The Bermuda codfish breakfast – salted cod, with potatoes, eggs and banana – gave me another idea of serving sautéed bananas with grilled fish, and delicious it was too. We would make a cedarwood fire on the rocks, sometimes first wrapping the fish in corn husks. I dried bananas in the sun for cakes and puddings; others I preserved in the pale gold rum for Christmas.

Mr Gilbert was a great cook and gave me recipes of the things they ate; I remember his pepperpot soup with great pleasure, as well as many fish dishes cooked with ingredients then unfamiliar to me. I learned the laborious way to prepare and cook shark. Jimmy asked us if we'd like to go out fishing with him sometimes. Coming back, one day, lying on our stomachs in the prow of the boat, looking down through the clear waters, usually so full of colour, we saw nothing but blackness. It was puzzling until, with a tightening of our muscles, we realized we were chugging, but so slowly, over a gigantic manta, or devil fish, as it was called in Bermuda. These triangular-shaped monsters, sometimes over twenty feet across, were frightening; they had a ferocious stingray whip tail, and all through August we used to watch them leaping high out of the sea and coming down with a thunderous splash. Many nights they wakened us with the nerve-chilling noise. As it happened only in the hottest part of the summer, we wondered if it was a mating display. It was always a relief when it was over. Another night I was out with Jimmy and we were anchored. I put my hand over the side to feel the water, but instead I felt something hard like a seaweed-covered rock.

'Jimmy, I think we're on the rocks, come and look.'

He came over with a lantern and looked over the side, said nothing, but quietly started the engine and moved slowly off. When we were some distance away he said:

'Lucky you put your hand over. It was a young whale. One sudden movement by him and the boat would have overturned.'

I never really saw it, but at least I have stroked a whale! When we caught a large sinister-looking moray eel he would cut his line.

'Never bring those things in the boat. My brother got his foot bitten by a decapitated head and was in hospital for four months with poisoning.'

After that I used to scan the water very carefully before diving off from the terrace steps! One of the most superb fish to eat was young barracuda, another man-eater. Steaks cut from it brushed with oil and herbs grilled over wood tasted like the finest kind of veal.

In theory we were supposed to put the live fish in the fish pond, then hook them out when we wanted to eat them. But they were so beautiful that we just left them to look at: angel fish with long blue-and-orange streaming fins and electric-blue made-up eyelids, parrot fish, and my favourite, cuckold or cow fish, encased in a hard shell, with huge cow-like eyes, little horns and a tiny mouth. They were almost impregnable to predators owing to their casing and would feed from our hands, little rosebud mouths caressing our fingers as they took a tiny piece of bread. They had the ability to change colour at will; most enchanting little creatures.

At one point the weather had been oppressively hot and still for days. At night before going to bed we jumped in to the sea, then lay on the bed, damp, with an electric fan going. Yet a little later we would be wet with sweat. The heat was surprising, since usually by the middle of October it was a little cooler. Work of any kind was an effort; all we wanted to do was lie in the shade on the terrace with a cool drink. Halfheartedly in an attempt to do something I lifted up the rope of the fish pot. It was so heavy it wouldn't come out of the water. I called to Con to help and we both tugged away until it was on the side of the fish pond.

'Heavens above, look at all these fish,' we said. 'Whatever's happened?'

We felt some were too large for our little family in the pond, and those we decided to eat: a yellowtail weighing about four to five pounds was detailed for a luncheon with Throck and Julie.

The refrigerator became over-packed so straightaway I set about making a huge fish chowder, which as it turned out was to be a godsend. Fred rang that evening saying he couldn't sail over as there was no wind, but would we bicycle over there? We told him about all the fish and asked them both over for an impromptu dinner from some of it, which we all agreed was the best ever. He talked about his new novel *The Saxon Charm*, about a Broadway producer who was, I suspect modelled on a real person – as he was saying he would have to be careful to avoid a libel action. They talked about Con's new book, and Fred thought it 'a swell idea'. Fred was musing about a novel of his which Gary Cooper had had for months. That evening he'd called him to find out if at last he had finished it. The reply went like this:

'Well, no, Fred, you see it's kind of difficult.' Cooper was a slow talker and hesitated before going on. 'I want you to know, Fred, I'm giving it a lot of attention. I'm reading it word for word.'

It was an unnaturally still night, very hot and humid as we all sat on the terrace, just the gentle lapping of the sea against steps and the fish pond. About midnight, Ted the taxi driver came to take them home, we went for our customary quick swim, and found the sea as warm as bath water.

The curiously deadening weather persisted through the next day, as more and more fish came into the sound and were trapped in the fish pot. That evening the announcer on the wireless (Bermuda Radio had just started in a very simple way) told us to 'batten down' as bad weather was expected.

'What on earth does he mean?' said Constantine. We rang up the Misicks to ask if they'd heard the news. They told us to close up the shutters and all the doors, it could mean a bad wind. We did that and it felt quite uncanny being in the house which was never normally closed up. Later that night we listened to the news and heard that a hurricane was approaching. We were warned to make quite sure everything was closed and locked, whilst on no account were we to go out. This was difficult for us, as to get to the bedroom below you had to go down the steps from the sitting room. We decided to get our things up quickly and sleep on a large sofa and divan upstairs.

Lethargy had gone as we sat waiting. It was a little like waiting for a bomb to fall and, as the wind slowly started up, a noticeable feeling of elation rose in us. As the wind determinedly got up, it shook every corner of the room and there were fearful, inexplicable noises outside. Early next morning we peeped through the slats of the bay window to see the most extraordinary sight. It was as though the sea outside had an enormous boiling cauldron under it, for it was almost as high as the window, not washing over the wall, but bubbling, bubbling and bubbling yet more. I had seen a distant typhoon in the Indian Ocean but it was nothing like this hellish brew boiling just outside the window.

'I wish I'd got my camera up here, it's fantastic. No wonder all those poor fish swam into the sound for shelter,' I said.

We were both in a state of high excitement. The dogs felt it too, for they started chasing each other round the room and throwing a ball up in the air.

'I feel full of life,' said Con. 'What on earth can we do all day?'

We played backgammon for hours, in the darkened room, winning and losing vast sums from each other. From time to time ominous cracks came from the front of the house and beyond the closed windows. Through the slats of the shutters we could see tall palm trees almost lying across the road from the force of the wind which was making a continual high whining noise. From time to time the solidly built house shook and shuddered.

'Let's ring up Throck and see how they are.'

The telephone was dead. By lunchtime the electricity was off, which meant no light or cooking, and no radio. How long would it go on for? We had a little wood in the house, so we lit a fire, although it wasn't cold, in order to heat up the soup and some water. Then we had to let it almost go out to conserve the fuel. We also had to go easy with the water, for it had to be pumped daily from the sea; there would be no pumping today. There was but little sleep that night on the improvised beds, and the whining noise continued throughout. In the morning Mouche decided she must go outside. No matter how much paper we put down, she went on making determined efforts with an 'I-went-through-the-war-you-know' look in her eye. We tried to entice her on the floor of the shower; no good. By late afternoon Con agreed the dogs must go out. They'd been shut in for nearly twenty-four hours.

'We want some more logs anyway to cook on, don't we? Which side is the wind noise?'

It appeared to be quieter on the sheltered road side, so slowly he opened the screen and front door and looked out of a crack.

'It's still pretty bad, but maybe for a minute or two.'

They slipped out, I followed to bring in more logs. Flotow was back in seconds but Mouche was determined to see what was going on and jumped up on the sea wall, almost immediately being blown over – luckily for her and us on to the road side.

Indignantly she stalked back to the house and we locked up once more. The hurricane persisted the next night but by the following morning all was quiet. Outside, there was destruction everywhere. Wood and large trees were flung across the road and on to the rocks like matchsticks. Luckily the old house had stood firm. We certainly didn't need firewood for some time and it was fortunate there were no other houses nearby. An unearthly feeling of quiet had followed, and with it came depression. It was also my birthday; as we had nothing but rather high fish in the inactive fridge, the soup finished, no electricity and no phone, Con said he would take me to Hamilton if the ferry was running and give me a birthday lunch.

The ferry was running, but all we got at the hotel was a club sandwich as they had no electricity either. Feeling even more depressed, we wandered along Front Street until we found an open bar called the Ace of Clubs.

'Come on, darling, I'll buy you an Alexander. An uncle of mine always had them instead of tea,' said Constantine.

Now, if you've never had an Alexander, beware, for the innocuous taste of cream disguises its lethal qualities. It consists of cream, brandy and crème de cacao, is perfectly delicious and makes you feel you could go on drinking more for hours – which is what we did, until the ferry went back to Somerset. By the time we got home I was a bit tipsy, at the same time hungover and dejected. I'd had a horrid birthday, I thought, and the dear dogs had been alone all day; there was no electric light, nothing but a pervading smell of rotting fish. We had bought a few tins, to have yet another makeshift meal. I burst into tears and ran into the kitchen to be greeted by Father Tom coming through the screen door. I flung myself at him, still blubbering. We had quite forgotten we had asked him to share my birthday dinner.

'Theo, dear.' He put his arms around me. 'What on earth's the matter?'

From the other room came Con's laconic voice:

'It's all right, Father Tom, she's only drunk.'

He let go of me. 'Oh, thank God,' he said. 'I thought something was the matter.'

CHAPTER FOUR

To someone from a northern climate, Christmas in a hot country seems very strange. It needs a fertile imagination to feel the cold winds of winter, or to contemplate frozen fields and leafless trees when one is alternately swimming, then drying off in the sun. I would have found this feat of imagination almost impossible during 1946–47, had it not been for the letters from my family during the hard winter known as the 'ice age' in England, where all major foods, even bread, were still rationed. In restaurants, I read with amazement, bread was considered one of the maximum three dishes allowed at any one meal. It was only slightly better than during the war years, except for cans of a weird fish called snoek. None of this appeared in the Bermuda newspapers. For some time, when we could afford it I had been sending back parcels of food which my grandmother said made her feel like a child at Christmas again. This Christmas I had sent a whole tinned ham. The golden-guinea rum I put into smaller bottles secreted in half-filled giant packets of porridge oats. It was the best packing ever; of about a dozen shipments not a bottle even cracked and the Customs (even if they wondered at the passion for porridge) never rumbled it.

With one of these parcels I had to wait one day at Mrs Skeffington's tiny post office on the bridge while a man produced his own letter scales and carefully weighed his airmail letters. He fussed and peered at the scales for a long time before he was satisfied.

'Are your scales broken then, Mrs Skeffington?' I asked when he had left.

Pushing back a strand of mop-like grey hair, Mrs Skeffington sighed:

'Oh, no, he always does that; says mine aren't accurate. He's very rich, you know, I suppose that's how he's got all that money.'

A week later I was at a party where the same man was as usual talking about his money. Remembering poor, tired, honest Mrs Skeffington I said to him almost involuntarily:

'Just how much money have you got, Mr Mott?'

He turned round, his heavy, rather dull face showing signs of interest. Without having to think, he drawled at me.

'At the last count it was $113,000,000.'

From then on he considered me a friend, always going out of his way to speak some boring platitude by way of conversation.

There were many such parties with many such people in the weeks before the end of the year. Why we went to them I can hardly remember: maybe because Constantine had just finished his novel and, with the subsequent post-birth depression, needed some stimulus. If nothing else we could spend hours afterwards remarking on the oddities of human beings. One elderly man, a director of General Motors in Detroit, appeared fascinated by me, for he always made straight for me and would invariably ask me the same question: had I been to eat at Pink Beach yet? The sand was really pink and the lobsters (there were not in fact any lobsters in Bermuda waters) swell, flown in from the States every day.

Now, Pink Beach was in Smith's Parish, quite an expensive drive away; the prices of the food were equally expensive. I grew very tired of thinking up excuses for not going. One evening I had had enough of the question. I told him we didn't have the sort of money to indulge in such extravagance; that we had free crawfish at the bottom of the terrace; that I enjoyed cooking them and asking our own friends to share them. My voice must have been unaccountably sharp and I began to regret my outburst. He looked at me shrewdly, the hard, blue eyes fixed on my face. Putting his head slightly on one side, he said:

'Say, you're not a communist are you?'

Oh! Eugene, I wonder whether they said that to you, too!

For Christmas Day we had invited Throck and Juliet, Fred and Margaret, Barney Fawkes (captain of HMS *Sheffield*, then on a courtesy cruise), his girlfriend Sue Watson, who was also a good friend of ours, Father Tom and two hard-up actors he had discovered would be alone on Christmas evening: a fresh crawfish each, half a ham roasted with guavas, cheese of an unspectacular kind, my bananas preserved in rum, and a rather heavy fruit cake which the Dutch oven had refused to appreciate. It was a beautifully hot day as we prepared the feast in our bathing suits. Our guests were to arrive around three o'clock, we would dine at the eighteenth-century hour of about four-thirty pm.

Making the sauces in the kitchen, I saw one of the huge spiders on the white wall above me apparently carrying a round white Christmas package on its stomach. As I watched, the package, like a huge white pill, the *cachet faivre* of years past, burst open and out ran thousands of tiny spiders, scattering in a thousand directions. So engrosed was I that the opening of the screen door startled me. It was Father Tom, carrying some huge parcels.

'You're early, Father Tom; we've asked the others for three o'clock.'

He was bubbling over with excitement.

'I've got us a turkey from the American base. Come on, let's get going.'

The parcel was enormous, the Dutch oven small, but to complicate matters when a the wrapping was undone it was frozen solid. His kind, mobile face lengthened visibly with disappointment. 'What on earth could we do with this lump of rock?'

'Salt,' I said, holding up a half-empty salt drum, 'and sun.' But that would take hours and it was now midday.

'I know, the sea, that's salty – and warm.'

So we tied string to one turkey leg and Father Tom sat on the edge of the slip and dangled it in the sea. There, this improbable dinner bobbed up and down, a curious Christmas captive. After a little while he called me: 'I can't read or do anything, holding this thing.' I tied the string round his ankle and told him to waggle his foot up and down, like the punka-wallahs in India. A turkey-wallah, I called him. Reports on the slow progress were shouted up; one wing was plumper and looked more natural. Then a cry of:

'Theo, Theo, come quickly!'

I ran down to find that a shoal of baby swordfish had arrived. They weren't more than a foot long, but the sharp, pointed snouts were prodding vigorously all over the turkey. Father Tom was hauling the bird up.

'Leave it, it's the best way of thawing it, they'll soften the ice with the constant darts.'

And so they did, the helpful little creatures. After an hour or so squashed in the hopeless oven, we lifted out the whole interior box and cooked it over the cedar fire, liberally basting it with lime butter and endlessly flambéeing it with rum. There never was, or had been, such a magnificent bird, the *pièce de résistance* of a Lucullan feast.

Dawn, with breakfast on the terrace after a swim – everyone agreed it had been the finest Christmas ever, which, as Father Tom pointed out had cost us very little, all the main items being free. While we had all been talking, Throck for once was silent, busily engaged in what appeared to be painting a picture.

'There's the dawn for you to remember this Christmas by,' he squeaked, holding up his work done on a sheet of typing paper.

The rising sun painted with cooked egg yolk was as brilliant as the scene in front of us. Splashes of red tomato sauce streaked across the sky, the shoreline of streaky bacon was most realistic, with houses dotted along it in mustard! The sea showed great ingenuity – ink mixed with a little mint sauce, it looked like seaweed; boats of coffee, with sails of sugar. As an example of modern art it was striking, but alas by the following evening, after two hot days, the smell was appalling. A pity, since there are many times when I would like to be able to look again at that dawn, Christmas 1947.

The Iron Hoop, for that was the name of Constantine's second novel, was entirely different in subject from *The Arabian Bird*. In the same lucid, simple prose it told of an unnamed ruined city in a defeated country, peopled by the victorious army, and those left of the population surviving in makeshift dwellings. The main character, called The Hero, was a kindly, understanding, poetic man, a victim of misfortune, who looked after two orphaned children, an older girl and a boy. He educated them through elaborate allegories, fairy stories told from memory and his imagination. The Hero's world was one of his own making, exquisitely described. It was a very haunting book, which showed great tenderness, sadness and understanding.

After it was sent to Rinehart, Constantine suffered for a long time the depression which afflicts most writers when a work is completed. He seemed very listless and complained of darts of severe pain at the base of his spine. The doctor diagnosed a fistula (a deep-seated abscess in the anal passage) and he was operated on. Several weeks later it appeared the operation had been a failure, so back he went for another one. It was a debilitating, painful period, and when he came home he couldn't walk far or swim. The dressing had to be changed by a nurse every day. Not only was this very worrying, but the vast expense of two operations, hospitals and nurses was beyond us. Georgette sent us a cheque to cover immediate expenses, but Constantine couldn't concentrate on writing. He had given up Saltus Grammar School, and we were living on a small monthly allowance from Rinehart, so even our frugal purchases of food had to be on credit. Father Tom, friend of everyone in trouble, was a great moral help, as well as bringing us food. His fertile brain kept turning out all kinds of impractical suggestions until one day he said I should get a job and he would give me a reference.

'What on earth could I work at? I've had no experience in anything except acting.'

They both sat and stared at me as though expecting me to produce a hidden talent.

'I know,' he said, 'you can work on a newspaper. I know the owner of the afternoon one very well. He'd be delighted to have you.'

'But, Father Tom, I've never even been in a newspaper office. I did see that film *The Front Page* years ago but I don't think I'd be any good.'

'Nonsense, of course you would, you're very quick at picking things up. I'll come and sit with Con while you go.'

So off I went on the ferry to see Mr Toddings of the *Mid-Ocean News* with my reference in my bag. I was full of alarm and apprehension trying to recall less frenetic scenes from the film that I might be able to do.

However, Mr Toddings was not at all frightening and seemed impressed by Father Tom's letter.

'Hm, hm, *Evening Standard*, eh? I think we can fit you in somewhere. Are you married?' I couldn't see what that had to do with it, but said yes, so he promptly said that if I was married I must look after my house for some time in the day, or I wouldn't be concentrating at work, so would I like mornings or afternoons? I chose the afternoons as the nurse usually came in the morning, also I could leave lunch and so on. I was to start on Monday at two pm. The entire interview was most urbane.

Madeleine, a Portuguese girl working there, was very helpful, also Brock, the editor. I was put on to doing headlines and Madeleine carefully explained what I should do. This I found quite easy and enjoyed selecting the various letters and typefaces. Unfortunately it wasn't as easy as I thought, or I didn't listen properly, because when my first page came out all the words were strung together; nobody had told me to leave two spaces between words. It looked something like this:

NORAINWATERSHORTAGEWORSE

I didn't lose the job, because that evening the paper sold twice as many copies, as people wanted to see the page of startling head-lines. I was, however, moved from that job to being society editress, which seemed much more in my line. It meant finding out which celebrities had arrived in Bermuda, then going to interview them. It was in this capacity that I found Romney Brent and his wife Gina Malo had taken a house there for a while.

Romney, despite his name, was Mexican and a very fine actor. He had just finished playing the Dauphin in *Joan of Lorraine* with Ingrid Bergman on Broadway, where he had had exceptional notices. I knew him quite well as he had directed the first play of Anatole de Grunwald in London, in which I had a part, just before the war. Gina Malo was extremely pretty and attractive; she had been the star in the musical *Anything Goes*.

They were just what Constantine needed: new faces, new ideas, full of original improvisation, and nothing to do with literature. Both were fairly small and dark, Gina with huge expressive eyes and a pert manner. Romney's face could assume several different expressions in as many minutes. He had quick graceful movements (I was told his manipulation of the Dauphin's train was a work of art), a puckish sense of humour, a ready wit and a rich granary of theatrical anecdotes which he told with great skill. We thought how well they would get on with the Throckmortons – alas, we were ignorant of an episode which took place during a performance of *The Streets of New York*. At a certain point in the play a hose was brought on stage, which Throck had connected to a water main one night. Romney Brent was drenched to the skin. Not the kind of incident an actor is likely to forgive easily; however, peace was made that evening and they became the best of friends again.

Leaving the office one day on my way to interview Jennifer Jones the actress, I met Father Tom looking very solemn and weary. His large Irish face brightened when he saw me but I could see he was worried so I asked what was the matter. He had found that Shane O'Neill, son of the playwright, was camping in a cave near Eugene's house, Spithead, eating practically nothing and drugging. Would I come with him to see what could be done? This request couldn't have been asked at a worse moment. I was new to the job, we urgently needed the money, Con was still ill, and my appointment already made. What good could I possibly do? Reluctantly I had to refuse, for I felt he needed someone like me to go with him, knowing the rather anticlerical feelings of the O'Neill family.

Jennifer Jones was staying with David Selznick the director near Throck's house, so after the rather exhausting interview I called on him.

'What should I have done, Throck?'

He said I had done the right thing as so many people had tried to help and failed. Shane had always loved that house, for the happiest part of his childhood had been spent there. His mother,

Agnes, had lent it to Shane and his wife Cathy after the death of their baby the previous year, but that had been a failure too. They had sold everything in the house right down to the bathroom fittings, even family mementos of James and Ella O'Neill.

I told Father Tom all this, but I still feel that I should have made some effort, even later on. As might have been expected it was Father Tom who took food and arranged for him to get back to the States. Dear Father Tom was constantly in trouble with the bishop, but as Constantine said, he was the best advertisement for the Catholic Church one could ever meet. He helped everyone who needed him, not only spiritually but practically.

In early March, *The Arabian Bird* was published in America and received a very good press, which naturally delighted us. Georgette came down to stay with news from New York and told us in how many bookshops it was and showed us more press cuttings we hadn't yet seen. It was a very happy time. Con's health improved more quickly than with any medication. Added to all that he heard that Desmond Flower of Cassell in London had bought the book for publication there. Our spirits revived overnight. Constantine was on the road to success; we were convinced our lives would be different from now on.

Having Georgette to stay made things much easier for me. Not that she was in the least domestic, far from it, but it was a relief to get back in the evening, find odd little jobs done I hadn't even thought of doing, also to share her delightful sense of humorous wisdom. On the occasional day I did complain bitterly about the difficulties of our life, she would give that silvery laugh and say:

'Imagine me with a FitzGibbon husband and four FitzGibbon children!'

Just the thought would make me stop. After living alone she enjoyed being with us and meeting the mixture of people who constantly came to the house. How some of them found out about us I will never know, it was as though there was a signpost pointing out a place of interest. Some came once and decided we were not for them, others became good friends. A great surprise was Archie Douglas turning up unexpectedly one day. We had met in London during the war but to see him in Bermuda in the same attire – sports jacket, flannels, beret and bicycle – was startling. Why he had lugged his wife and three children all that way I don't know, but there he was, eyes sparkling behind the spectacles and talking in a kind of bad imitation of his father Norman Douglas.

Archie was endowed with a permanent optimism, so far-fetched that it was both amusing and endearing. He behaved as if we were owners of large properties there instead of a small rented cottage, proclaiming it 'not a patch on Provence' which indeed it resembled not at all. He wanted a house and a job and introductions. 'Three children to provide for, you know, and then there's Marion' – as though we could magically provide it instantly. Nevertheless when Con gave him a letter to Bobbie Booker at the school he seemed delighted as if it would solve everything. After a brief swim and a drink he bicycled off, leaving us all a bit stunned. Georgette broke the silence first:

'He's like an enormous St Bernard puppy bouncing all over the place. Not a bit like Norman.'

Nevertheless he did get a job very soon and also a pleasant house right on the beach in Paget which we visited from time to time.

A carriage drove up one evening and out jumped a fair-haired, fresh-complexioned young man, immaculately dressed, unmistakably English. He had a ready smile and a pleasing manner as he came towards us, hand outstretched. After enquiring if we were the FitzGibbons he introduced himself as Emerson Bainbridge.

'Shall I keep the carriage?' he asked, but we replied we could telephone later on for one. Maybe it's just as well he didn't keep it, as he stayed for four days. Emerson was delightful company, giving out good nature and bonhomie extravagantly. Nobody would have thought that he was experiencing frightful marital difficulties, his wife having arrived on the island with their small son and a large, overbearing man she introduced to Bermuda's staid society as her lover.

That, of course, was the reason he was only too delighted to stay with us; he dreaded going home. He was rather rich, so the lady wanted to hold on to both of them. Luckily we lived a distance away, so Emerson often escaped when things got too unbearable, and enjoyed being with us and our friends. When the lady and the lover took trips to America, we were asked over to stay with him which didn't endear her to us at all. The situation got very bad, so I suggested Emer and I write an historical novel together (it was the time of *Forever Amber*) as some sort of therapy. We worked out a very gusty plot, each wrote a chapter and were each convinced our own chapter was better than the others. Eventually the manuscript was packed off to a publisher, only to be lost in the post. Foolishly we only had notes and no second copy. Nevertheless it did Emer a lot of good, taking him over the worst time with his problems, for the lady and the lover departed for another country shortly afterwards. Emer behaved all the way through as a most kind, gentle and generous man.

Georgette said it was too much for me, working and looking after everybody as well, and as she was contributing very generously to the household expenses why didn't I give up the job? With over six hours' work, the cooking, sometimes late hours, I was a bit over-tired, although I had enjoyed my time with the *Mid-Ocean News*.

The news about *The Arabian Bird* was very good, the new novel was with Rinehart, and Cassell's offer had been very heartening. It had been a long time since Christmas when we had last entertained, so with all the change of fortune we decided to celebrate the good news. Giving a party was not expensive with our free fish and fruit; the rum was cheap; I now had time to prepare the food, and the weather was nearly always perfect.

New and old friends came, the food was laid in the outside dining room as a buffet, the night was as soft as sixteenth-century satin. It was nothing like the sometimes frenetic London parties, but leisurely and relaxed. We had all night to eat, drink, swim and talk. Fred had just come back from Hollywood and was glowing with gossipy stories; Father Tom was talking about going to Antigua to build a church there; Emer, who also did a superb imitation of Queen Victoria after eating a duck dinner, vied with Throck's impersonation of her; Georgette was regaling Sue and Barney with tales of prohibition, and of coming to Bermuda at that time with four cabin trunks and the four children. On their return she had said to each child:

'Now, children, when we get to New York, I want each one of you to sit on a trunk and not to get down until I tell you.' The Customs man had arrived, moving along the trunks, marking them as he went, saying:

'That's a swell bunch of kids you got, lady.'

'You can get down now, children.'

And that's how she got four large steamer trunks full of honest-to-God booze back to New York.

The next day, there was a letter from Rinehart saying their chief editor was coming to Bermuda to see Constantine the following week. We were all overjoyed; imagine sending someone down especially to see him. They obviously thought very highly of him. It seemed that nothing could ever go wrong again. That evening we sat on the terrace, full of love for each other, looking out over the calm, pellucid sea, amid the scent from the luminous pale blue plumbago, and the slender wand-like lilies. We watched the sunset with its explosion of colours like the palettes of a myriad celestial painters, and were replete with happiness.

Chapter Five

Walter Pistole, for that was the editor's name, was tall and slender with large dark eyes which looked over your shoulder rather than at your face. He was impeccably polite with a serious manner. After dinner he said he would like to talk to Constantine, so Georgette and I busied ourselves clearing up and speculating on the conversation. Whatever speculations we made we did not foresee the outcome; it was in fact the last thing in our minds.

Briefly, it was that Rinehart thought the book a beautifully written, original story, but it was not for them. It was too different from *The Arabian Bird* and they couldn't see a US market for it. Constantine was very subdued at first when we joined them, then a false, brittle gaiety took over. As long, and over-familiar anecdotes were recounted, the bottle got considerably lower. Pistole looked nervous, but said very little. Georgette and I were apprehensive and glad when the evening ended.

Writing seemed to me to be a vocation for unhappiness. Authors, I had discovered, were like Aunt Sallies at a fairground; as soon as someone put them up, a sideswipe knocked them down again. Did it happen to all of them? I wished Fred was here and not in the States. What on earth were we going to do now, eight hundred miles out in the Atlantic? The nearest land port was Jacksonville, Florida, which seemed a very unlikely place for a penniless writer. Why had I given up the *Mid-Ocean News* just when we were likely to need every penny? These unanswered questions chased round my mind during that long, hot night.

The next day I went with Pistole into Hamilton, and over lunch he made apologies which had a depressing effect on me. I would rather he had said nothing. He caught his plane, then I went disconsolately home, not knowing what to expect. Georgette and Con were playing backgammon, at which they were both very good. Con looked up:

'Mummy's been marvellous. She's advanced my birthday and given me this huge cheque.'

A thousand dollars.

'I'm going to write a short story about the visit and send it to the *New Yorker*. Can't think why they had to waste money sending him down. Why couldn't they have written? Better to have sent me the money.'

The wound had been cauterized but it was not to be easily healed.

Throck and Juliet seemed less ebullient too, as there had been no definite news about starting the theatre in over a year. Throck picked up a thriller I had tossed aside – 'Gene (O'Neill) used to love thrillers,' he remarked, 'always read them for relaxation.'

I couldn't help commenting that there was a bit too much relaxation about at present, telling him about Rinehart. Yes, he knew all about it. He'd seen rejection affecting so many brilliant young playwrights. At least Con didn't go on three-day benders, disappearing so nobody could find him. He remembered helping Agnes Boulting, O'Neill's second wife, check all the dives for days at a time.

I caressed Mouche's ears; Flotow was sitting by Juliet.

'He just adored his dogs. Gene, I mean,' said Juliet; 'liked them better than most people. Do you remember that enormous Irish wolfhound he brought to Bermuda, Throck?'

Throck chuckled.

'I don't think they'd ever seen such a dog here before. It made headlines in the *Royal Gazette*.'

'Did they ever see him now?' I wanted to know, but I was told his health was poor and Carlotta, O'Neill's third wife, didn't approve of his old friends.

Constantine was writing another novel about a dominating woman seen from different points of view by the people with whom she had been most closely associated. He no longer read aloud to us every evening, and when he did the old spontaneity and pride were absent. It was a clever book but the humanity shown in the first two had gone. However, criticism was not encouraged, so the readings which we used to enjoy so much became a sad affair which we sat through with solemn faces. I no longer even thought I knew what would sell and what wouldn't. Con became touchy and irritable.

'You want to expose something,' said Father Tom. 'Expose the Catholic Church, I'll give you some pointers. That would sell.'

However, he continued with the novel, now called *Cousin Emily*. Bob Giroux, a New York publisher, arrived one evening, a charming, avuncular man who radiated friendly feelings, read what was written and pronounced it a *tour-de-force*, which secretly I thought was like saying of a painting that the colour was striking.

Most of our friends were leaving the island, or, like the Ullmans and the Wakemans, had gone already. Father Tom said he was going to Antigua to prospect; he would let us know what it was like. Georgette went back to New England and the gap they both left was immeasurable. I was lonely as well as worried when Sue Watson said why didn't she rent the schoolhouse for a month? Barney could come over from HMS *Sheffield* when he was off duty.

This worked out quite well, Sue and I taking turns with the cooking, which made Constantine remark that every man should have two wives to get a good change of menu. She was a charming companion – a quiet and introspective girl of original thought – and I enjoyed her being there. Barney entertained us to dinner on the *Sheffield*, a grand affair where we were piped on and off. He was a marvellous host, his smiling face and kind brown eyes always gave a gentle easiness to occasions.

Father Tom wrote and said he was enjoying Antigua, land was £1 an acre and he had bought seven acres: with the help of three reformed Canadian alcoholics, he was building a church. Why didn't we come down? The money was getting scarce, however, and, although tempted, we thought it was that much more primitive and even further away from the world of publishing. A little money trickled down from *The Arabian Bird*; my grandmother sent me a cheque which I hid for a bit against the day when we had nothing, which came only too soon. By September we realized we must leave. Where to was now the problem.

Georgette now had a small apartment in Irving Place, near Gramercy Park in New York. It was decided that I would go up to New York with Mouche, stay with Georgette and try to get a job. Constantine would follow in a week or so with Flotow when he had cleared up what he could in Bermuda.

Throck gave me a letter to Laurence Langner of the Theater Guild, a very glowing letter, and he was sure Laurence would find me something. An Englishman was anxious to take Graysbank over and pay any back rent. I hated to leave it, for despite all the anxieties we had had during the past two years, it still remains the most beautiful and *sympathique* house I have ever lived in.

Although Georgette's apartment, a first-floor walk-up, was very small, it was a charming quarter with friendly shopkeepers and the delightful green square of Gramercy Park around the corner. Gramercy Park was very dignified, surrounded by elegant nineteenth-century houses, one of which was the famous Player's Club. At night I would let Mouche run free in the park, and there met a white-haired gentleman with his dog. We got into conversation and I found it was Norman Thomas, the head of the small Socialist Party in America. He was most interested in England (the Labour Party was in power) and we would sit there talking, seeing each other's faces only by the light of a street lamp. I looked forward to those park-bench chats.

The traffic in New York was frightening after our almost car-free island, and getting used to town shoes again was even worse. I had no warm clothes, so had to wear Georgette's, which were far too old for me. However, she did voluntary work for the Quakers, sending parcels of clothes and food to Europe, and sometimes she would see something that would suit me and buy it cheaply.

'After all, you are a sort of war survivor,' she would say.

Jobs: I rang Laurence Langner, a leading figure of the Theater Guild in New York, but he was away. I rang Romney Brent, who said he would let me know if he heard of anything. I scanned the *New York Times* ads; stenographers or secretaries – no good. I rang our Bermuda friends the Ullmans, but the only idea they had was to hire Constantine and myself as butler and cook. Somehow I couldn't see Con as a very good butler. Sue Watson said she would try to get me a job with an eccentric Russian professor who wanted his art objects catalogued. Everyone else said I must go to Columbus Circle and get a work permit. I sat there for two hours one day and didn't see anyone at all. I rang Bob Giroux the publisher, who took me out to dinner but couldn't suggest anything. Constantine would arrive any moment and I'd achieved nothing. We heard of hurricane warnings in the Atlantic and wondered if it would catch Bermuda. It was all unsettling. I spent the days going round museums, for I was starved of good paintings and sculpture. There was a ramshackle cinema at the bottom of Irving Place where they showed old undubbed foreign films. It was a fleapit of sorts and cheap. I remember seeing *Les Enfants du Paradis* twice and Cocteau's *Orphée*, which for a brief time made me think I was back in Paris.

Constantine just appeared early one afternoon, taxi bulging with luggage but no Flotow. Where was he?

The hurricane. The boat wasn't sailing, he had rung some friends, the Ivanovics, and had been staying with them. Vladimir had arranged a seat on the last plane out, but they wouldn't take Flotow, uncrated. So he was with them, and when the hurricane had passed they would have a crate made and put him on the plane. Constantine seemed very bright and cheerful. Pleased to be in New York, he delightedly told us *The Iron Hoop* had been accepted by Cassell in London.

The following week a cable came from Vladimir; Flotow was on such-and-such a plane, so out we went to La Guardia to fetch him. After waiting until everyone was through Customs, we saw there was no dog. Constantine waved the cable about to be answered by shrugs. Somehow we got through to the tarmac, wandered about, and were just leaving, walking past a hangar, when we heard a bark.

'That's Flotow's bark,' I said and we went to the door.

It was quite dark but fortunately the huge door wasn't locked, and there inside, still in his crate, just large enough for standing in with no food or water, was a dazed little Flotow. There was nobody about, so we just broke the crate open, it was only loosely held by nails, and took him out on his lead saying not a word to anyone. Nobody ever contacted us to find out what had happened to him. I dread to think of the state he would have been in the next day, standing up in the crate on a hot night with no water, but it ended very happily for all of us.

It became obvious that we couldn't all live indefinitely in Georgette's tiny apartment. We went to the Irving Hotel on the corner where they had tiny apartments with kitchenettes. No dogs. I brought Mouche in, the best mannered animal I know, and put her to sit, stand, open the door and close it; so they relented. There were two entrances to the hotel, and for the whole time we were there they never knew we had two dogs, as one of us would go out one door with one dog, and then use the door at the back with the other dog.

The Ullmans asked us to dinner several times in their grand house on 66th Street, always arranging that there was a publisher or someone who might be useful there. We wandered around nearby Greenwich Village, browsing in secondhand bookshops where we were surprised to find several Norman Douglas books we hadn't read. When Norman had escaped from Italy during the war he had been able to bring only a few belongings with him. It was reading *Looking Back* that made Con remember the letter Norman had given him in England to Muriel Draper, with the words:

'Get her to tell you the story of the wood ashes.'

In *Looking Back*, which is based on his going through a large bowl of visiting cards, under the name Muriel Draper he says, 'the story of the wood ashes will have to wait'.

Muriel Draper was an extraordinarily alive woman, very cultured, with a striking head and face like an Aztec sculpture. She was delighted to hear news of Norman and to meet us.

'The old rogue,' she mused, 'Mmm. . . I had to forgive him. Yes, I'll tell you the story of the wood ashes.'

It appears that early in this century she was spending the summer in Berkeley Square, London, with her scholarly husband, enjoying the season, then at its height. She found she was pregnant, and the last thing she wanted was morning sickness and other accompanying *malaises*. All her friends were consulted, but it was Norman who came up with the remedy. It was an old Calabrian folk remedy, he said. You half-filled a hip bath with wood ashes and sat in it while it was topped up with hot water. After a number of hours you were lifted out and the inevitable happened. It was high summer, so the servants were given days off while endless wood fires were burned and the ashes retained. The hip bath, such as Marat was murdered in, she said, was purchased and filled. Friends were asked to attend this levée; Henry James came and read a short story; George Moore came and talked of his newest attachment; Arthur Rubinstein, the leading musician of the time, came and played a piano piece, especially written. The contemporary Rose Bertin designed a hat for her. Meanwhile, she sat in the hip bath, a delicate lace jacket round her shoulders, while Norman saw to the hot water. It was all very *dégagé*. The time was up, she was lifted into the linen sheets (filthy, she said, with ashes), champagne was brought and she waited. The party went on.

The next morning, Norman called.

'Nothing's happened,' she said, and then he laughed and laughed until she thought he would have a paroxysm, tears trickling down his cheeks.

The child born subsequently was to become Paul Draper, the magical dancer who had so entranced us at the Plaza Hotel when we first arrived.

Harold Strauss, then with the publishers Alfred Knopf, was at one of the Ullmans' dinner parties and it was no doubt our preoccupation with Norman Douglas that made Con suggest to him that he go to Italy to write his life. He readily agreed that it was an excellent idea and he would put it up to Alfred Knopf and Blanche, his wife. The idea was just as much a surprise to me as I think it was to Strauss, perhaps even to Constantine. The next thing we knew was about a week later Alfred Knopf asked us out to lunch at his house in the country, at White Plains. It was a fairly large luncheon party, Alfred a charming host, his portly suave figure solicitous to his guests. After lunch he showed me round his large garden, explaining the origin of every plant and tree.

Meanwhile Constantine wrote to Norman in Capri, asking his permission, which was given by return of post. He also wrote putting the idea to Desmond Flower of Cassell in London. We didn't dare to be too hopeful, tried not to talk about it, and were very close at that time, almost every thought either of us had being anticipated by the other. We did things to take our minds off the subject, explored unknown parts of New York; we went to the cinema. We saw Laurence Olivier's *Hamlet* and were amused to hear the man behind explaining the plot to his girlfriend while the film was running.

'Then she goes nutty, see, and drowns herself; that old guy gets killed,' and so on.

'How marvellous,' said Con, 'to reach that age, and *not* know the plot of Hamlet.'

Both publishers agreed to commission the book almost within days of each other. There were terms to be arranged, and as it came about the Knopf advance was to finance our trip there; the Cassell advance would be sent to Italy to keep us while the book was being written. Alfred Knopf also liked *The Iron Hoop* and bought it for publication the next year. It was all perfect. Thus it was that early in October, Constantine, myself and the two dogs set sail on the SS *Saturnia*, third class, for Naples.

Most of our friends came to the boat to take farewell. Bob Giroux and his friend Charlie Reilly brought a huge bunch of roses, others brought wine, some a little keepsake. At almost the last minute Emerson Bainbridge, whom we didn't know was in New York, arrived with a massive box and more wine. The little third-class bar was full of our friends, who looked like birds of paradise amongst the many drably dressed emigrants returning to their homeland. It was an emotional send-off. As the hooters sounded for our departure there were tears in our eyes. Turning away as we cast off we saw Emerson had left his brand-new hat and raincoat behind. They were to last Con for years.

Our departure had been very simple, no last-minute alarms such as there had been when my father and I left India. Not that our departure then hadn't been simple, but my father had a friend who also wanted to leave India but, unfortunately, owed a lot of money to tinkers, tailors and no doubt candlestick-makers too. Manny, as I will call him, was what used to be known as 'the black sheep' of an extremely rich Middle Eastern family. The name alone gave traders a misplaced confidence; he was often sent things

he hadn't ordered, things which somehow or another were absorbed into his household.

'I don't like to hurt their feelings,' he would say to my father,
'and it is very beautiful.'

Nobody could quite understand why Manny and my father
were such great friends. To look at together they presented an odd
picture: my father, tall, vividly blue-eyed, handsome and always
impeccably dressed; Manny, small, dark, untidy, his body seemingly put together from odd pieces, a large head and face on top of
a small body with big hands and feet giving him the appearance of
being drawn by a good cartoonist. He walked like a racing duck if
such an animal could be imagined. The characteristics they had in
common were a love of the outrageous and the desire to explore
all the good things of life, preferably together. They seemed to me
like a new music-hall team, making me laugh so much sometimes
that the tears would pour out of my eyes. They would bicker
continuously, always ending up the best of friends. I loved them
both.

Two days or so before we were to take ship, Manny came to the
house late one night, imploring us somehow to smuggle him
aboard.

'All my creditors will be waiting on the dock. You know what
happened to young Ernesleigh. I'll be thrown into that dreadful
debtors' prison. Do think of something, Adam, you're so
resourceful.'

The large black eyes seemed to turn into liquid orbs, as the
heavy, sad face looked up. It was such a recognizable face, not
easy to camouflage, as my father pointed out. They drank large
glasses of beer whilst working out the problem. I went out to
bring in another jug from the huge barrel we ordered every week,
to find that was the last of it.

'The barrel's empty now; shall I get Hari to tap another?'

'My God!' My father slapped his knee hard. 'That's it. You're
only a little fellow and you're always boasting about being
double-jointed. Come on, let's go out and measure up. Everyone
knows I always have a barrel of beer.'

Manny looked a little apprehensive as we stood him beside the
large barrel.

'My head's outside,' he complained.

'Oh, that's easy, you can sit down.'

'Won't it smell terribly of beer? I'll get all wet, won't I?'

My father pointed out it was that or face the creditors. The top
would be lifted, the barrel well washed, and air holes punched in

concealed places. It would only be for the most about an hour. It seemed the only way, so for the next two days Manny practised sitting in the barrel, the top being left on for longer and longer periods.

'I might be starting you in a new career,' my father said delight-edly, 'if you get in this situation again you can do it at fairs, and then, when you're more proficient, there's Niagara Falls.'

I was detailed to take care of the luggage and the animals, including my tiny monkey and the barrel. Hari was the only member of the household to be taken into the secret and would be with me. Since our journey across India we had become firm friends, and many was the time he had covered up for me if I was out too late, or where I shouldn't be.

Sure enough the weasel-eyed creditors lined the dock. My father swept majestically on board with an imperceptable greeting, to be followed by his numerous friends for the leave-taking. Hari and I saw to the luggage with special instructions; the barrel, for the time being, was to be put in my father's stateroom. I accompanied it and was alarmed when I saw it being rolled, very roughly, up the gangway. When we were alone, I prised out some of the bungs and whispered through them.

'Are you all right? You're on board now. I'll try to get Hari to take off the lid. Wait a minute.'

Try as I did, I couldn't find Hari, so I went to my father, who was in the middle of a circle of admiring – mostly women – friends.

'The beer's getting very hot,' I said. 'I can't find Hari to settle it.'

He waved his arm, and cheerfully said it would be all right for a while. I hoped so for it was airless in the stateroom. I didn't know what to do, for I couldn't ask a steward to release a stowaway. Poor Manny, would he survive? I wandered about for some time; it seemed as if the ship would never sail. I looked over the rails feeling as though I were taking part in a murder. After a while, someone touched my arm; it was Hari who walked as silently as a cat.

'Barrel-Sahib whistling,' he said.

'Whistling? Whatever for? He'll be discovered.'

'Wanted to get air, missy. I lifted off top and put him in bathroom. Now top is back so beer is all right.' He looked sad. 'Will you come back to India?'

I hoped I would. Taking off a small turquoise ring I had, I gave it to him for his bride. I watched him go down the gangplank, and as the engines started up and the ship pulled away, I waved at the thin figure with the purple shirt until it was just a speck.

On the *Saturnia* we had a four-berth cabin, somewhere down below to ourselves. The dogs were to travel on the top deck in large separate kennels. This was in the first class. They both looked horrified at being put into a kennel and took no comfort at the fact other dogs were travelling too. I didn't feel at all happy about it, for Flotow was prehensile and could open almost any door, a talent which had much impressed the poodle-clipping shop in New York.

Down in our cabin we opened our cases and the presents. Emerson's massive box contained twenty cartons of Chesterfield cigarettes, about 4,000. The Italian steward came in as we had them open. His eyes glistened at the sight, so I gave him a carton, which proved a very good investment, for later on he let us bring the dogs down with us; we had the top bunks and they the bottom ones. Their exercise deck was the one adjoining the first-class deck so it was through the dogs that we met Sinclair Lewis, the first American writer to get the Nobel Prize in 1930 for his novel *Main Street*.

Sinclair Lewis was at that time in his early sixties, a tall thin man with scant, greying red hair and a skull-like face which was mottled in colour, as if he had at one time had a skin ailment. He was travelling with his ex-mistress's mother, an ingenuous American lady called Mrs Power. Her daughter, Marcella, had apparently, in Lewis's words, 'Gone off with that son-of-a-bitch Mike'. Also in first class was an American doctor, Dr Camp, a party of young American girls who were the first contingent to go to Myron Taylor's newly opened Academy of Arts in Florence, and a dashing Brazilian called Prince Oliviera. Every morning I would sit on deck with Mrs Power and the dogs, Constantine and Sinclair Lewis usually having drinks in the bar with Dr Camp. Later we would join them; it was all very enjoyable.

After a while, I asked if I could call him Sinclair, he having called me Theodora from the first.

'You can if you like, but you'll be the first person since I left second grade school who has. Why don't you call me Red like everyone else?' So Red he became.

He was loving the journey and longing to get to Italy. Mrs Power was an ideal travelling companion, interested in everything.

'Different from my first wife, Dorothy Thompson. When I

travelled Italy with her and would admire a view, she would answer; "Yes, and you see that factory? All the workers are getting a slave wage. No proper trade unions!" '

He enquired who Constantine's publisher was, and on being told Alfred Knopf, he screwed up his mouth and mused:

'Hm, Alfred, hm . . . when I was a young man we always had to have the *mot juste* for everything. Alfred, yes, we decided he wasn't a personality, or even really a person, so we called him a *personage*. Hm. Alfred. I hope you're getting good terms.'

The young American girls were picked, I think, more for their piety than their talent, a noisy, chattering, pretty little crew, who were asked occasionally to sing or play the piano in the evenings. We all grew very fond of them, none more so than Prince Oliviera. This infuriated Red Lewis, whose face would scowl when he saw the prince dancing with first one then another. He also had his eye on me, which is what brought Red to boiling point. I must say Oliviera's line was pretty good. I was the fulfilled young woman, which is attractive to any man, he said; '*Les pucelles* are charming, but . . . in a few years maybe. They have money, no?'

I reported this to Red during one of the evening dances and his face swelled up like a bull-frog.

'Son-of-a-bitch! I tell you what I want you to do, Theodora. When those girls go to the powder room you go in and say I want them, *all of them*, to come and see me, at once.'

This I did, and we all agreed to meet back there afterwards. He got them grouped around in a circle. Ten youthful, expectant faces turned to his.

'Now, listen to me, girls. You're all coming to Europe for the first time, and a lot of princes and other so-called nobility will pay court to you. Sooner or later you're going to go to bed with one of them and in the morning you'll find you have nothing in common. This won't hurt you, but by God, it'll hurt me. I'm not proposing you don't go to bed with anyone, but for God's sake make it someone you can talk to, and laugh with in the morning. Now you can continue your dancing.'

'But we all knew that,' they said, giggling with me afterwards. 'Still, it was nice of him, wasn't it?' One, rather more advanced than the rest, said thoughtfully:

'I hope I don't remember it all my life.'

On October 21st it was my birthday, so Red invited us up to a posh dinner in first class. He was very funny about certain New York characters, particularly Alexander Woolcott the writer and critic whom, he maintained, went out for a drink after the first act of a particular New York play (all theatres were dry at that time) and went back to the wrong theatre for the second and third acts. It was quite a stimulating if mystifying review, he said; nevertheless the first play ran for a long time.

'Never took any notice of my reviews after that,' he said. 'In those days, just to be noticed by Woolcott meant a success.'

I always felt it was a bit hard on the second play.

After dinner Con and I took the dogs for a turn around the deck, and looking out to sea thought there were lights in the distance, Sardinia maybe. We sat down enjoying the balmy night air, sitting close to each other in silence. There was no need for words; we were completely in harmony, our hearts full of hope and love for each other.

Downstairs in the third-class bar the Italians were singing their local songs, the air was thick with smoke and wine fumes. The barman on hearing it was my *festa* gave us a bottle of Asti Spumante, which we shared with a young Italian couple about the same age as us who had been working in America. Now they had enough money to get married. We, too, were starting a new life; the past was behind us.

Packing up I realized we still had far too many cigarettes to get past Customs, despite the packets we had handed out as tips. So I unpacked the large canvas sack of books and put a lot on the bottom, then systematically went through our luggage tucking them into suit pockets, sponge bags and so on, until I had a reasonable amount left. I put two cartons in the bottom of my hand luggage and two on top.

'You're optimistic,' Constantine remarked. 'Don't expect me to stand by you. I'll look after the dogs while you deal with the Customs man.'

My Italian was very limited and as we got there I gave the Customs man the top two cartons. Con was some distance away, holding the dogs. We chatted as he marked our cases; suddenly he pulled my bag towards him. I pointed out his mark on it, yet still he persisted. All was up, I realized. But to my surprise he brought one of the cartons I had given him out and popped it back on top.

'For you, *signora*.'

'*Grazie, grazie molto*.'

Red Lewis and Mrs Power were staying at the Excelsior, and asked us to dine with them. We were in a smaller hotel a little distance away. Looking out of our bedroom window I was amazed at the vast destruction all over this area from the war. Even two and a half years later whole blocks of buildings had been

blown up and there was nothing but large empty spaces. I took a
photograph from the window.

'Let's take the dogs for a walk and look around; it's good to be
back in Europe again. We are, after all, Europeans,' Constantine
said.

Which was exactly what my father had remarked when we
landed at Naples over thirty years ago from India, prior to he,
Manny and I starting our Grand Tour of Europe.

CAPRI AND
ROME

CHAPTER SIX

The *vaporetto* to Capri was small and battered. It badly needed painting and smelt of grease and oil. Downstairs there was a small bar set in a tiny cabin with slatted wooden seats around the walls. It was a fine day with a brisk wind, so I took the dogs up and we walked round the deck. Over the rails on the port side a priest was hanging his head over, so I asked if he was all right. He answered me in a heavy Limerick accent:

"'Tis terrible I feel,' he said. 'Would there be a drop of whisky anywhere?'

I went down and got him an Italian brandy, the nearest drink to his request, which he swallowed gratefully, without apparently noticing the difference. What was he doing in Italy? I wondered, for he didn't seem to be a very good traveller. He told me he had come over for his niece's wedding in Rome, and was seeing a bit of the country before he went back.

I said how much he must have enjoyed it, what a good idea of his.

He shook his head sadly, before continuing:

'Ah,' he said, 'it t'was all very strange. Not a bit like an Irish wedding.' He hadn't enjoyed it very much at all. He would be glad to get back home where he understood the life. I left him sadly shaking his head.

From the harbour the island looked much larger than I had expected. Unlike the flatness of Bermuda, the mountains were quite astonishingly high, and everywhere, sometimes in the remotest places, villas were precariously perched, dotted over steep slopes. There were a few men at the port, and some small cafés set back against the rock walls, in which was situated the little red funicular to take us up. Norman Douglas was waiting at the top when we arrived, looking much happier and about ten years younger than he had when we had last seen him in London at the end of the war.

'Hello, duckums,' he chuckled as we came out with the dogs and three young men struggling with our luggage.

'Come on, we'll all have a nice drink.' He spoke fluently to the porters and they disappeared with the luggage around the corner.

'They'll take the stuff down to the *pensione*, then we'll join them.'

As we sat down at the funicular café, the familiar voice rapped out:

'Giorgio, *subito*,' but Giorgio was already at his elbow.

'Norman, I do hope it's absolutely all right my writing your life,' Constantine said almost at once.

'I don't mind what you write so long as you tell the truth.' He hesitated for a moment. 'But I don't know how you're going to get over Eric.' It was to prove a prophetic remark. Our seats had been carefully chosen at the café, not immediately opposite the railings where tourists took photographs of each other with their backs to the sea, but where we could look down on the last traces of megalithic walls built to protect the upper town from invasion. Norman recalled having seen other remains on his first visit to the island in 1888. On our right was the higher part of the old town, studded with ancient houses. With Norman was all the paraphernalia I remembered as always being with him: his pipe, the old tobacco tin, the snuffbox and his stick, but on his head instead of the out-of-shape hat, a beret.

'Are those American cigarettes?' he asked. 'I'd like to try one, please.' After a few puffs he put it out with the solitary words: 'Muck, dearie, M-U-C-K.'

After several drinks we wandered across the piazza and down tortuous lanes lined with stone walls.

'They were built twisty like this to confuse the Saracen invaders,' he said.

Stopping outside a modest establishment called the Pensione Floridiana, we saw the porters patiently waiting.

'Here we are, dearie, you'll be all right here for a bit. We'll all have dinner in a little while when you've settled in.'

We walked into the small hall where the first person we saw was Emlyn Williams, the actor, talking fluently to the proprietor. It seemed as if we had come home. The dogs were delighted to be in a house with a garden once more. Mouche, with her proprietorial sense, greeted visitors in the hall.

Every day we would meet Norman at the Café Vittorio, which we called Giorgio's, about noon, when the campanile bell would boom its chimes and the church bell opposite would ring for the angelus.

At one pm precisely Norman would say:

'I must toddle off now, dearies. I'll call for you at four o'clock.'

Then there would be a planned expedition, so that before long we'd seen all over the island. At eighty years old Norman was still an amazing walker, thinking nothing of walking several miles up to a cave-like tavern above, the Arco Naturale, drinking one or two bottles of wine, and coming back to the piazza before yet another long uphill walk home. Of all the places he took us to I think Peppinella's cave was his favourite spot on Capri. It was literally an inhabited cave, the earth floor scrupulously swept, wooden tables and chairs, with fresh, cold wine made by Peppinella and her husband. Or sometimes we would go on the stiff walk up to the Villa Jovis, the ruined pharos nearby, where we drank with Carmolina, then nearly ninety, in her youth the island's most famous tarantella dancer, whom Norman had known for over fifty years. Her old tarantella costume was always to hand and, when she got bored with talking to us, she would dress us up in it. Then there was the old ruined Bishop's Palace in the middle of a huge vineyard where Norman would chat volubly to the inhabitants. Or perhaps it was the Piccola Marina, the small café there closed up for the winter, but always opened for the *signor Inglese*.

Sometimes while walking we were companionably silent; at other times he would tell of the history of the place, or some personal reminiscence, always in his erudite, crisp style. He peopled the places with ancient characters. On the occasions I didn't accompany them, Constantine would ask Norman about his early life, and as soon as he came back to the *pensione* he would make copious notes.

On one of our walks I remarked I hadn't seen any birds, which was strange.

'They shoot them all,' he said. 'The quails used to fly over here on their migration, but so many were slaughtered, they learned sense and now take a different route.'

We were sitting at Peppinella's one day when a young boy with a gun and a small haversack approached. Norman asked him in Capresi dialect what he had in the bag. He brought out a beautiful hoopoe.

'Surely he's not going to eat that?' I asked.

'They'll eat anything that flies,' Norman answered. 'Pity about that hoopoe, though, it's a rare bird here.'

Capri seemed inexpressibly beautiful: a livelier more colourful beauty than Bermuda, the limestone hills and mountains with their ever-changing colours, the Faraglione Rocks where Norman had found the first blue lizards in 1888; the sea shimmering, sometimes blue and often when the hot sun blazed down on it silver-gold, as if lit from underneath; the multi-coloured old and new houses, the peaceful symmetry of the Certosa; the Punta Tragara, and out to sea, the large island of Ischia would appear as if floating on the water. It was all breathtaking, spiced with Norman's sparkling conversation, 'a sun of laughter'.

We met Norman's friends, too – the dear gentle lawyer Arthur Johnson and his beautiful wife Viola. He had been a great friend of Guillaume Appollinaire in Paris in the 1920s. The Johnsons lived in Rome but also had a gracious house, Molino a Vento, in Anacapri. Arthur Johnson was extremely well read, a good foil for Norman's pungent wit, and could be relied on to intervene with a quiet, amusing comment, always well taken by Norman. There was the musicologist Cecil Woolf who was to write a good bibliography of Norman's books for Nancy Cunard's book *Grand Man*. We were to see a lot of Cecil later on. Edwin Cerio, an impressive-looking man, who always appeared deep in thought as he walked about the island, wrote an excellent book about Capri (*L'ora di Capri*) and wrote also with great perceptive finesse about Norman's own work. Then there were the two Prince Caracciolos; one tubby and gossipy who knew everybody's life story, or if he didn't, invented one; he was known as the 'day' Caracciolo. His brother, Prince Stefano Caracciolo, only appeared in the evening and was known as the 'night Caracciolo'. He was small and frail-looking, always dressed in a black cloak, which went well with his silver hair and fine features. Gracie Fields, just about to marry her Boris and long before she built her Lido, always used to call him 'Uncle', and was as cheerful and outgoing a person as you would wish to meet, sometimes breaking spontaneously into song as she walked up from the Piccolo Marina.

Baron Schack, the incredibly tall German who had lived in Capri for many years, looked the epitome of the German cavalry officer (he had been an Ulhan) with a sabre scar on his face, but was the gentlest of souls, whose principal occupation was searching for rare wild flowers which he would bring to Norman. When Goering had come to Capri during the war, Schack, being the senior German resident, was asked to lead a deputation to greet him. This he refused to do, saying he didn't see how Herr Goering had been promoted from Captain to Air Marshal in peacetime. On the Kaiser's birthday he would put on his helmet and what was left of his uniform and drink a toast to a photograph of the Kaiser. After knowing him for many months, I still called him *Herr Baron*, and as he called me by my first name I suggested maybe there was something less formal I could call him. He thought for a moment, then said:

'Yes, you can call me Schack.'

Then there was perhaps most important of all Norman's

friends, Kenneth Macpherson. Tall, with fine brown curly hair, a kind, sensitive, smiling face, Kenneth was the staunchest and truest of people. In an unobtrusive way he saw that Norman's last years were comfortable and agreeable, giving him every attention and consideration. In 1947 Kenneth bought the Villa Tuoro, high up on Tuoro or Telegrafo Hill overlooking the serene Certosa, a charming villa which he divided into two. The larger top floor with a large terrace he shared with his friend Islay de Courcy Lyons, an extremely good photographer. Below was a bedroom, sitting room and bathroom in perpetuity for Norman. Nancy Cunard has described the Villa Tuoro thus:

> . . . elaborately beautiful as the result of perfect taste and lavish development of natural resources, its terraces embowered, its rooms ideally coloured and furnished, spacious and comfortable . . . the enchanting company of Kenneth . . . when so disposed. Long, low rooms, shaded or light at will. Book-filled, everything in perfect order.

To begin with, Ettore, a little Naples urchin Norman had befriended, came as cook and to run Norman's messages. By the time we arrived late the following year Ettore had gone back to his parents; installed in his place was Antonino, or Tonino, a major-domo of a man, who according to Norman 'got a cabinet minister's salary'. There was also the maid Rita, and Peppino the odd-job boy.

Many are the perfect meals we had on that terrace, enjoying Tonino's home-made ravioli Caprese followed by exquisite veal, or Norman's favourite dish, tongue.

'Afraid I'm going to punish your tongue, my pet. I'm rather heavy-handed when it comes to tongue,' said Norman, always sitting with his back to 'all that ridiculous water'.

Those lunches particularly are like etchings done in pure shimmering crystal in my memory: the sun, the silver glinting waves far below us, the profundity of the many-coloured flowers, the good food, wine and charm of the witty, carefree company.

Then the cool, nectar-like drinks in the evening. Shall we dine here, or in the town? In the town tonight, duckums. Where shall it be? Gemma's in the cloister-like passages by the church? No, too hot. What about the Sett'Anni or the Savoia? We decide on the Savoia because it has a large door open on to the street and tables outside.

'Might be a bit nippy for that, later on,' says Norman. 'Don't forget, I'm beginning to break up.'

After three weeks at the *pensione* we decided to rent a villa, as we would be there for some time. The day Prince Caracciolo, of course, was the person to ask and he put us in touch with Contessa Delafeld, who lived in Rome, and who owned the Casa Solatia on the via Mulo, once a twisty mule track, which led down to the Piccola Marina. It was a lovely house, large and well appointed with a huge terrace looking over the sea. A green patch of rough ground was in front opposite and it nestled below Monte Solaro. Behind the house lived Concetta, the permanent caretaker and housekeeper employed by the contessa, and her fisherman husband, her son and her daughter Rosetta. There were five bedrooms, two bathrooms, also a large *salone* opening on to the terrace. We paid the first month's rent and found that it was just about all we had left. The money from Cassell had not arrived despite constant enquiries. It began to get worrying, only too familiar. I was taking Italian lessons, so I was left to deal with the shops.

'*Prego, vorrei aprire uno conto, per favore?*' ('please may I open an account?') was repeated in many places, at first with ready agreement, later with '*non e possible, signora.*'

I wrote to my family and asked them to go to Cassell to find out what had happened. It was simple: the Treasury were taking their time deciding to send sterling out of the country. An impossible situation, the money there and we were unable to use it. My mother sent us small cheques, some of which never reached us; Kenneth lent us a little; and fortunately the very handsome butcher in the piazza fell in love with me. We could have any amount of the choicest meat, and when I said plaintively that our money still hadn't arrived he would wave his hand nonchalantly and say it didn't matter.

However, you get very tired of eating nothing but meat, with nothing except the occasional slice of bread to accompany it. I suggested Constantine might try his charms on the girl at the wine shop. He did get a few bottles, but nothing like the continuous amount of meat I got. The butcher was apparently a cousin of Concetta's, so when he asked if he could call one afternoon, Concetta produced a bottle of wine and entertained us very grandly with little cakes too, as though it was her house. She also found some wood for a fire.

Everything was made much worse by the weather – the coldest winter for thirty years. There was even snow, and all we had were light Bermuda clothes and few blankets. Stepping on the ceramic tiles when we got out of bed in the morning was like putting our feet in an ice bucket. We couldn't afford wood, only a little charcoal for the cooker, so we made do with some of those tiny charcoal braziers that you have to huddle over.

Fortunately, at a very critical moment we ran into two old friends, David Tennant (a cousin of the owner of the Gargoyle) and Peter Elder, a classics don whom we had met in London when he was in the American Army during the war. Both lent us what money they could spare, without any hesitation. It was a godsend. Peter Elder was an optimistic, outgoing man, whose learning sat lightly on him. Sometimes he was very boyish, always adventurous; his enthusiasm would often envelop me as well.

'Come on, Theodora, let's explore. I'm tired of passing that enormous hill on the way to the piazza and not knowing what's at the top of it.'

Never a mountain climber, I was apprehensive, but he persuaded me it would be easy. In fact it wasn't too bad, but it took all one's concentration, the small stones wretchedly and treacherously slipping when you thought you had a firm foothold. We made for a house at the top.

'They'll probably be delighted to see us,' he said. 'Must be almost shut off from all Capri life up here. Might give us a glass of wine.'

Eventually we reached the top, steadying ourselves on a sturdy stone wall before we looked over. A strange sight greeted us: a tall, very white-faced woman dressed in the style of about 1912 with a long black skirt, high collared blouse and a large straw hat. She walked up and down continuously, her hands clasped in front of her, apparently talking to herself on a long bare terrace. Behind her, at what seemed like a respectful distance, was a man also dressed in old-fashioned clothes. On a bench outside the villa sat a female servant in cap and apron and a male servant wearing a green apron. We watched, fascinated, for some minutes, the walking up and down never ceasing for a second. The house behind was grey in colour; there were no plants of any kind. It was like looking at an eerie black-and-white film.

'They look like crazy people,' said Peter, and I agreed. After a minute or two, he gasped:

'My God, they are. I've just remembered hearing some sort of story. Nearly forty years ago they murdered a close member of the family, I can't think who right now, and were shut away up here for life, with their keepers. There's no prison on Capri, you know.'

We stared at each other, wide-eyed, turned and went down the hill considerably faster than we had come up. Norman was at a café in the piazza when we got breathlessly down.

'That's right,' Norman replied when we told him of our adventure. 'They poisoned their father to get hold of his money. Very *cinquecento*, my deeaws. You should go up to Barbarossa's castle next. It's safer if you don't go too near the edge.'

Talking to Norman was like being in a magic circle of his creation. For brief moments you were allowed into his treasure house of past enjoyments. 'The pleasure of memory and reconstruction at a distance,' as he wrote in one of his books. Everything he saw or heard which interested him was carefully filed away in his mental storehouse. Sometimes he would shoot very unexpected questions at me.

'You were in India, weren't you? Did you ever go to Rawalpindi?'

'Many times, Norman. I loved all that part and Kashmir.'

'Is the regimental library still there?' he asked, and I replied it had been there in 1933, as my father was fond of using it. He was very interested in that.

'I spent three weeks in that library in 1898. I think the reading I did there gave me the idea of becoming a writer; I felt I gained a true understanding of literature in that library'.

I tried to learn more but the sudden flash of revelation was over. As he wrote himself in the Maurice Magnus pamphlet (or *A Plea for Better Manners*, a pungent essay Norman wrote to D. H. Lawrence), he liked 'to taste his friends and not to eat them'.

By February, over three months since we had arrived, the money had still not been released by the Treasury and we were desperate. The once-kindly shopkeepers were very demanding, all except the butcher. Concetta, too, had been very kind, often leaving us little cakes and sometimes small fish from her husband's catch. At Christmas we had been asked to the Villa Tuoro and when we came home a tiny little tree had been put in the *salone* – little branches of fir to resemble a tree – and underneath little fritters of apple rings. She was such a dear little woman, round and short with fat little legs which moved at an amazing pace.

Then I remembered my father's advice: 'If you're broke always go to the best hotel. Not only do they never ask for money until you leave, but you might see someone you know.' Constantine thought it an excellent idea – we could sleep there until the money came – it couldn't be long now, surely – and come home during the day. Concetta would look after the dogs at night. So we packed our best suitcase with a minimum of things, night clothes and toilet articles, and set off for La Palma Hotel, the larger

Quisisana being closed for the winter. They were delighted to see us.

What a night we had: expensive cocktails, something we usually avoided, in the bar, then we ordered a soufflé, followed by a whole fish grilled with herbs and excellent wine. We sat on our little balcony with a night cap, saying what a capital idea it had been, before having a most comfortable night with plenty of blankets on the bed. The next day we went home and towards evening looked forward to a repeat performance. The following evening when we ordered our drinks at the bar, we were asked to pay for the previous two days, as the bar did not belong to the hotel, but was a *concessione*. This was certainly something that never arose in my father's time. Constantine explained, but it made no difference – no more drinks until the bill was paid. By the next morning, after an uneasy night, the news had percolated to the hotel manager who greeted us sternly.

He was sorry, but we would have to leave and we must leave our luggage as surety.

In melancholy manner we trudged home picking up yet another parcel of meat on the way and telephoning the American Express at Naples to see if by any chance . . .?

'*Niente, signor.*'

The next few weeks were very hard. I was beginning to think we had starved in some of the most beautiful places in the world. True, we were invited out a few times, but there was no coffee for breakfast, only an occasional loaf of bread which got stale very quickly, so sometimes I would fry it in dripping which we would sprinkle with salt. It was better than nothing at all. I pawned my ring, the last thing of value I had left, but got very little for it. By now the whole of Capri must have known we were penniless; news travels as quickly there as in Ireland. I did hide enough money for the ferry to Naples, just in case. Towards the end of February, the note came from the American Express to say money was there. Over went Constantine jubilantly on the early morning ferry. I waited expectantly and went to Giorgio's to wait for his return that evening, sitting with Norman, a new lightness in my step as I walked up. No Constantine. I waited for several hours, then trudged miserably home in the dark. The next morning early, a telephone call, and a sad small voice saying:

'Can you come over? I've been drugged and I'm frightened. What shall I do?'

I said I had no money left and whatever had happened?

Slowly, and in a voice very unlike his own, he told me it wasn't

Cassell's money at all, but $50 in royalties. He had gone to a bar, had a beer and got talking to some Italians at another table. He remembered having another drink with them, which must have been drugged, and much later, early this morning, waking up in an unfamiliar quarter of Naples in bed in a huge room with a painted ceiling and a muddle of women's clothes about. Nobody else was there, but almost all the $50 was gone. He felt dreadful. I advised him to go to the American hospital in Naples to have a check-up, then if he had enough left to come home.

While he was talking there was a knock at the door. Telling him to count what he had I turned round and opened it. The postman. Quickly I ripped open the envelope and turned back to the hall phone.

'It's here darling, Cassell's money – it must be that. Go quickly and get it, then go to the hospital, just in case. Darling, darling, don't worry, I'll meet you this evening at Giorgio's. Oh! Thank God!'

CHAPTER SEVEN

After all our debts had been paid there was still enough money left for us to live comfortably for several months, so we had a certain peace of mind. Various friends had written saying how much they would like to visit. Mimi, Constantine's sister had also suggested coming to stay. It was a warm and sunny spring, the hillsides glowing with the golden glory of *ginestra*, the prolific broom, and a mass of fragile early flowers on the mountain, plants of which Baron Schack liked to bring me little bunches. We had closed some of the bedrooms up in the winter; now, with the huge vines of bougainvillaea starting to bloom, the windows were flung open, the rooms prepared for guests. It was while going through an old handsome chest of drawers, removing bits of fluff and lining them with paper, that my eye caught a glint of metal stuck down one side. It took me some time to extricate; then I saw it was a small holy medal of the Virgin Mary. Examining it more closely, I thought the writing round it was in Greek for they were not Roman characters.

Norman's customary knock on the hall window with his walking stick disturbed me. I went to answer it; I still had the medal in my hand as I opened the door.

'Look what I've just found in one of the drawers, Norman. I think it's Greek.'

He examined it closely in the bright light of the terrace.

'Not Greek, duckums, it's Russian. Probably belonged to Gorki's summer wife. They lived in this house for a time, you know.'

'Gorki? Maxim Gorki the writer lived here? When, for heaven's sake?'

Norman was chuckling, then he stopped to take some snuff before replying.

'He settled in Capri about 1907, I think it was. He had a summer wife here, and a winter wife somewhere else. I only met the summer wife. Hm, hm, that would be hers; very holy she was, living in sin and feeling guilty about it. All humbug.'

I wanted to know much more, but Norman was always a bit miserly about revealing scandal, telling you only so much. He took a swallow of his wine before continuing.

'I remember calling one morning in the 1920s, the maid took me upstairs and he called to me to come in. He was standing naked in front of a cheval looking-glass, admiring himself. I heard him say:

' "Ten books, one play, twenty-seven women, fifty-five years old today. Not bad, not bad."

'Then he turned round and we had a birthday drink. Polished off a good bottle, duckums!'

Try as I would nothing more could be gleaned about Maxim Gorki, except that I gathered Norman must have liked him very much.

Constantine took his daily stroll with Norman and would go through his notes most evenings in his charming work room which opened out on to a small balcony. In the mornings he would write until a little after noon, when he would join me if I had been shopping, in the piazza; also Norman and any of our friends who were there. Always at Giorgio's Café in the morning, but the piazza in the evenings. Everyone always bought their own drinks unless it was a particular celebration. Few houses had telephones, so messages were carried by young boys glad to earn a few lire. Grubby little notes would be pressed into one's hand: 'Can you come up this evening at 6.30 pm?' Which would be answered by the same method. Norman produced a very sickly-looking child to run my messages, called Eduardo. He was suffering from severe undernourishment with consequent ailments. I must look after him, Norman said.

My first step was to entice him into a bath, firmly resisted to begin with, but once in he refused to get out for some hours; then good, regular meals and a new suit of clothes which a tailor made from an old suit of Constantine's. He looked a different child in a few weeks, becoming very devoted to me and the dogs. Norman walked me for miles, past Peppinella's cave, to where Eduardo's mother and a younger child about three, called Carmine, lived. This, too, was a cave but so clean and homely-looking, with one huge double bed covered with snow-white sheets, a table, a few rickety chairs and a cupboard.

'Never give her money,' said Norman. 'We'll take food for them. Otherwise she'll spend money on a bedspread or some damn-fool thing.'

So often we would walk up with pasta, flour, cheese and perhaps some fruit. They all spoke only Capresi dialect, difficult for me to understand, but through Eduardo I learned a little. I grew fond of the family and wondered what would happen when the baby she was carrying was born. Concetta didn't approve of Eduardo at all. *Cattivo*, naughty, she called him, but when pressed could give me no details. Also the family were *straniero*, foreign, which I found difficult to believe as the mother was obviously a native of Capri. I found out later that their name was *Albanese*, which is of course 'Albanian' in English, but that must have been a very long while ago. In any event he stayed as 'my boy' all the time I was on Capri. One morning he arrived handsomely dressed in a new suit and handed me a packet of sugared almonds. But where had he got the new suit and everything?

'From my uncle in America for my first communion.'

Oh dear, I thought, how much better to have sent small amounts regularly to help them. I realized how right Norman had been about giving money.

Our first guests were Roy and Lotte Sworn. He was a surgeon from Stafford, his wife an amusing Austrian girl. Both were our good friends and had been very kind to us before we left England. Almost immediately Con's sister Mimi arrived with plans for an indefinite stay. The Treasury allowed tourists only £50 at that time; however, her allowance from Georgette came from America – not that, as long as I knew her, she was ever able to manage on it. They all revelled in the beauty and interest of Capri and felt very relaxed after the rigours of England. Apart from the long and fascinating walks with Norman, we all went with Concetta's husband in his boat to the Blue Grotto which Norman had written a monograph about in 1904.

Lotte wanted to go to the Swedish writer Axel Munthe's house, then not at all like the industry it is today.

'Oh, don't be so German, Lotte,' Roy said in his sad voice.

But to Munthe's house, Materita, we went, a rather boring little villa with brown paintwork inside, most of the cramped rooms in disarray, but not much to display in any event. The garden had a few rather poor pieces of statuary, and all in all I found it very disappointing. Even Lotte found it difficult to enthuse about it, so when talking to Norman she also talked about 'the wonderful book *San Michele*'.

'Hah! Wonderful book,' said Norman. 'It was written by Rennell Rodd, you know. Munthe was very good at getting people to do things for him. Especially rich and titled women; even persuaded the Queen of Sweden he was related to her husband.' Here he paused and mimicked an adoring woman:

' "Poor Doctor Munthe, his sight is going, you know, we must raise a subscription for him." Funny thing, I was lunching with him just about then and he was able to pick a minute fly out of his pasta which I could hardly see.'

His dislike of 'the dear doctor' was apparent in every word.

'Those statues he dug up in his garden, quite true, dearies, but he forgot to mention he bought them in Naples and had them buried there first. Well, I must evaporate now.'

I often thought Capri resembled a great big beautiful railway station, people coming and going all the time. However, there were also colourful characters who paid longer visits. Mimi stayed on and decided to settle in Italy. David Jeffreys, a great friend of Norman's, was vice consul in Naples. He had a small place in Positano called La Brescia, which he used for some weekends and offered to lend her. Mimi and I took the ferry to Sorrento, then a very rickety bus to Positano along that fearsome coast road with its low, then very much decayed walls at the top of the cliffs. The long drop down was only too evident. We soon found the top of the hundreds of steps which lead down to the beach, to the then only café there, the Buca di Baco, where we had been told to go. Positano is like a giant amphitheatre; the beach the stage, with a permanent backdrop of the ever-changing sea. Villas were dotted about the curved cliffs, not very many then, with just a few hotels mixed amongst them. The beach of grey-brown volcanic sand was the focal point on which many dramas were enacted.

The scene which greeted our eyes at the Buca could have been from a Buñuel film: tables set out on a small terrace with, as we found, a very cosmopolitan group of characters drinking and talking on a variety of subjects. Mimi was extremely attractive to look at and we were the object of much attention. We, too, were quite interested in them, for like many parties at another table, everyone appears to be wittier and more amusing than oneself. After lunch we decided to look for La Brescia, so we asked the attentive waiter where it was. A rather languid English voice coming from the next table was accompanied by an arm waved to his right.

'It's quite near, along there. Isabella will show you.'

A very beautiful Italian girl with long, glossy dark hair stood up and we followed her along the beach, past many paint-flaked houses with small terraces. At the end was La Brescia, a charming little house with a few rooms, simply furnished. It was just right.

'Come back and join us,' said Isabella. 'I hope you are coming to stay here.'

We were introduced to the rest of the party. The possessor of the languid voice was an Englishman called Alex Smith who lived in Positano with Isabella. A very jolly, rotund American with a laughing face was Reynolds Packard, a journalist who lived in Rome with his equally large wife, Pibe. There was an elderly English couple, whose names I never discovered over the months; also an attractive young man, very blond, called Pinky, sitting next to a woman addressed as Franca. It was all very easy and pleasant. The thought of the long walk up the steps to catch the bus because daunting. A swim, maybe, would freshen us up. Coming back from the sea a tall, dark, bearded man had joined the table and was standing by Packard's chair. He had an extremely arresting face.

'Wow,' said Mimi; 'Look at that.'

I looked up to see an amused yet slightly arrogant expression on the handsome face as he said 'Hello' and vanished around the corner. On the bus he was sitting in the seat in front of us. The damp bathing suits we had hung out of the window were flapping about his head, so we took them down, exchanging a few words only.

At Giorgio's, Constantine and Norman were having their evening drink while we enthused about Positano.

'Positano. I was staying there last year with David Jeffreys when I was homeless. People used to go there when they got turned out of Capri. Nobody's ever been turned out of Positano. Well, dearies, I must evaporate – I've had a tiring time with Graham Greene – ruins my whole morning,' Norman said as he toddled off.

Graham Greene had arrived in Capri early in the month, accompanied by a blonde woman and three or four of her blonde children. He had bought a charming villa, called Rosaio, in Anacapri, where Compton Mackenzie and Francis Brett-Young had also lived and worked. I think he had been instrumental in getting the Italian Lux Films to sign a preliminary contract with Norman for the rights of his book *South Wind*, which was to be filmed on Capri. Graham was to write the script, hence Norman being with him for consultations. However, as with many films, difficulties arose before filming started.

'I just want to see Norman gets his money,' Graham confessed to me one evening.

The film proceedings fluctuated throughout the summer. There were about three film companies already working on Capri, and it was, as Norman pointed out, 'in danger of developing into a second Hollywood, and that, it seems, is precisely what it aspires to become'. It was due to these film companies being there that I first met Vernon Jarratt, then working with the film lighting company Moles Richardson, having been film attaché in Rome after the war. Vernon was a very professional, painstaking person at whatever he did. Jovial and pink-faced, he appeared a typical Major Thompson type of Englishman, but underneath he was far from blimpish, being outspoken and amusing, with a sense of fun. He lived just outside Rome on the via Appia.

Vernon Jarratt was at the house one evening with Mimi, Peter Elder and Norman. Norman kept on about some poor people from Trani he had asked here to meet him. A knock came at the door, which, when I opened it, revealed a small Italian man standing there in an odd assortment of mixed clothes, a beret and a pair of sneakers. I didn't catch the name, so I assumed he was part of the poor family from Trani when he asked for Norman. I asked him to wait in the hall while I fetched Signor Douglas. A burst of laughter came from the hall as I was going back into the drawing room. After a moment they both came in and Norman introduced the quaint little man as Mario Soldati, the well-known Italian film director who was to direct *South Wind*. Mario never allowed me to forget it, but it was a fortunate meeting for me as time went on.

My mother wrote that she was coming for a visit in April, so Mimi and I decided to go to Rome to meet her.

It was not the first time I had been to Rome; that was almost ten years earlier. On the journey back from India with my father and Manny, the ship called in at Naples and we went ashore. There were large notices up indicating that Mussolini was offering very reduced fares for those travelling to Rome.

'What a capital idea,' said my father. 'I've done this journey so many times before, I'm weary of the ship, let's get off and go to Rome.'

After our luggage was brought up from the hold, we set off on a long, extraordinary expedition. At once I felt Rome to be familiar, for brightly coloured prints of St Peter's had decorated the walls of several convents; at home, long-dead relations had left water-colours of the Colosseum and other buildings as mementos of their visits. However, in reality the sights were breathtaking. Even all those endless books about the Gallic wars which had bored me so much at school came to life amidst the ancient dust and stones of the Roman Forum. What impressed me most as a young girl was that it all mingled so well with modern Rome. On every street corner or in some alleyway were traces of earlier civilizations. I had seen some very beautiful buildings in India of different religions and culture; here, walking along the via Sacra under the Arch of Titus, I could share in the glories of Roman triumphs. Who was it who said, 'Go to Rome first and let all the rest follow?'

Every day we visited a new wonder and marvelled. We would sip coffee or a *granita* at the eighteenth-century Café Greco, shop in the via Condotti, perhaps dine at Casina Valadier (built by Napoleon's architect, Valadier), gazing out over the magnificent panorama of the Eternal City. My father and Manny visited monasteries, more for tasting the wines than any religious experience, it seemed from their condition when they returned.

Arrangements were made for a papal audience, with all the excitement of buying new clothes and, for me, a veil. This was one time when my father was adamant: Manny was not to accompany us. He was of another religion; this was to be a personal and private visit for him with his daughter. However, Manny displayed as much excitement as I did, taking the greatest interest in the preliminary proceedings, buying new clothes, too, when we shopped. The day arrived, the maid at the hotel helping me to dress and to arrange my veil; it was a fine, fair Roman morning. On the way Manny was left at a nearby café and told very firmly to wait for us there.

The Swiss Guards in their colourful costumes, the crowded, ornate anteroom, the atmosphere one of expectation and solemnity – after a little while we were ushered into the presence and told to kneel on a cushion which was provided. There were other people behind us, but not too many. I tried to compose my thoughts, think of holy things and not let my gaze wander about the room. I looked to the ground. Then behind me I heard a slight clearing of the throat, a little cough, which was only too familiar. I half-turned, my father frowned at me, but in that second I caught a glimpse of Manny's swarthy face and black hair. A voice was talking and I could see white vestments in front of me. In a mysterious way Manny was back at the café before us, looking as angelic as he could.

'This is the end between us, Manny. I particularly asked you not to come with us, to leave us alone for once, not always to be padding behind. I'm very annoyed indeed, this is the last straw and I'm finished with you.' My father stopped suddenly in the middle of his tirade, saying:

'But how on earth did you get in without an invitation?'

Manny beamed, for he knew my father's lightning moods.

'I said I was with you, that *you* had it.'

'I think it was very clever of Manny; and what harm has it done?' I asked.

There was very nearly a rift in their friendship, but humour prevailed in the end. From then on Manny came everywhere with us, kissing St Peter's toe in the basilica like the most pious of Catholics.

Mimi and I were advised to stay at the Hotel Inghilterra in the Bocca di Leone just behind the beautiful and historic Piazza di Spagna. It was the most perfect old rabbit-warren of a hotel which in the past had housed a good many writers, painters and musicians. It was very cheap with an old-fashioned comfort and few amenities such as private baths and so on. To me it was not unlike the Cavendish in London, and I loved it. There was little service, no food, and only a small bar to the left as you entered where you could also get coffee and sometimes a roll or a packet of biscuits. That bar, small as it was, catered for a most interesting selection of people of all nationalities. If you wanted to meet someone in Rome you went to the Hotel Inghilterra, for the bar had the atmosphere of a club. It transpired that Reynolds and Pibe Packard lived at the Inghilterra, although they usually drank at the press club, the Stampa Estera in the via della Mercede, a few streets away.

In a matter of hours we were talking to Tennessee Williams, looking a bit dazed, with a young golden-haired, boyish Truman Capote; Eugene Deckers, an English actor who was acting in a film there; an American photographer called Carl Perutz; sad-looking Gerald Osborne, a young, slightly mysterious Englishman who lived in the via Babuino; and a handsome, rather shy German called Reinhard Woolf, whom I had met briefly before, with his ebullient friend Count Bendi Esterhazy. Reinhard was a tall, slender young man with kind brown eyes and straight black hair brushed back. He had been studying law before the war, and had been in the north of Italy in 1945. They usually ate at a nearby trattoria called Toto's, now alas no more, which served excellent, cheap and good food.

Something unexpected always happened when you were with Mimi, for she was irrepressibly full of fun and high spirits. This time was no exception. Our new friends seemed delighted to take us around Rome, Gerald Osborne appointing himself as my guide, while Eugene Deckers appeared taken with Mimi. Gerald took us to the Flora Hotel, where the airport bus arrived, to meet my mother, who looked very pale and not at all her exuberant self. The next day we showed her a little of Rome, Gerry bringing us to St Peter's, and the little-known coffee bar in the basilica, then taking her to Toto's for lunch; there we saw the handsome, dark stranger of Positano sitting with a very slim young woman, not pretty but extremely striking, her large sad brown eyes seeming to dominate her small pointed face. As I looked over, smiling, he nodded, his companion's face showing an expression of surprise.

'Who's that man?' I queried. Gerry looked in my direction.

'Oh, that's Peter Tompkins and his wife. He's supposed to be an illegitimate son of Bernard Shaw. He did something frightfully brave during the war. Don't know what he does now.'

The small restaurant was full of people who all knew each other, and who I was to know well later, such as the writer Sybille Bedford and her friend Esther Arthur; Reinhard and Bendi; and an American painter called Gabriel Cohn. It was very like the atmosphere in a Paris café before the war.

My mother went to bed early to prepare for the long journey the next day. So when Mimi and I went down to the bar, Reinhard and Bendi suggested we should see some of Rome's night life. Eugene Deckers came as well, as he wasn't working the next day. I have only the vaguest memories of that long night but I do remember a very sparkling dinner at the exclusive Whip Club, late drinks in the rather squalid all-night Café Notturno, frequented by journalists and many others, also Mimi driving a *carozza* down the via Veneto, a wildly protesting driver sitting beside her. It was about four am when we got back, the bus to Naples leaving at eight-thirty am. Three hours' sleep, then a quick bath and the packing. The porter knocked at eight am to collect our bags for the bus. We sat on the bed feeling pleased with ourselves while the luggage was all whisked away. Everything was ready. Then we looked at each other, both in open kimono-like dressing gowns.

'My God! We've packed our clothes!'

My mother appeared, saying 'not dressed yet', and we told her. Heavens knew where our bags were, as the bus first made a tour of the hotels for the luggage. Another knock on the door:

'*L'autobus e qui, signore.*'

What on earth could we do? I thought of Reinhard who lived at the Inghilterra and whose room was just along the balcony on our floor.

'I'll go along the balcony and wake Reinhard, he'll know what to do.'

Roused from deep sleep, he took over immediately.

'Don't worry, Theodora, we'll manage. I'll put on some clothes and come along to your room.' In minutes he was there, then downstairs on the telephone, and he traced the bags to the bus station, where they would be left. Within half an hour he was back with them, looking as imperturbable as ever.

'You can take a later bus, I've arranged it. Get some clothes on and we'll all go and have breakfast.'

When we were ready he called a taxi and we all went off to the bus terminus, where he checked us in. The bus would go in a few hours. Then he took us to a small café within an easy walk, which was nothing more than a room in a house with a large wooden table in the centre. There we had freshly baked bread, hot from the oven, farm-fresh butter and boiled eggs with the most delicious very slightly sparkling white wine. The most exquisite meal ever, and we too were all sparkling by the time it was over.

We caught the ferry to Capri easily; nobody to meet us, so we had a drink while we found some boys to bring our luggage to the house. Nobody there either, except the dogs.

About nine o'clock Constantine came home rather drunk and aggressive. He hardly addressed my mother at all, only saying to us before he left the room:

'Have a good time?'

We had been away for four days but it was obvious that something had happened during that time to bring about the change.

CHAPTER EIGHT

My mother's visit was not a success, for Constantine's aggressive mood lasted almost all the time she was there and was extended to me when he saw that I was spending time with her which he felt should be given to him. I hadn't seen her since I had left England in 1946 and it was her first holiday abroad since we had both been in France in 1939. I was determined that she would enjoy at least part of her time with us. She had known and liked Norman in London, Baron Schack amused her, but she grew very fond of Reinhard, who had come down to stay in Capri. He was always charming, and I came to rely on him as a calm, civilized person who was helpful and easy to talk to.

Constantine seemed reluctant to talk to me, which had never happened before; he showed only hostility if I tried to find out what was wrong. Even the good news that *The Arabian Bird* had been sold to Denmark didn't change him, except to make him spend more on drink, and more and more nights in a newly opened club called Tabu, with Mimi, an American girl and her friend, a young sculptor. The house was divided in a way, as we only met for occasional meals and drinks. Through Reinhard we met a Swedish painter called Harald Klinckowström, a very engaging personality, with a fierce Saxon wife called Blanca who first thing took me aside and said Harald mustn't drink as he was ill. He seemed very lively without it and we all enjoyed his company.

My mother and I were sitting one morning in the piazza – Constantine had gone to Naples – when we were joined by Reinhard and Harald, who said Blanca had gone to Naples for the day too. It was late when we all decided to have lunch at Sett' Anni, which had a tiny balcony overlooking the terraces down to the Marina Grande and the funicular. During lunch I asked Harald what was the matter with him that he couldn't drink, and he replied:

'Nothing at all. Blanca just says that to stop me drinking.'

'Right', said Reinhard. 'You had better start now. You have to catch up with us.'

Another bottle of wine was ordered as we all grew happier every moment, then yet another and maybe another too.

'Siesta time,' we said, looking at the late hour on our watches. 'Leave that bottle, we can drink it tomorrow.'

Reinhard got up to go and settle the bill. The door to the main restaurant was locked. We shouted, banged and rattled, but it was obvious the owners had shut up and gone for their siesta. Our table had been against the main wall, and looking out we wouldn't have been seen by them.

'They'll be back soon,' said Reinhard.

'I don't care if they never come back,' cried Harald.

'It's the nicest day I've had here,' exclaimed my mother.

I said nothing just then, hoping they would return before the ferry.

But they didn't: we saw the ferry come in, the funicular disgorge, Constantine and Blanca on the terrace outside. They were talking and looking around, even up. It was a little nerve-racking.

'My God! Blanca, and I'm drunk,' said Harald.

'Constantine! Whatever can we say?'

'We were only having lunch,' said my mother. 'It's not our fault.'

Reinhard was calmer than usual. We heard the door of the restaurant unlocking, saw the owners' amazement when they saw our faces pressed to the glass. They started to laugh and laugh and laugh, and approached our doors with another bottle of wine.

'Just one glass,' said Harald.

'I need something,' echoed my mother.

I took just one. Reinhard swallowed his quickly.

'I'll go out and find out where they are. Then you follow when I come back.' The owners were quite hilarious and begged us to stay for dinner. Reinhard returned.

'Constantine's drinking with Norman. There's no sign of Blanca. I think it's quite safe to come out.'

We were all halfway across the piazza when we saw a carabinieri approaching; he stopped in front of us and, addressing me, said:

'The Countess Klincköwstrom wishes to see you at the station.'

Bewildered, we followed him, having sent Harald back to his hotel. It appeared Blanca had caught sight of us on the balcony, the table covered with bottles, and had at once gone to the carabinieri and reported that I was trying to poison her husband. What had I to say?

Reinhard, with his most urbane manner, took over in fluent Italian. There seemed to be a certain amount of argument; then, quite suddenly, the carabiniere were apologizing, Blanca was ushered out firmly, and they shook hands with us, smiling broadly.

Harald was kept in close confinement for a few days after that, then managed somehow to escape. My mother and I walked home and looked the picture of domesticity when Constantine returned.

The time came for my mother to go home. In an impulsive moment she had given Constantine most of her travel allowance soon after she arrived and was now left with very little. He disappeared after dinner before I had time to ask him for some money to get to Rome. Mimi had finally gone to Positano, so there was no appealing to her. Late that night we found him at the night club, Tabu, looking very annoyed at our appearance. On being asked for some money, his reply was:

'I have very little money and what I have I need for myself.' It was very uncharacteristic.

Could we appeal to Reinhard yet again? It was almost one o'clock in the morning and vital my mother returned in a few days. When I woke him yet again he said he too was going on the *rapido* to Rome in the morning and would meet us at the boat. It wasn't easy at seven-thirty am struggling up the via Mulo with our luggage, as the boy hadn't turned up. We had a little over a thousand lire left. There was no sign of Reinhard at the boat, but over a cup of coffee we decided we were better in Capri with no money than in Naples. Later I plodded up the steps, saving the lire on the funicular, to look for Reinhard to see what had happened. He too was distraught, having had most of his money stolen the previous evening. He would get more when the only bank opened, and meet us at five-thirty pm. Did I need a little now? It seemed a very long day; we were reluctant to go up to the piazza, and spent it at the Marina Grande, wandering about, eating very little and waiting, waiting.

When we finally got to the Inghilterra in Rome very late, we found it was booked out owing to the Rome Horse Show. Reinhard offered us his room there, saying he would find somewhere else. It was only a single room, however, so it meant more telephoning, another taxi, until well after midnight when we got a hotel and gratefully got to bed.

At a tearful farewell the next day, my mother pressed a cheque into my hand.

'Try to find someone to cash it and keep part of it for an emergency like this. I wish you would come back with me for a little while. You have to pay Reinhard back, too.'

I looked at the fifty-pound cheque, wondering what to do with it, for it was quite impossible to cash it in the normal way. Wandering about the nearby streets, I passed the Ambasciatori Hotel, where my father, Manny and I had stayed when we departed from that eventful passage from India.

For old time's sake I went into the crowded bar and ordered the cheapest drink, mineral water with lemon. Again I remembered my father saying: 'Always go to the best hotel, you're bound to see someone you know.'

The bar itself was packed with men in uniform. I looked closer; yes, it was some of the teams riding at the horse show. The uniform at the end was familiar, and wasn't that . . .? I moved over to see more clearly – the Irish team. The laughing face of my father's old friend Captain Dan Corry turned slightly towards me.

'I suppose you don't remember me?' For an instant the weathered face looked at mine.

'Begod, I do,' he said. 'You're Adam's daughter. A great little girl on a horse. Not so little now, though. What'll you have? Coming to the show? Tomorrow's our big day.'

As drink after drink was put in front of me, I thought more and more about the cheque in my bag. Could I, would he, be able to cash it? I must do something quickly, now.

'Could you ever cash me a cheque? I've run out of money. It's my mother's, so it's all right,' was gabbled very quickly. Within minutes my bag was stuffed with pound notes.

'Sure that's enough, now? Here, take this too. Many's the time Adam's helped me out.'

I left to find a *cambio,* the banks being closed by that time. I changed it, luxuriously took a taxi to the Inghilterra, repaid Reinhard and went back to my hotel. I rang Vernon Jarratt, who asked me to dinner, and I told him briefly a little of what had happened.

'Give me half, Theodora, I'll keep it as a safety valve for you. You know if you take it all back you'll give it to Con.'

I gave him the half I had left. I also wrote a cheerful letter to my mother.

Travelling back to Capri, I was in an optimistic mood. Now, with the house to ourselves at last we would get back to the old comradeship. No more of this exhausting hostility. Concetta was the only person in the house when I got back. She burst out of the kitchen with a voluble flow of Italian which seemed to be about the dogs. Where were they? La Signora Mimi had taken Flotow to Positano and the old dog was ill. She had made a bed for her in the *salone*. Mouche, who had never had a thing wrong with her, was certainly ill, but with what? She looked sad and dejected and was unable to stand up. Her back legs seemed paralysed. I rubbed them and lifted her on to her feet and she wagged her tail feebly. Where did the vet live? Another flow of Italian, from which I gathered there wasn't one on Capri, but a Neapolitan vet came over once a week. There was a German woman who looked after sick dogs; Concetta would find her tomorrow. No, she did not think Il Signor would be here for dinner. Perhaps he was with Signor Douglas? I stayed with Mouche a little while, giving her something to eat and helping her out to the terrace. She seemed a little better.

Norman was dining alone at the Savoia, so I asked if I could join him. Constantine might look in later. He looked at me quizzically: 'Mummy gone home? I like her, not always fussing. Didn't seem to think the pins and needles in my hand was much to worry about. I'm just breaking up I suppose, my dear. Enjoy Rome? Archie said he couldn't find any pretty girls when I found him that job in Rome. Bah! Rome's *full* of pretty girls. Damn fool.'

It was the night for settling his monthly *conto* at the trattoria. I always dreaded this, being very bad at arithmetic. He would make everyone add it up, to make sure they 'hadn't cocked it on, dearie'. He himself was equally bad at addition – 'those infernal mathematics', he called it. When he took his examination for the Diplomatic Service in 1893 he had been top in everything and next to bottom in mathematics. Both our totals would end up differently, but always in Norman's favour. I got to believe the restaurant did it deliberately, for they seemed to enjoy it thoroughly. Telling him about Mouche, I said I would go back now, but not before he had promised to come to dinner the following evening. He would never dine with us more than about once a week, as he said, 'I know what an infernal nuisance entertaining is, my dear.'

About midnight I went to bed; much later I heard Constantine come in, and feigned sleep when he came to bed. He came down to breakfast just as I was finishing, with what looked like a hangover; I said I was going up early to try to find the animal woman, also to do some shopping as Norman was coming to dinner. Would he join me at Giorgio's? A quiet affirmative was given.

Having our lunchtime drinks with Norman, the American girl and a tall, blonde Englishwoman greeted Constantine affectionately. I was introduced to the English girl; her name was Gavrelle Verschoyle, her husband being at the British Embassy in

Rome. I mentioned I was in Rome for a few days and that I had been to the horse show, a great mistake on my part for it led to endless questioning and acrimony later that evening because of Constantine's mistrust and jealousy.

Several days later he said he wanted to talk to me, which I was glad about, for we had discussed many things in the past and he was obviously worried about something. We sat on the terrace after breakfast, the early, yet hot, May sun warming our shoulders. He didn't see how he was going to finish the book about Norman, honestly discussing his sex life and its great influence on his writing. What on earth could he do? He'd written about four chapters and was now irrevocably stuck. In the 1940s society's attitude to sexual misdemeanours was not as liberal as today. It would have been impossible to persuade English-speaking countries that it was quite common practice for poor Italian families to 'loan' their older children, girls and boys, to rich (as they thought) foreigners, in exchange for money which went for their dowries, or their education. Alas, too, he couldn't 'get round Eric', now a happily married chief superintendent in East Africa. Did he have to be explicit about it? Couldn't he write round it? To which the answer always was, not if he was to tell the truth, as Norman had insisted. I suggested he talk to Norman to see if he couldn't think of a way. But all his life Norman had defied authority, both in lifestyle and in some of his books. It wasn't the sort of idea to appeal to him.

Indeed it would be easier to persuade many that there was in Norman an affiliation with the wise old centaur Chiron who spent much time advising and instructing the young. It was not difficult, either, to be certain he would have infinitely preferred to renounce immortality for some modern-day Prometheus rather than suffer long drawn out, incurable pain.

We were in a strange country, with very little money, unable to work, with the awful prospect of being penniless once more.

'Why don't you finish *Cousin Emily*, the novel you started in Bermuda? You can still go on with your walks and talks with Norman just in case you thought of a way, yet you would have another book ready to sell.'

He nodded, looking glum, showing no enthusiasm at all for my idea, and wandered off, saying he was going up to the piazza.

The German woman, to whom Mouche took an instant dislike, arrived with the vet, who didn't seem to know what was wrong with the dog, but gave me some pills for her and a prescription. She seemed a little better but still could only take a few tottering steps. It was an added worry. I sat on the terrace for some time. Was it true, then, what Goethe said: 'Beginnings are always delightful; the threshold is the place to pause'? I paused to remember how many knife-pangs of hunger I had known, in Paris, London, Bermuda and in this beautiful, sun-filled villa where we had searched in vain sometimes for even an edible crust of bread. There was not even a scrubby tree or bush to bear fruit in this planned, pretty garden. I walked up to get the prescription filled, later joining Constantine and Norman at Giorgio's. A tall man was leaving as I arrived, apparently someone attached to the British Council in Naples.

'British Council twaddle,' said Norman; 'coming over here to teach the Italians how to build houses. They were building magnificent houses when the English were still painting themselves blue and living in caves, bah!'

I enquired how he was after our late night, as I hadn't seen him since.

'Decidedly squimpy, my dear.'

'We did consume eleven bottle of wine, Norman. I didn't feel all that good either.'

He affected not to hear what I had said.

'The doctoressa was there this morning. Insists I have to drink a lot of liquid and do the goosestep. Goosestep, duckums, whatever next? Get up my circulation, she says. Ever hear such rubbish? Takes me off whisky to wine, didn't dare suggest water, anyway it can't be good for arterio-sclerosis, can it? Most of this wine is water, hah! Goosestep indeed, as well as walking about five miles a day.' He slapped the empty glass down on the table.

'If that muck's able to check arterio-sclerosis, dearie, it's time to put your trust in God! How's that dog of yours? Vet come yet?'

I told him what had occurred and he made that loud 'hah' noise which sounded like a cross between a growl and a muffled bark.

In the two weeks that followed, Mouche made no improvement; neither could Constantine think of any solution to his book. The only cheering news was that an Italian publisher had bought *The Arabian Bird*, a welcome and unexpected bonus, but as Constantine now had no agent, it would be up to him to get the money here. He did very little writing, mainly going through his notes, sometimes lengthening them.

One day a very handsome young German arrived saying Norman had asked him to call to look at the dog. He examined her, injected her, and the treatment seemed to do some good. I told the little German woman about it; she seemed mystified, making me

describe him in detail, asking where he was staying. When I told
her, she started to laugh, then speaking rapid German, which I
asked her to repeat more slowly, she told me he wasn't a vet at all,
but the Shah of Persia's psychiatrist. Could it be true or was it just
Capri gossip? I begged her to find me a better vet, but she shook
her head, and said the only good place was an animal hospital in
Naples run by the old blind Princess Pignatelli, who used all her
money and her house for sick dogs mainly, but also some cats.
Would I let Mouche go there? Con and I talked it over, and after a
week of no improvement I said I would take her over and spend a
night to see how she liked it. I rang David Jeffreys, the vice
consul, to book me into a hotel. It is not difficult to imagine the
nightmare of a journey with a sick, heavy dog, on the ferry, then a
taxi out to the Posilipo, where Norman had built a house in 1896
and lived with his wife.

The animal hospital was in a large *palazzo*; it had a pleasant
atmosphere, a resident vet, the dogs housed in the large rooms
with covered mattresses on the floor. The old blind princess was
kind and gentle, grey hair framing her serene face as she sat in an
elaborately carved chair. She caressed Mouche and asked what she
looked like, her colour and so on, the sightless eyes looking ahead,
not down at the dog. I went back to the large Londra Hotel,
having said I would go out again in the evening. It seemed an
endless tram journey, looking out all the time so as not to miss the
house. Mouche seemed quite at home, comfortable on her linen-
covered soft mattress, somehow pleased to be in a place which
might make her better. I stayed until it was quite dark, talking
quietly in my limited Italian to the princess, still sitting in the
chair. I felt quite relieved.

On the way back I got off the tram a stop too soon, so walked
along the quays in the warm night air. Then I saw three men
advancing, a black American sailor being held up by a man on
either side. He appeared very drunk. Not wishing to tangle with
drunks, I hid in a gateway while they passed. As I came out I
turned to see how far up they had gone and saw the sailor collapsed on the ground, the other two men bending over him.
Quickly I slipped away, almost running until I reached the hotel.
The next morning when the maid brought in my breakfast, she
moved over to the window and stood looking out for some time.
What was she looking at?

'*Omicidio, signora.*'

'*Omicidio?* Homicide? Where?'

It was difficult to follow her rapid Neapolitan accent with all the ends of the words chopped off. Murder? It seemed unlikely on that May morning. An American sailor had been knifed and robbed. This was accompanied by dramatic gestures. Along the quay, last night. It didn't take long to connect what I had seen, and the murder. What should I do? I couldn't identify anyone. I telephoned David Jeffreys and he invited me to lunch. Upset as I was, I still remember the exquisite pasta with fresh basil and his cheerful attitude.

'Don't say a word, Theodora. As you say, you can't identify anyone and you'd be kept here for weeks of questioning. What good would it do? Come on, have some more wine and take the evening ferry back. It's happening all the time in Naples.'

Back in Capri that evening telling Con and Norman about it, Norman said:

'Hum, don't forget Naples is halfway to Baghdad.' A somewhat cryptic remark, nevertheless somehow applicable.

Towards the end of the month, yet another problem occurred. The Contessa Delafeld called and very politely, so delicately, said she must raise the rent to double for the summer months. She hoped that would be in order.

It was of course impossible.

More and more, one's tired brain thought in clichés or adages, words which over the centuries had been well used for similarly repetitive events. 'The more things change, the more they are the same.' Was it La Rochefoucauld? Did it matter? We went to Positano, where Mimi had settled, now with a young Italian lover, and explored the possibilities of living there, as it was much cheaper, though at that time much more primitive. We had no furniture, no pots and pans, nothing but books, and there would be no chance of doing any more research into Norman's life. Mimi was delighted to see us, Flotow overjoyed by our visit. Mimi said could we take him back with us, as he had been asked to leave.

'Asked to leave? By whom and what on earth for?' we queried; 'He's the gentlest dog ever.'

'For chasing boys on the beach; the mayor has requested he leave,' Mimi answered. 'I told him straight. You can't blame the dog, he's only copying everyone else in Positano!'

Constantine was rather pleased: no person had ever been asked to leave, it was rather a distinction when one's dog was.

During most of May we searched Capri for a suitable house at the right rent, but many places which had been empty all winter were filling up with families or lovers from all over Europe and

America. We could not help but resent most of them, for what they engendered – as Norman wrote in a postscript to *Footnote on Capri*, published in 1952, four months after his death:

> The island is too small to endure all these outrages without loss of dignity – the pest of so-called musicians who deafen one's ears in every restaurant, roads blocked up by lorries and cars, steamers and motor boats disgoring a rabble of flashy trippers at every hour of the day.

However, it is probably true that everyone who has known Capri when it has been quiet and almost peopleless feels the same and has complained, from the days of the Roman Emperors onwards. Eventually we took a house in a remote part of Anacapri. We were sad to leave Solatia; Concetta was almost in tears, insisting her daughter Rosetta accompany us, to see we were *comodo*.

The large, old, open taxi couldn't come down the via Mulo, which had many wide steps; it was waiting outside Concetta's small house on the road. Constantine, Flotow and I sat in the back, Rosetta in front with the driver. A sad leave-taking, Concetta's face unaccustomedly downcast. At the last moment little Eduardo came running up, begging to be brought with us. Alas no, but we would see him tomorrow. It was as though we were going to another country.

CHAPTER NINE

In 1949 Anacapri was very rural with a few old houses, lanes rather than roads, which converged on to a road leading to a small piazza dominated by a church. The church was not large but had an extremely attractive ceramic floor. Around the piazza were some little houses, joined together, and some shops, the largest being a grocery on the corner; it was pleasant inside, with old wooden counters, wooden shelves and drawers. For such a village-like community it was remarkably well stocked. There was also a small café. A bus to Capri and back ran several times a day but stopped running quite early in the evening. There were few *pensione*, no hotels, except about halfway up from Capri, the Cesar Augustus, then in the course of being completed. The only restaurant, I remember with pleasure, was called Mingetti's, small with a garden; it was cool and shady in the summer when tables and chairs were set outside.

Mingetti was squat and square, remarkably like the actor Edward G. Robinson to look at, which no doubt gave rise to the story that he had been a gangster in America. If he was, he was also one of the kindest men I have ever met, capable, always helpful and most interesting to talk to. He loved to speak what passed for English, words like 'boids' 'goils' and 'dames' peppering most of his anecdotes.

He was very pro-American, especially with regard to Marshall Aid, but said quite firmly: 'Every guy oughta end up in his homeland.' He did all the cooking himself with only a girl to help him; it is with great pleasure I remember his superb *pizza rusticana*, the size of a small wheel, filled with ricotta cheese, eggs, herbs and just the suspicion of nutmeg it needed. Anything you wanted to know, or have done, you asked Mingetti, and that was enough. The Anacapresi were a superstitious people: the postmistress was reported to have the evil eye, so nobody dared to complain when her five-year-old grandson, who couldn't read, was made the delivery boy for telegrams.

Our house was quite a long way down one of the lanes, past small houses owned by peasant farmers, who kept the cow or the bull on the ground floor (the poor bull was led all over Capri to serve the cows); a vineyard at the side or back, some chickens and maybe a pig or two. Graham Greene's house, Rosaio, was down the lane and at the end was Arthur and Viola Johnson's beautiful villa, Molino a Vento. Baron Schack had two rooms in a *pensione* on the other side of Anacapri. He would walk down to Capri and back every day, quite a few miles. Sometimes if he was tired coming back, or after a lot of wine, he would go to sleep on the stone shelf under the statue of the Madonna about halfway up the long, winding hill.

After the Casa Solatia we felt as if we had been imprisoned, for the house, Casa Carracciolo, was in two parts; the ground floor had two not very large rooms, downstairs a primitive kitchen and small dining room. Outside the ground floor were white-painted steps winding around the house to another floor of two rooms with a bathroom and a terrace. In effect, two flats, one on top of the other. To begin with we thought it rather amusing to with-draw to the drawing room above, for it had wonderful views of the surrounding country, with Ischia in the distance. This novelty soon palled, especially as it meant carrying up books, glasses and bottles. Another irritating thing was three twittering little girls with a much older woman in charge, who were sent by the owner to clean the house. It was all impossible in a small house, four extra people scurrying about, moving everything daily, even Constantine's writing paper. If we went out while they were there, things were successfully hidden. For instance the bedcovers were removed, nowhere to be found, and when asked where they were it turned out they had all been put under the mattresses. Either they went or we did, was our ultimatum to Mingetti, who under-stood completely and sent down a sad, sweet, madonna-faced girl called Ilda instead. After two days she didn't come; apparently the three girls and the woman had waited for her on the road and intimidated her. Mingetti again soon put a stop to that, but we had provoked almost a vendetta and Ilda was sometimes nervous.

Between Graham Greene's house and ours, a plump, pop-eyed Dutchman called Tony Paanaker was building a house to be called Casa della Madonna. He strutted about Capri, always with a silver-topped stick which he twirled when he stopped to talk to you, joining your party unasked. He was certain that Graham, also Constantine and myself, would be interested to see the mag-nificent place he was erecting – we must all come *now* to see it. The building was certainly extensive with Madonnas everywhere – outside, in niches up the stairs, over the doors, in the rooms. It was more like a temple than a house. Halfway up, Graham and I got the giggles and had to sit on a stone bench underneath one of these appallingly modelled statues. We were almost helpless with laughter. Paanaker appeared round the corner twirling his stick, Constantine with an expression of exhausted helplessness behind him.

'Ah, I see the beauty has overcome you both. Rest awhile, then we will see the top floor.'

'But I couldn't, Tony, it's all so overwhelming. Another time, don't you think so, Graham?'

Graham was mopping his eyes with his handkerchief, gratefully agreeing with me. Constantine, quick to latch on, said.:

'Theo will tell you, I can only look at a few pictures in a museum. Too many makes me dizzy.'

'What an extraordinary man,' Graham said afterwards. 'Is he very religious?'

I replied, I didn't think he was, certainly not a Catholic, as he was never in church.

Although Graham lived nearby, we didn't see very much of him. He was writing a lot I think. He came to lunch and sometimes we had a drink together. I was a little in awe of him, those pale blue eyes with a slightly tortured expression worried me a little. I wondered if since becoming a Catholic he was finding it too difficult. Born Catholics have had longer to get accustomed to the rigidity. Did he have feelings of guilt? At this time the only books of his I had read were *Brighton Rock* and *Ministry of Fear*, for *The Heart of the Matter* and *The End of the Affair* had yet to be written. If he did have feelings of guilt, it was something I didn't understand, for I firmly believe that every thinking person knows, maybe even for only a few seconds, before they do something wrong, and therefore have a choice. If the doubtful one is taken, it is permissible, even essential, to have a conscience, but never guilt. My father was a good example of this principle, and to a lesser extent my mother and grandmother.

We talked on many subjects; he told me he always tried to write a thousand words a day.

'It's amazing how much you get done if you do.'

Of Norman we talked frequently; he was beginning to think *South Wind* wouldn't be made into a film now, but he was determined Norman should get some money from it. He seemed a very concerned person. We spent one curious evening at Rosaio with Graham and a very small dark woman with a masculine, Scottish-sounding name. I think she wrote plays. The blonde and her blond children had left some time past. It was a very hot night, the drinks much stronger than the wine we were accustomed to; I don't remember having anything to eat either. At some time, fairly late, Constantine said he was so hot he would take a walk in the garden. Graham and I were talking in his work-room when I realized we must go home. The time had passed very quickly, none of us thought it was so late.

Graham and I picked our way through the garden looking for Constantine. Then we heard a faint voice calling, 'Theo, Theo.'

We intensified our search, the voice, sometimes fainter than others, still calling from time to time.

'Where on earth is he?' said Graham.

'He can't have gone home, for we can hear him,' I replied.

We went on looking, stumbling and holding on to each other through rockeries, prickly cacti and small bushes. The moon 'was having one of her fits' as Norman used to say, capriciously there one moment and gone the next. The leaves whispered as we brushed past them.

'My God, there's a well in the garden. I hope he hasn't fallen down that', Graham cried. He ran off to look. I stood, completely perplexed, straightening myself for I was cramped from bending over, looking where I was going; then I looked up at the sky.

'Theo, Theo.'

I called back: 'Where are you?'

As I looked up I thought I saw something moving in the sky. Impossible. Graham came back saying thankfully, he wasn't in the well.

'Look up, there, Graham. Isn't something moving, or am I going mad?'

For some minutes we stared. Yes, there was something briefly, then it would disappear.

'He's on . . . no, he can't be, he is . . . he's on the roof. How in God's name did he get there?'

We hurried over, found a small but convenient tree, which Graham said wouldn't hold him. I scrambled up a little way.

'Here I am, darling, Come on, I'll help you down.'

He came over, bent down, then stood up again.

'No, I don't trust you. You'll let me fall.'

We tried to persuade him; no good. Like a frightened horse he would veer away as we got closer.

'It's no good, Graham, he won't come down for me. What about your friend? She's small and we could be behind her.'

Constantine was more against her then me, refusing even to stay that end of the roof. We were getting annoyed with him.

'Who will you come down for, then?' I called up. A faint voice answered:

'Graham wouldn't let me fall.'

'You'll have to try, we'll hold you, Graham. He can't stay up there all night.'

So Graham crawled up the very flexible tree, supported by the two of us. Very slowly Constantine lowered himself on to Graham's shoulders. Together they were very heavy, we had to hold on very tightly to keep steady. With much crackling and snapping of twigs he was down in the garden. We all reeled back with exhaustion. The first thing he said was:

'How did I get up there?'

Every time we passed Graham's house we looked, first at the roof, then at the slender tree.

'I couldn't possibly have gone up that, could I?'

I asked him where he'd thought he was going when he left the garden.

'I thought I was going home,' he replied instantly. 'It was a funny way to choose, wasn't it?'

As long as we lived in Anacapri the riddle was never solved and we were never asked again to Rosaio, although we did meet occasionally in the piazza.

From time to time we had a few friends to lunch, for if they lived in Capri it meant they could get back by bus. Sometimes we met at Mingetti's, where we could eat very cheaply. The kitchen at the house only had a small charcoal brazier, difficult for cooking any but the simplest food.

The Johnsons entertained us a few times, the elegance of their villa contrasting greatly with our rather unpleasant one. Occasionally, if Kenneth or someone asked us to lunch we would go down to Capri, sometimes walking one way. It was a very different existence in Anacapri, perfect for those who came from a city for a few months' peace and relaxation; or if you wanted to get away to write. However, writing was one thing Constantine was quite unable to do at this time, so he became more and more disconsolate and restless. He started to go down to Capri on his own, quite early, spend all day there, catching the last bus back. Gradually the last bus was missed, so an expensive taxi was taken. He would sometimes arrive early in the morning, go to the upper part of the house and stay there until the following evening. Money was getting perilously short again; the Italian publishers of *The Arabian Bird* hadn't paid their advance despite repeated letters. I

asked Mingetti if there was any job I could do for him. When he
saw I was worried he would wave his hand and say:

'Sit down.'

Then a bottle of wine and a plate of food would be put in front
of me, with always a dish of pasta for Flotow.

'Everyboda feela better on a full stomacho.'

I tried not to harass Constantine but our life together had to be
discussed, for I began to dread being hungry again, apart from
worrying about his writing. It was Mingetti who said one day:

'You live in all that house down there?'

I said, no, not really, for we only occasionally bothered to go
upstairs.

'Why notta get good rent for that part? You know people.'

But we didn't know anyone who wasn't already living in either
their own villa or a *pensione*. Yet the very next day when I was
down on Capri in the morning I met the Swedish woman who
lived with Norman's great friend Cecil Woolf. Usually very placid, she looked flustered, and without my asking she volunteered
the reason. The owner of their apartment wanted it for his nephew
who was getting married. Where could they find something
reasonable in summer? Timorously I suggested that we had the
very small apartment in our house. Would she like to look at it?
We took the next bus back and she thought it was just right.
Quiet, and far enough away from the fatal piazza with its teasing
charms to get Cecil working on his book. She would talk to him
and I to Constantine.

It turned out very well, Cecil and his friend being perfect
tenants, quiet yet amusing and interesting to talk to. He told us
Norman had at one time been an accomplished pianist, having
studied years before under Rubinstein; this surprised us, as he had
appeared to dislike some German music, but maybe it was only
Wagner, of whom he said he had had a surfeit when young. I
should have remembered his words at the end of *Alone* as he is
walking in Italy near Ferento, not far from Viterbo, and 'a wistful
intermezzo of Brahms' comes into his head: '*It seemed to spring out
of the hot earth. Such a natural song, elvishly coaxing! Would I ever play
it again? Neither that, nor any other.*'

However, I was not to enjoy Cecil's conversation for very long.
Alone most days, with money getting very low, I suggested I go
to Rome, try to get the advance from the Italian publishers and
look about for work. Acting was about the only profession I had
any real experience in and there were many films being made in
Rome then, not only good Italian ones but British and American,

using blocked sterling and dollars. Rather to my surprise this idea was accepted immediately. Had I had a suspicious mind, I might have realized why. I suppose I was preoccupied with the immediate problems.

Friends gave me telephone numbers to ring in Rome, including that of Gavrelle Verschoyle, who was leaving that week. I arranged for a German girl, who also had very little money, to cook Constantine one meal a day. Mouche was still with the Princess Pignatelli in Naples.

Would I take Flotow with me? Constantine asked, as he might be out a lot.

I took only the minimum amount of money, for I thought of my 'safety valve' I had left with Vernon Jarratt. So early one morning Flotow and I, with a little luggage, took the bus down for the ferry, then on to the bus for Rome. I was glad to have my loving little travelling companion snuggled under the seat.

Chapter Ten

Arriving at the Hotel Inghilterra, I found that the usual hall porter, Cipriani, who knew me, was off duty. A strange man was there who asked for money in advance which I hadn't got. Reinhard was out and Vernon Jarratt didn't answer his phone. After waiting for some time, I left the luggage there, deciding to take Flotow for a walk in the Pincio Gardens. It was late afternoon on the hot July day. We walked up the elegant eighteenth-century Spanish Steps, by the house where Keats died, along the path so many people of note have walked. As we passed the Trinita dei Monti church, I wondered if the nuns were still singing vespers as they had in Mendelssohn's time. I thought of Lucullus, who had lived on these slopes, and from the platform of the Pincio Terrace, once the favourite promenade of Roman aristocracy, looking out over the superb panorama of Rome I thought too of Nathaniel Hawthorne's *Notebooks in France and Italy* which I had read at Aunt Maud's house in Bermuda, what seemed so many worlds ago:

> Here are beautiful sunsets; and here whichever way you turn your eyes, are scenes as well worth gazing at, both in themselves, and for their historical interest, as any that the sun ever rose and set upon.

As I gazed at the view there came over me a love of Rome which would last for ever. I walked through the gardens under the shade of noble trees; there was a small hut-like café, my money just enough for two large sandwiches which I would share with Flotow and a fresh lemon drink. I sat under a tree with the picnic and read my book for some time, feeling more peaceful than I had for ages, although little twinges of apprehension would dart through my mind, then disappear, as I went on reading some Turgenev. It had been a long, emotional day; the food, the quiet and the warmth combined to make me feel sleepy. I dozed, woke up, then putting my bag under my head thought a little sleep would be a good idea. Alas, when I woke it was pitch dark, Flotow lying beside me, fast asleep too. I wandered about a little but was completely lost, so I returned to my tree and slept the night through. My watch had stopped in the morning so I had no idea of the time, but it was gloriously sunny and I felt refreshed and full of energy.

We walked through the leafy groves towards the Spanish Steps.
'*Buon giorno, signorina,*' a voice said.

Turning, I saw a small, undernourished man with a camera, one
of the many who earned a precarious living photographing tourists. He snapped his camera. I explained I had no money. He said
he had none either but was hoping to get enough for breakfast.
Putting into my hand a grubby piece of cardboard with his name
and address on it he walked along with me. He looked even
hungrier than I was; it was nearly eight am. I said to him:

'Stay with me, we'll have breakfast together.'

At the Inghilterra, he waited outside, sometimes taking a
photograph, while I rang Vernon. Yes, he would meet me at the
café in the via Frattina. I was to have breakfast and he would bring
me the money as soon as the banks opened. So my new friend,
Luigi, and I went and had the most delicious *caffe latte* and fried
eggs with crusty, fresh bread. Flotow had a bowl of milk with
some rusks. Even with my limited Italian I was able to follow the
conversation about Luigi's family. My troubles seemed minimal
compared with his. By the time Vernon came we were in a replete
stupor. Luigi said he would leave the photographs at the Inghilterra – no, I was not to pay for them. Vernon said he would
telephone me that evening. I retrieved my luggage, and Cipriani,
full of apologies for the previous evening, gave me a far better
room than I would have taken myself, with a balcony.

I rang the publisher, but he wasn't in. Reinhard seemed pleased
to see me, and when I told him about getting the money he said:

'There's only one way. You must go and sit there, all day if
necessary. That way you will catch him. It's no use telephoning.
I'll come with you tomorrow.'

However, it took about three days of camping in the office,
with sandwiches, before I got the cheque. But I felt an enormous
sense of achievement. What would I have done without Reinhard?
Once again I was reliant on him, that kind, gentle man whom it
was difficult to believe had ever been the enemy. Vernon too
seemed concerned about me; what sort of job did I want? And
why did I go on staying at the Inghilterra which was depleting my
little store of money? Why didn't I come out and stay with him?
He had a house on the via di Porto San Sebastiano. It was a bit far
out, but he could bring me into Rome when he went in the
morning and I could get a bus back.

'I've got a permanent girlfriend,' Vernon went on, 'so I haven't
got designs on you. You'll meet her later.'

It was very rural at Vernon's house, for it was set far back from the road and had a lot of land in front where he grew globe artichokes and sweetcorn. Flotow loved it, for he had plenty of freedom, and he became a good guard dog. To begin with I didn't know how or to whom to go for a job, so I helped Vernon by working in the garden – setting up sort of sunshades for the artichokes against the strong heat. I got tanned and felt very healthy. Enrica, his Italian girl, would come out at weekends. Later they were married and together started the well-known George's restaurant in the via Marché. She was an excellent cook then, subsequently becoming highly qualified professionally. Some days I would go in early with Vernon, wander about Rome exhausting myself with its beauty, then go to Toto's for a bowl of soup, where I was sure to see someone I had met on earlier visits and find out what was going on. Everyone, even the waiter, knew I was looking for work. Peter Tompkins and his wife Jerree became very good friends and were always asking me to meals.

Vernon's house was near the Terme di Caracalla, where they were staging spectacular open-air opera in the ruins. I went along there one evening but couldn't get a seat, so I wandered around the back hoping to see something, or at least hear it. A young mounted carabinieri saw me, offered me a seat on his horse and lifted me up. So that is how I saw *Aida*, elephants and all, sitting on the front of the carabinieri's horse. Vernon thought it was very brave of me.

'I'm not frightened of horses,' I replied.

'I wasn't thinking of the horse, just that you might have been in too close contact with the carabinieri,' he said, laughing.

One evening quite soon after I went to stay there, Vernon came back, his blue eyes dancing with pleasure.

'I think I've got you a part in an English film being made here. We're doing the lighting. Soldati's directing. You've met him, haven't you? I'll give you a letter to him.'

In the old wartime jeep he had been given, Peter drove me out to the studios to see Soldati. But at the last minute I got cold feet. I hadn't acted for years. Would I, could I, do it? He more or less frog-marched me into the studios, almost into Soldati's arms. He looked up, his face not unlike Groucho Marx's, smiled and said:

'You want the part? Go and see Mario right away.'

Bewildered, I asked where Mario was, found him and was told to be there for rehearsals in a week's time. No money was mentioned and I was too scared to ask. It seemed unbelievable. Peter was waiting in the hall, talking earnestly in Italian to an official-looking man. He had found out much more than I had. He told me it was a splendid cast: Margaret Rutherford, Gordon Harker, Jean Kent, Robert Beatty, Walter Crisham, on and on he went. I couldn't take it all in.

'But why me, then?'

Apparently the actress they had engaged had fallen ill.

I felt in my handbag for a cigarette. Vernon's letter was still there, I had forgotten all about it. With excitement I cabled Constantine, as well as telling my friends.

It was a long journey from Vernon's house to rehearsals and often I would be too late for the bus. Later they would be filming at a variety of locations around Rome and I had to be living somewhere central. Without hesitation, Peter and Jerree asked me to stay in their apartment in the via Gregoriana, although they had little room for guests. Jerree too was working all day as a sort of custodian of the Palazzo Antici Mattei, one of the places in Rome where Peter had lived as a child. Peter did all the cooking and was extremely good at it. Jerree was the daughter of an American diplomat, so had travelled widely since early childhood. She spoke several languages and had been a very gifted pianist as a young girl, but unfortunately had had a breakdown in Milan just before a concert. She had never played again. She did, however, do exquisitely fine ink drawings, as delicate as her sensitive and original nature. She had eloped with Peter during the war, in East Africa when he was a war correspondent, but that is their story, not for me to mis-write.

Peter was tall, with a fine-shaped head and a handsome face, yet with a touch of devilry about it. Jerree had told me he was Bernard Shaw's son. Peter neither denied or confirmed this; yet once when I was talking about Ireland, he said quickly:

'I suppose I'm half-Irish.'

Whatever the true story, Shaw certainly felt great affection for Molly Tompkins, wrote her numerous and interesting letters proclaiming it and paid for Peter to be educated at Stowe, in England. Peter found the letters in a trunk hidden in a Roman *palazzo* during the war and published them in 1960. To Peter nothing was impossible; he reminded me of a late eighteenth- or nineteenth-century adventurer or an aristocratic traveller. His quick-thinking mind was at ease with many subjects and some of his abilities were very practical, for instance breaking down one wall of the via Gregoriana flat to make a large room with an archway. He was to a certain extent mysterious, and although I learnt a little from Jerree, nothing but occasional hints emerged from Peter. There were trunks everywhere; Jerree said they were full of diaries and notebooks.

'Get him to show you them,' she urged, but he never did.

Yet when those trunks were opened he wrote his book, *A Spy in Rome*, and I realized that I wasn't wrong in thinking I had been in contact with an extraordinary person.

Peter had arrived (in his early twenties) in Salerno while it was still under German fire. He then recruited and trained democratic Italians to carry out espionage behind German lines. By the time Naples was captured he had a sizeable and enthusiastic, almost personal espionage service. It was from here with a few trusted friends that he made the perilous journey to Rome, where he remained until it was liberated on June 5th. He managed to keep a remarkable diary of these events, which was smuggled in parts every week or so into the Vatican, where it was hidden in the room of an ageing cardinal.

Donald Downes of American Special Intelligence, whom I met in Rome then, wrote in the preface of Peter's book:

> To land on a hostile coast and go into Rome, with no one prearranged to receive or hide him, required of Peter Tompkins a courage beyond that of charging up San Juan Hill or planting the flag atop Iwo Jima. To live for months on end as a fugitive from justice (or injustice) believing, rightly or wrongly, that your own side are betraying you, to hide in the uniform of the political police who are hunting you, to be in terror of meeting your boyhood friends on the street lest they turn you in, to have your agents caught, tortured and killed – that takes something beyond mere courage; it requires fool-hardiness, determination, bravado, and a lusty appetite for adventure and danger, all sharpened by a taste for the cold sensation of fear.

This was 1949, however, and acts of bravery had been soon forgotten. Now we were all more or less penniless, but no two people could have been both kinder to me and more fun. Our problems and our money were often shared. I loved them both deeply for themselves; also because they, as much as anything, gave me back a feeling of warmth and belonging.

Constantine and I exchanged many letters; his took some time to reach me. Telegrams got hopelessly muddled and became incomprehensible, sometimes amusingly so. I still have one, of which part says: 'stop fianning'; neither of us ever knew what he had said originally. He wrote that he had been writing a film script of the July 20th plot to kill Hitler, as well as going to a lot of parties, and he generally seemed to be having not too bad a time.

He was, however, beginning to show signs of jealousy. There was an English newspaper then, called the *Rome Daily American*, which had a gossip column about who was seen where and with whom. I was often reported as having been with a party of people, when perhaps I had been at the next table, or maybe just saying a few words to them in a hotel foyer. This was read avidly by Constantine, who commented that I seemed 'to be spending a lot of time in the company of some very unsavoury people.' As he knew none of them, I wondered how he reached that conclusion. I decided to go down for the weekend before I started filming. I also realized it would be difficult leaving Flotow all day, and maybe Constantine would take him for a few weeks. Full of hope, I sent a telegram saying I was coming.

I arrived in Capri on the afternoon ferry, to be greeted by the day Prince Carracciolo, who of course wanted to know how long I was going to stay, his round inquisitive eyes searching my face. When I told him, he said Constantine wasn't there but in Positano, as Mimi had been ill. I wondered if it was true; if so I had wasted a day. I saw a friend who confirmed it.

When I arrived in Positano about lunchtime the next day, everyone was in festive mood; Mimi had completely recovered, Constantine was sparkling and delighted to see me (no telegram had arrived), and there was a very jolly pre-luncheon drinks party going on at the Buca. Some of the Sadler's Wells Ballet Company were there: Robert Helpman, Margot Fonteyn, Freddy Ashton and Brian Shaw, all bubbling and delightful. Their conversation and company made it easy to forget things, which I did for the rest of the day. That night Robert Helpman and Margot Fonteyn did a superb dance on the beach, by the light of a full and sparkling moon. Then, the water shimmering and enticing, everyone went swimming without their clothes. Our laughter must have been heard all over Positano, for when we came out, there was a semi-circle of armed carabiniere, waiting to make arrests. Unfortunately our clothes were behind them so there was no chance of getting to them. I felt very defenceless trying to argue with no clothes on, and trying not to laugh, for all this time Bobby Helpman was making very funny quips. I was glad Flotow was with me, otherwise he would undoubtedly have been growling at them, and he wasn't popular in Positano anyway. However, help was at hand, as they used to say in early films, once the Mayor and the tourist chief arrived and bailed us all out. Nothing more was heard of the incident.

As I had to get back for rehearsals, there was only time for a hurried conversation with Constantine before I climbed all those steps for the bus back to Sorrento, and then Rome. He would keep Flotow for a couple of weeks before bringing him up to Rome. Mouche apparently was a little better but still not well.

Rehearsing, rehearsing, rehearsing. My small part was with Margaret Rutherford, Gordon Harker and Robert Beatty, and I found it very enlightening to be working with such fine professional actors. To begin with I felt awkward, for they had been filming for several weeks; it was like being the new girl at school. Soldati put me at my ease, as did the Italian work crew. In a day or two I was one of them. There was, however, a problem. The actress originally engaged for my part was considerably shorter than me, and the budget didn't run to more clothes being made. It was evening dress. Surely I had one I liked particularly? The trouble was I hadn't. We'd been so poor in Bermuda that only the minimum wardrobe was possible, and formal evening dress never played any part in our entertaining. Esther Arthur, a friend of Sybille Bedford, said she had a trunkful of evening clothes; I must come to their rooms at the Inghilterra and select one. Sybille was making grimaces at me, but I didn't know why and so a time was fixed.

Yes, certainly Esther did have several trunkfuls of evening clothes, but she was about six feet tall – 'they can be taken up' – and all the clothes were Chanel models of the early 1920s. Nevertheless I had to try them on. It was very comical, for I looked like something out of a Twenties magazine, except all the dresses were looped about my feet. Sybille and I got the giggles, but Esther remained unperturbed, picking out one, in violent yellow and mauve with a waist around my hips, as being particularly suitable. She remained adamant I must wear it. I took it, hoping to think of some excuse for never appearing in it, except as a fancy dress. I returned it later, saying the director thought it too similar to the leading actress's dress. I hoped she would never see the film, and I'm sure she didn't. The problem was solved very unexpectedly by some friends we had met in New York, a sculptor called Harold Ambellan and his wife, Elizabeth, turning up. She lent me a very suitable dress, which I promised to send back but couldn't as it turned out.

It was the happiest production I have ever worked on; everybody seemed to be en fête . Soldati was a tireless director, kind but very certain of what he wanted. He lived in the via Gregoriana too, so we became friends. At one point in the script of the film, a large party was given; extras were wanted, so I immediately went to see Mario the production manager and said I could find several very suitable people. As the film was British they were looking for non-Italian actors. He was therefore delighted when I turned up with the distinguished trio of Peter, Jerree and a friend called Richard Brookbank. By this time we were filming in a large house just outside the city; it was a night party scene so we worked all night from six pm on to eight o'clock in the morning. Peter produced a small bottle of spirits which, judiciously poured into the coloured water, kept our morale up. It was all great fun, acting and dancing all night for about four days. One mystery for me was never solved: how Peter had lived in Rome all those months, even in the enemy's ranks without being discovered – for he was, without any doubt, the worst actor I have ever seen. A very small scene had to be rehearsed and shot endless times. He would be the first to admit it. Then Jerree, too, had to have an evening dress, but that was easy. Peter disappeared to one of his resistance friends, now an *haute couturier*, and arrived with a most beautiful filmy model dress. Unfortunately it was almost exactly the same as Jean Kent, the star, was wearing, so of necessity all Jerree's scenes were very distanced.

After filming ended, Peter and Jerree gave a real party for our friends in the cast. All those people remain in my memory very affectionately. Coming back through the busy, sunny streets to the via Gregoriana at about eight-thirty in the morning, having a large breakfast, then closing the shutters against both the sun and Roman street noises, sleeping until about three-thirty, was the pattern of those lovely working nights and days. When the film was finished, other offers came in, some of which I accepted. Through Vernon I met many of the well-known Italian directors, such as Alberto Lattuada, who made *Il Molino del Po*; Vittoria de Sica, director of *Ladro di Bicicletta* (*The Bicycle Thief*) and *Sciuscia*, the superb film about the shoeshine boys.

I played a small part in an Italian film, a comedy with Mischa Auer, which to my relief I found would be dubbed afterwards by someone else, so my accent didn't matter. I did a fair amount of dubbing, myself – Italian films into English. Here I found that if you were a pretty girl you got paid more than a plain one, or a man. I mentioned this to Peter, who immediately started to organize a dubber's union.

I had also been lent a large apartment in the via di San 'Costanza off the long via Nomentana. The apartment belonged to a girl in the British Council who was going back to England for a month and wanted someone reliable to look after her cat, Figaro. This

came about through Derek Verschoyle, Gavrelle's husband, who
was at the British Embassy. I had been to several dinners at their
house. Derek was in fact an Irishman from County Sligo, which is
no doubt why we got on so well together. He was very mondaine
and charming, with an unusual face of regular features, a very
attractive mouth and smile. His manners were impeccable, putting people at ease immediately. He talked in a slightly muffled
voice on a variety of subjects – sometimes, as I was to find out
later, Irish-fashion; that is, he tended to please rather than be
factually correct. His walk was quick, but with a gliding motion;
one almost felt he could disappear at will. His manner too was
sometimes guarded, to cause one to think his life held many
secrets, but this was undoubtedly part of his attraction to women.
I had known several Irishmen of similar secretive attitude, so I was
never in any danger of falling under his spell, although I was
extremely fond of him.

Derek was chivalrous towards me at that time, doing what he
could to help. He would call from time to time, always with some
wine or a bottle of Saccone and Speed gin, the old firm of wine
and spirit merchants that usually supplied embassies. We would
talk about Ireland, books and many other things, as if we had been
lifelong friends. I had no work at that time so I spent my day
telephoning likely people, going into the city to the Inghilterra, or
to Toto's to see what was going on.

One day Derek said in his muffled voice, scarcely opening his
lips, that he might have a job for me. I was to meet a man at a café
one evening, carrying a walking stick. Because of the stick he
would know me. After that I would report to Derek all that took
place when he called at the end of the week. I duly did this, feeling
a little stupid sitting at the café for several hours alone, for nobody
ever arrived. However, Derek seemed quite satisfied, nodding
knowledgeably, and paid me quite handsomely for the service.
Several other little missions were entrusted to me, but never once
did I ever make contact with anyone. I felt like a spy without a
cause. Each time I got paid very well, so I didn't complain. In
retrospect, I think he had made the whole idea up, and it was just a
way of helping me out without embarrassing me. I rather enjoyed
it and will now never know the truth of the matter.

I had a number of other jobs at this time, so with my new-found
wealth I gave dinner parties in my large apartment for the friends
who had helped me, such as Vernon and Reinhard, also Bendi
Esterhazy. Bendi lived in a *pensione* somewhere in Rome on a very
small allowance, difficult to manage on. He had had a hard time

since leaving Hungary. He had been in prison there and he told me that what really kept him going was the amazing fortitude of the elderly, aristocratic ladies who were in prison with him. He had never been trained for earning his living, so his life was hard. Yet he showed amazing resilience, never complaining about his present life, often imparting a wonderful middle-European gaiety to the evening. He was very dark with a slightly pointed nose, large eyes with a quizzical expression, and wavy black hair which seemed to grow almost straight up from his head, having to be tamed to make it lie flat. He always walked very quickly and his voice was inclined to be high, as though coming from the top of his throat rather than his chest. His well-shaped hands were used expressively. As we walked around my apartment with its many bedrooms, Bendi exclaimed that we could all live there comfortably. Impulsively I said:

'Why don't you stay for a few days, Bendi?'

He readily agreed, as he was weary of his small, cheap room. The days lengthened to weeks, but I have seldom ever been so well looked after by anyone. The place was kept immaculately, accounts made of what was spent on food, my appointments arranged in perfect order. He was also interesting to talk to, for he told me of his early childhood, with an English nanny – all European aristocratic families had them – which explained why his English was so good. He'd had early attachments to young women, but none for many years. That was as far as he would go.

One day I was summoned to Scalera Studios. Bendi was as thrilled as I was, pressing my clothes and being very emphatic as to what I should wear. For if I ever disagreed or did something unusual, which seemed very often, he would raise his thick eyebrows and say:

'Theodora, I find you very extraordinary.'

One film I was in was called *La Strada Buio* (*The Dark Street*); I never found out the entire plot, but there were a lot of scenes with hands going into medicine cupboards, and taking out of bottles. One leading part was played by Eduardo Ciannelli, an Italo-American actor who usually played 'baddies' in Hollywood, so I assumed the hands were up to no good. I didn't have much of a part; there was nothing like the cohesion and pleasure of working with Soldati, although Sidney Salkow the director was a pleasant if uninspiring man.

The English actress Binnie Barnes (her husband was producing) was in the cast; we got on very well together, for I think she was a bit homesick for England and English voices, as she asked if I

would like to be her stand-in, with the promise of a part later on. I
accepted. As a young woman I had seen her in various stage plays,
also in Korda's *Private Life of Henry VIII*, and I had quite admired
her forthright style of acting. I didn't know many women in
Rome, and Binnie seemed a congenial person. She and I became
quite friendly and often she took me to their apartment for tea, or
drinks when she wasn't working.

The late August weather was stifling hot. When filming, we had
to sit with moistened chamois leather around our necks and
sometimes on our foreheads to stop the make-up running. Binnie
had the first fixative aerosol hair spray from America, which she
sprayed over her hair to keep it in shape, and she lent me some
too. It seemed very ingenious then. We all suffered tremendously
from the heat, none more so than Bendi who was forever dabbing
his forehead with a spotless white handkerchief. I told him about
the chamois leather.

'But, Theodora, I suffer from the Esterhazy complaint, heat
about the head, we all have it. Some years ago my uncle, the
cardinal, was in conclave to elect a new pope. He had it so badly
his handkerchief soon became very wet. So he opened the window, to shake it out to dry.' He dabbed away more furiously as if
even the memory made him hotter. 'People watching in the piazza
saw something white, immediately jumping to the conclusion it
was the puff of white smoke.' He smiled wistfully. 'It was very
embarrassing for my uncle.'

When I came home early one day he was coming out of the
bathroom after a shower wearing my black velvet dressing gown,
his hair standing on end, the long bell sleeves trailing at his side. I
collapsed with laughter, saying:

'Bendi, you look just like the Widow Twankey!'

'And what, Theodora, is the Widow Twankey?' He glared at
me.

One of these days when you have nothing better to do, try
explaining the Widow Twankey to an Hungarian count.

'You see, it's a character in English pantomime, you know like
commedia del arte. She's a washerwoman, always played by a
leading male comedian, the principal boy's part is played by a girl.
The Widow Twankey's son is . . .'

I couldn't go further; his expression ranged between annoyance
and mystification. Sweeping my negligée around him, he said:

'Really, Theodora, I find you very extraordinary.'

The best thing about the film was that they shot it on location
all over Rome, both inside buildings and out of doors, so I was

able to really savour Rome as never before. They even filmed at Castelgandolfo, the pope's summer residence, one night.

Bendi was invaluable; he knew Rome far better than I did, so he always directed me the best way to get to the locations, often coming to the bus or train with me when they didn't send a car. Food would be ready for me when I returned, and if I had a late morning call, he might have asked a few friends for a simple meal. However, certain friends were not approved of and were *never* asked. He was very correct most of the time and expected me to behave accordingly.

Films and filming were the rage in Rome in those days. Even Bendi was delighted when I suggested to him he become an extra (in a rather grand scene), and Sidney Salkow, who had Hungarian connections, seemed thrilled at having a Count Esterhazy on the set. Most of the extras were just called *generica,* and they were led about together, but with Bendi it was a case of, 'Count Esterhazy, would you please come this way?'

Constantine wrote frequently. He had finished the film script and wanted to come up to Rome. Having the large apartment made it simple, so we made arrangements. Bendi took the whole matter in hand at once.

'Should I stay here, or leave, do you think? Will he be jealous?'

I had told Constantine of Bendi's stay with me and of his great help. No, he wasn't at all jealous; he had made enquiries about Bendi, everything pointing to the fact that we were not, and never would be, having an affair.

'There's no need to strip my bed, Bendi, it was only changed two days ago.'

'Theodora, of course it must be changed. What are you thinking of? I will also make up the bed in the other small room.'

'Whatever for? We always share the same bed.' I replied.

'Theodora, I find you extraordinary; of course Constantine must have a dressing room!'

It would have been much better if Constantine had waited a week until I had finished filming, for my hours were irregular, but I didn't want to appear to be putting him off. Fortunately he arrived on a free evening, but with Flotow. I had forgotten to mention the cat. It was all right for a few hours or a night, as there were so many rooms, but not for a week, for Flotow had never been close to a cat and would surely want to investigate the frightened Figaro. The Tompkinses said they would take him, providing one of us exercised him.

In other ways the week was a disaster: my part came up, which meant learning lines, as well as rehearsing, so Constantine was left alone most of the day. He apparently went in to get Flotow, then spent most of the day in bars with Gerry Osborne, who also had nothing much to do. By the time I had finished working, sometimes very late, he was quarrelsome with drink. Being tired, I was not always tactful when we met. The climax was one night when Rome had had one of its violent thunderstorms, always guaranteed to make me hyperexcited and rather headachy. We were going up the Spanish Steps with the Tompkins, back to the via Gregoriana, Constantine berating me for leaving him alone all day. To avoid answering, I hurried a little ahead, not easy on those steps; he leant forward, pulled me back by the dress, which ripped right down the back. I had hurried from the set, not changing, so it was a serious problem for me, as for continuity I had to wear the same clothes throughout the filming. Jerree, fearing I would be pulled backwards, and be hurt, quickly whipped round and hit Constantine sharply over the head with her umbrella to make him let go of me. Nobody said a word. He wasn't hurt, but sobered, and he stopped the verbal assault. Jerree also sat up until nearly three o'clock mending the dress, painstakingly, so I could wear it that day. We were filming at the Teatro Argentina then, and wearing a jacket over the top it passed unnoticed. But that was the reason Elizabeth Ambellan never received back her dress.

Two days later, about ten at night, one of the grips came to me and said there was a man in the foyer who was demanding to see me. I hurried out after the scene ended. As I rounded the corner I saw Constantine arguing with the producer; never a good idea, particularly not for an unasked visitor. I was deadly tired, and somehow feeling I should support him, I too got into the argument in a very hot-headed fashion. It was a very bad mistake on my part. There was never another call from that company. I wrote to Binnie Barnes apologizing but there was no answer. Scalera Studios became wary of engaging me, as they said I had 'a difficult husband'.

It was very depressing on every count; we were both dejected. But for Bendi giving us both moral and practical support, I think I too, would have been inclined to drink rather too much. These violent scenes were occurring frequently, but only when Constantine had been drinking. They exhausted both of us, but for me they were tinged not with anger but with sorrow. I could feel the helplessness of his rage which particularly thundered against anyone or anything that gave me work and money, and thus made him to a certain extent reliant on me. I was in the impossible position of starving with him or trying to make my own way. Many times I wavered but my sense of survival proved too strong. Ultimately, I felt, he must find the strength of will to moderate his drinking and write. I had known several painters and writers in Paris as a girl and knew that in order to survive they had had to be single-minded in purpose. He knew I loved him with the same certainty that I knew he loved me.

I would have gone back to Anacapri with Constantine for a few days, but I had a dubbing session and a photographic job coming up. After that nothing, and the month's stay at the apartment was coming to an end.

CHAPTER ELEVEN

It was Bendi who solved the problem of where I was to live. A young friend of his, wanting, I think, to escape the close proximity of his stern mother, decided to rent out his Rome apartment. 'Apartment' is rather a grand word for the place in the Piazza di Spagna. It was on the roof of a tall building, about five storeys up, at the end of a large terrace, the front of which looked over the American Express, Keats' house and the Spanish Steps, and had a view of the Trinita dei Monti; a stone and brick bungalow with a flat roof (on which Rossellini had set the opening shots of his film *An Open City*), with pottery vases, pretty creeping and climbing plants around it, and a vine trained over a section as a shelter from the sun. There was a large L-shaped room with two divans, a bookcase separating a dining area, a pleasant little fireplace, a small hall with cupboards, kitchen and bathroom. It was most agreeable and cosy. French windows led out to the flower-decked terrace, which also had a table and chairs. The Inghilterra and Toto's were just round the corner, the Tompkins just up the steps. I took to it at once.

Constantine worried me, especially as he had written that Mouche had been sent back from the old Princess Pignatelli's, so I wondered how he could cope with her. I decided to go for a week to Anacapri. As I was leaving, my agent rang to say Pabst, the German film director, was in Rome, contemplating making a film of Homer's *Odyssey*, with Greta Garbo playing Circe. He had suggested to Pabst that I be tested to play Penelope, therefore I must return at once if I was called. It was an exciting project which helped to take my mind off more pressing problems.

The house was sad – Mouche really not much better, although delighted to see me; Constantine jittery, alternately depressed and elated. He had heard nothing from any of the people he had sent the July 20th filmscript to, was writing very little, just occasionally rewriting parts of the novel *Cousin Emily*. His money had mostly been spent. But for Mingetti feeding him from time to time I don't think he would have been eating at all. I had very little money to spare but he said he had written to his mother in New York; he was sure she would send something. When he heard about my little place in the Piazza di Spagna he became determined

my youth, riding at Annesgrove, County Clare

stantine's mother Georgette in Bermuda, 1946

By the tree at Tranquillity House

With the two dogs, Christmas 1947

Throck and Constantine on Somerset Beach

aysbank Cottage viewed from the sea

er Tom and Constantine in 1947 at Graysbank

Constantine writing at Graysbank

Casa Solatia, Capri, 19

Baron Schack in his old uniform on the Kaiser's birthday

Constantine and Norman Douglas in 1948 at Giorgio's, Capri

In rehearsal for *Her Favourite Husband,* 1949,
with Margaret Rutherford and Gordon Harker

Gerald Kersh in the Hotel Inghilterra, 1949

With Constantine and Flotow on the terrace of my apartment in the Piazza di Spagna, 1950

Sacomb's Ash, 1950

Giles Playfair and Constantine on board MV *Grebe* on the way to Bordeaux in April 1953

Constantine, Diana Graves and Minka in the garden at Sacomb's Ash, 1954

Mimi three months before her death in London
1956

On a lonely walk with Minka and the cat
along the 'engine path' in Allen's Green,
Hertfordshire, 1958

Arland Ussher in Wicklow, 1958

George Morrison in his cutting room in Dublin,
1959

to pay all the bills here, give up 'this horrible villa' and join me. I made it very clear that, if he did come up, he must work regularly, also respect my working hours, no matter how trivial he thought the work was. I was surprised, as he didn't really like Rome, saying it was too noisy; somehow I felt there were other reasons for leaving Capri, that he was withholding something. We had always been very close to each other, sensitive of each other's emotions. We both agreed that he must, from now on, drink only wine or beer and not too much of either.

'But you know, darling, I want to work. If only something would be accepted to give me a bit of encouragement.'

The Iron Hoop had come out in New York, and he showed me some very good notices, one particularly by the Irish writer James Stern in the *Saturday Review*.

'Didn't you get the publication advance money?' I asked.

Yes he had, but that too had been spent. There was a little money to come from Cassell but that was all. We also came to the reluctant conclusion that Mouche wasn't going to get any better. Since there was no vet on Capri, it meant taking her back to the best vet in Naples. The sadness at parting with my old friend from the war years was great, but I saw the cruelty and futility of keeping her alive. While down in Capri we had dinner with friends who introduced us to Admiral Manfredi of the Italian Navy, who gallantly said he was driving to Rome in two days' time and would be happy to have me as his passenger. My agent had said I was wanted back there shortly.

At Kenneth McPherson's we met Harold Acton, the aesthete and writer, who lived with his many beautiful treasures in Florence. He had been much influenced by Norman Douglas in his younger days, and was in good form that evening, reminiscing about things Norman had said to him in the past. One subject was D. H. Lawrence, and how Norman had considered that Lawrence was a sexual adolescent who never recovered from the shock of puberty, never outgrew it, remaining a frustrated schoolboy, who persuaded himself, and many others, that he was a pioneering genius in a *terra incognito*. Norman, however, always maintained to me that Lawrence was a superb travel writer; he particularly admired *Etruscan Places*. Harold Acton not only invited me to Florence but also gave me a letter to his friend Baron Paolo Langheim in Rome.

Everything about Mouche's last journey was distressing, from carrying her to the bus, the ferry, and the journey with Manfredi to the vet. Both Con and I were in tears, but Admiral Manfredi was very helpful, interviewing the vet for us as we sat in the crowded waiting room, then seeing that everything was carried out properly. Afterwards we went to the Hotel Excelsior for coffee and a drink, before starting on the long drive to Rome. In the bar, Lucky Luciano (the American gangster who had returned home after he was freed from prison in America) sat in his usual corner, alone. Then we heard our names called, turned round to see Vladimir and Scarlet Ivanovič, our friends from Bermuda who had looked after Flotow during the hurricane. They were on a tour of Italy, so I was pleased to be able to leave Constantine in such congenial company.

The Piazza di Spagna apartment was perfect for me; also for Flotow, as it had the terrace. It was just right, not unlike Grays-bank Cottage in charm, central for my friends as well as being near some of the most beautiful places and parks in Rome. If only I could make enough money to live there without too much worry. Physically I was exhausted after the last weeks; so much so, my tired body seemed relaxed. Now I had to go through the slow process of unwinding while the brain still worked double time. Being alone for a little while helped me to do this, sitting on the terrace in the lazy September sun. Georgette, Con-stantine's mother, in her generous fashion sent me a hundred dollars, which meant I had another month's rent in hand and a certain respite from worry. One weekend Peter drove Jerree, Reynolds Packard (always known as Pack) and me in the jeep to the island of Guilia, some miles north of Rome, once the watering-place of rich Romans until malaria made it unsuitable.

'Let's get away from tourists,' Peter had said. 'I know a very remote island.'

It did seem remote – a dark, forbidding mountain in the centre, with what seemed a collection of houses on the top. There was a primitive *albergo* near to where the ferry got in, where we booked large bare rooms furnished with enormous country-style wooden beds, a chair and a washbasin. We had certainly got away from the tourists, I thought. Old black ovens stoked with wood cooked home-made bread; and there was always a pot of coarse salt on the table to eat with it. Vast saucepans bubbled with home-made pasta, and fishermen and boys would come into the kitchen with small fish of the kind Norman Douglas used to call 'floating pincushions, duckums'. We wandered along the rocky shore, occasionally finding little sandy bays, and towards the end of the path a large hall adver-tising a dance on Saturday night. There was also a small, simple *trattoria* we decided to try later. We gazed up at the seemingly unscalable mountain.

'I wonder how you get up there?' I asked. 'They must need food. How would they get it?'

'Probably, from the other side,' Peter replied. 'We could no doubt go round by boat.'

But neither Jerree nor Pack felt like an expedition, so Peter and I wandered off behind the sea-front habitation. It was very over-grown once we had left the few houses, but a path winding up the mountain was just visible. Finally we came to some crumbling steps up which we started.

'They have been here since Roman times, I would think,' said Peter. 'I hope they don't get any worse.'

They did get much worse before we reached the top. Many times I thought I couldn't make it, but Peter would then hold my hand and pull me up. I didn't dare think about the return. Once there, the atmosphere was extraordinary. There was quite a large town with shops, larger houses, quite good roads, even a few vans or rickety motorcars. However, it wasn't like an Italian village, where everyone nodded, smiled or said '*Giorno*'; the inhabitants left their shops and stared at us without a word.

'Go and talk to them, Peter. I don't like being stared at like thus. It's almost hostile.'

He went over and with his usual fluent Italian talked to one of them, but I saw the man just shrug a reply.

'I don't like it either,' he said. 'They're obviously not anxious to have visitors. I wonder why. Come on, let's go back.'

It was one of the worst journeys I have ever made. The crumbling steps crumbled even more as we went down. It would soon be dark, which wasn't the gradual process it is in colder countries. My sandals were far from good walking gear. At one point I decided I'd be better without them.

'You can't go down in bare feet. The sharp edges will cut into you.'

'My soles are quite hard after running over rocks in Bermuda. I think I'd be better off, for I'm frightened of turning my ankle in these sandals.'

'No. Here, put my socks on over the sandals, they'll give you some protection.'

So that is how, some hours later, we arrived back at the *albergo*, to find no Jerree and no Pack. We wandered along, it was now quite dark, to find them comfortably seated outside the *trattoria* drinking wine. Pack laughed his infectious fat person's laugh;

Jerree glared, her dark eyes brooding. I knew at once what had happened, for had I not known so many heart-clawing tentacles of jealousy in those months with Constantine in Capri? The still, hot nights lying almost rigid, with torturing thoughts, actual pain around the area of the heart like a cold hand squeezing it hard; listening, holding one's breath, waiting for the sound of footsteps or the steady throb of a motorcar engine; then an exhausted sleep, the bedclothes knotted like string underneath – no, never would I want to be the cause of anyone feeling like that. Not that there was the slightest reason. Peter told them of our adventures; I said nothing for there was nothing to say. He started to dress the salad.

'Don't put too much salt on mine, Peter, please.'

Quickly, like a chameleon's tongue darting out, Jerree picked up the salt cellar and poured a pyramid of salt over the top. I burst out laughing.

'Oh, Jerree, how wonderful! There have been so many times when I wanted to do just that.'

It broke the tension; we all felt better after that contretemps. It was far better than any wordy recrimination.

'I'm going to that dance,' Pack stated firmly. 'Just as soon as we've eaten. Coming, anyone?'

It's a mystery how any film ever gets made with all the variables: not only the cast, but an army of technicians, then perhaps the biggest hazard, finding all the money. The director, his head full of ideas, must each time be like a conductor with an entirely new orchestra and a new sponsor. However, music can be played, whereas a film often starts in somebody's head, the script having no significance on its own. Pabst's idea for *Ulysses* seemed to me wonderful. How sublime Garbo would be as Circe; could I sustain Penelope against such magnetism? It was better not to think about it, but that was difficult too.

I telephoned Baron Langheim, who appeared pleased I had called, asking me for dinner in two days' time. His house was near the Villa Doria Pamphili, a part of Rome I didn't know, but a sleek, long, low car was sent to bring me there. Paolo Langheim greeted me, a fairly tall, suave man, with a smooth skin, almost like a child's, bright enquiring eyes behind his spectacles, and brown hair receding on a domed head. He walked silently through a sumptuously furnished hall bringing me to the *salone*. It was with the greatest difficulty I kept my eyes from looking around the room, which had many beautiful sculptures and paintings. It was a loved and comfortable room with luxurious sofas, chairs and a *chaise-longue* which was so beautiful I involuntarily stroked it with my hand.

'You like beautiful furniture, I see.'

I withdrew my hand quickly.

'There is something upstairs I think you would appreciate,' he purred, 'if you like to accompany me?'

It was a bedroom of unbelievable opulence, the magnificent bed taking pride of place, glowing in gold and clear azure blue colours to take my breath away.

'It was the bed of Pauline Buonaparte . . .' He lingered over the words. 'A fitting monument for a beautiful woman, is it not? But, come, I must see if my other guests are ready. It is a small, very private dinner, as you will see.'

I followed, not knowing what to expect, still enfolded in a maze of colour and richness. It was to contrast sharply with the clothes of the woman sitting on the sofa, who was dressed in a dark grey suit with a large-brimmed hat, her head turned away. Then she moved to smile a greeting: I almost gasped out loud, for it was Greta Garbo. She took off the hat, shaking out her hair, then smiled up at us. It was breathtaking to see such cool calm eyes above perfect features. A very blond young man, like an Adonis, came into the room and leant on the back of the sofa. He was introduced as Lord Montague. I thought as I looked at them both how right they were for the surroundings. Each in their way magnificent jewels in a superb setting. Garbo ate very little, using her large spatula-topped fingers elegantly. I found no difficulty in talking to her and was longing to ask her about the Pabst film but couldn't think how to phrase it. We talked about Rome, remarking our surprise that there were no theatres open in a city where so much drama had been enacted.

'They are all actors here,' she said in her inimitable voice. 'I've never seen such beautiful gestures.'

I enquired how long she was staying, thinking that might lead to my finding out more, but alas she was leaving in two days' time.

'For good?' I enquired; maybe she would be returning?

'Alas, no.' I couldn't help thinking it didn't augur well for the film.

The time went all too quickly; I could have spent hours just looking at her. Garbo was staying at the Hassler Hotel at the top of the Spanish Steps, so we went in the same car. It had been a fascinating evening for me even if it was tinged with apprehension.

Instead of hanging around Rome doing odd dubbing sessions, I decided I would go down for a few days to Mimi in Positano, where it was much cheaper, and maybe Constantine would join me there. I didn't want to go to Anacapri, for if I was wanted it always meant at least a day's extra delay getting the ferry to Naples.

Arriving in Positano to Mimi's rooms in the early afternoon I saw only Assunta, the large motherly woman who used to get the very odd stove working, make huge pots of soup and tidy up. The signora, her brother and the other signora had gone to Amalfi for the day, she told me, offering to make some coffee.

I went upstairs with my bag to find the room Constantine and I usually had littered with woman's clothes and make-up, as well as various things of his I recognized. Envelopes were scattered here and there so it was easy to see with whom he was sharing the room.

I felt quite numb, particularly so as that morning I had had a letter from him assuring me of his love, also saying he was coming to Rome shortly. Supposing they all came back and found me here? In panic I picked up my bag, muttered to Assunta I was sorry to have missed them, then made my way up to a small hotel near the bus-stop. The bus had just left but there was one more in a few hours.

I had seldom felt so dejected, almost hiding lest they should return by bus and see me there. What was the point of my trying to earn money for us to be together again? I kept Flotow closely by my side so he wouldn't give away my presence. I ached to be comforted.

The journey back seemed interminable; I had no appetite, and no doubt drank too much. The thought of being alone terrified me so much that I was alternately stifling hot, then cold. From the station I made a telephone call; it was late at night but I was welcomed. I did not spend the night alone; the anxieties and humiliations were washed away for the time being, in a warm embracing sexual ocean.

CHAPTER TWELVE

It was a bleak period made tolerable by my friends. There was no news about Pabst and in my bones I knew there wouldn't be. Meeting Garbo had been a dream; reality was a future of little hope. The Tompkins, too, had financial troubles, yet their apartment was a haven. It reminded me of Bermuda, when so many people came to our house. Martha Gelhorn, Hemingway's wife, was sometimes there; Janet Flanner of the *New Yorker* called, as well as many other congenial visitors from all over. There was wine and often one of Peter's prodigious, inventive pasta dishes, a big salad and fruit. To add to everything they had heard rumours they might have to move, but somehow one never doubted Peter's ability to find something else.

Constantine wrote several letters to me, apparently unaware I had visited Positano. He was unable to settle down to writing any kind of book and had no good news of the film script. His letters touched me, for I knew that although he had a fiercely possessive love for me, his first love was writing. Had I done any good in coming to Rome, apart from being able to support myself and occasionally help him out? Mimi sent a telegram that she was coming to Rome and would I meet her at the Inghilterra? As I sat alone in the tiny bar waiting for her I turned over these questions in my mind. Tennessee Williams came in and I thought, as I had when I met him briefly before, what very tortured eyes he had, set in the determined face of a businessman. He had a curiously set facial expression, yet the eyes betrayed the agonies of a different person. He put his coffee on the small table next to mine and nodded. We sat in silence for some minutes, then abruptly he said:

'Why don't you go home, honey?'

'Do I look as gloomy as that?' I replied quickly.

Then I thought, home – where was home? I couldn't go back to my mother at almost thirty years old, or to Ireland. Both were unthinkable. My home was with Constantine, no matter what. I had been behaving like a tragedy queen about very little. Of course if I left him alone he was bound to go to bed with another woman. What on earth was I making all the fuss about? It happened all the time: look at my father, whom I adored. He did cause a certain furore from time to time but it settled down eventually. It was the shock of seeing that squalid little room with the unmade, rumpled bed that had so disturbed me, turned my thoughts inwards so they focused entirely on myself. Georgette's words came back:

'Imagine me with a FitzGibbon husband and four FitzGibbon children!'

Yes, indeed, she must have known several similar situations. I smiled across the table.

'Maybe you've got a good idea,' I said.

Forthwith I wrote to Constantine asking him to come up, to leave Capri altogether, if he thought it was a good idea. The bar was filling up; Carl Perutz, a young American photographer who worked in Paris, came in, possibly to photograph Tennessee Williams. Behind him was a man of most impressive mien, who had a young dark girl by his side. He was in his late forties, of sturdy build, just above average height, with strong almost Middle Eastern features, black hair, a small, trimmed black beard, and the most compelling dark brown eyes, which seemed to flash sparks. His voice was surprisingly very English, deep-throated, almost booming yet muted. Everyone looked up, for he was impossible to ignore. Carl seemed to know him and introduced me. He was an English writer called Gerald Kersh, with his stepdaughter Ann.

Today when people meet someone they have seen on television they feel they know them. In pre-television days, if you had read an author's book, you too assumed that knowledge. As a girl I had greatly enjoyed his book *The Night and the City* about London with its Soho prostitutes and their pimps – what used to be called the 'seamy side' of London. Kersh wrote about it with great understanding, tenderness and humour. They were sad human beings to be looked after not hounded. The book stayed in my memory long after it had been confiscated by a pertinacious schoolteacher. To me, Kersh looked just as the creator of such books ought to be, for one could believe that, behind the extraordinary face with the penetrating eyes, an amazing imagination explored many depths.

Despite his looks, Kersh's manner was extremely English, rather guarded and polite. He asked Carl and me to lunch with them, saying he was tired of veal; where could they get a good hearty beef dish? I mentioned Carlo's in Trastevere, where writers like Moravia and Carlo Levi often went, famous for its Roman speciality of *coda di bue alla vaccinara* – oxtail simmered in wine. He almost jumped from the chair.

'My God, let's go. It's my favourite meal.'

I explained about Mimi, but he said couldn't we leave a message asking her to follow? She was just arriving as I went into the hall, and she looked somewhat hungover. No, she must have a drink, then she had to go and see Pibe Packard who was ill at the Anglo-American Clinic. I told Kersh to go on and start eating; I would try to follow, but it seemed unlikely. Mimi swallowed several brandies one after the other but repeatedly refused lunch, saying she had had something on the train, which I doubted. Would I come and see Pibe with her later on? Apropos of nothing, she said:

'Con should have come up with me. Have you heard from him?'

I said I had just written asking him to join me.

'He's in a bad way, drinking far too much, you know.'

I nodded and thought it must be too much if Mimi said so. She seemed to be unaware I had visited Positano. Assunta must have been very discreet, or more probably simply said a signora called, for she could never pronounce foreign names.

Constantine arrived unannounced, about three days later, in his most charming mood. He repeatedly said how glad he was to be there, particularly to see me again; he had missed me more than he ever thought possible. He'd borrowed money from Vladimir, paid all his debts and 'was heartily glad to be off that confounded island'. Looking around, he said:

'What a nice place you've got.' Then: 'Is Mimi still in Rome? She's drinking far too much. You don't know the trouble I've had with her.'

I nodded thoughtfully, waiting tactfully to approach him with an idea I had. We talked about his work and how we were going to live. I told him I had only a small reserve left until I got more work of some kind. He had next to nothing apparently, but thought he could soon finish the novel if he was in a tranquil atmosphere. I asked him who was still on Capri. He mentioned several friends, telling amusing stories about them. Then he said:

'A lot of Americans too. I can't think where they all get enough money to live on. Some are quite interesting, ex GIs mostly.'

This gave me my opportunity to broach the topic I was bursting to put forward.

'If they're ex GIs I know what they live on,' I replied quickly. 'They're all here on the GI Bill of Rights studying something or other. Why don't you get on it? It would give you a small regular income to write on.'

He said nothing for a few minutes, then:

'What on earth would I study that wouldn't take all my time?'

'Your Italian's still very limited but you have the groundwork, and what about French, which you speak so excellently?'

'Mmm, mmm . . . I might, at that. It's not a bad idea. But how do I apply?'

I had made enquiries. It was all remarkably easy to arrange and within a week he was off for a few hours a day for his lessons, for which he was allowed about $120 a month, paid weekly, quite enough to live quietly on. The Italian teacher he loved, she was an elderly contessa who passed on most interesting Roman gossip. The French instructor bored him as he constantly had to keep pretending he didn't know what he was being taught. Nevertheless the regular money was a great attraction, for he could work for several hours a day on his novel. *The Iron Hoop* was coming out in England in a few months' time, there would be a little to come on that. I was working very little so for a brief period we shared a tenuous happiness.

As the place was small I tried to leave him alone when he was writing. I had many friends, so it wasn't difficult. Some Constantine liked very much and he enjoyed talking to Kersh about books. Carl Perutz took many photographs of us, Kersh and others. I think Carl was attracted to Ann Allward, Kersh's step-daughter, an extremely bright and attractive young girl of about twenty.

As there was only one large old key to the heavy wooden outer door, I tied it to a piece of wood, so when the top bell was rung we always went out to the terrace and threw it over, for five floors down and up was too much at one go. Luckily there was good street lighting in the piazza, particularly outside the house. If either of us went out separately we would either arrange a time to return, telephone each other to make arrangements or, failing that, leave the key at the Inghilterra. One evening, over dinner, Constantine said the novel was going well and he would work again afterwards. I decided to go to the cinema to see Visconti's film *La Terra Trema* which I had missed earlier on. It sounded fascinating, an impressionist film about a community of Italian fishermen, made on location with a mainly non-professional cast. The cinema was on the outskirts of Rome, therefore I told him I would be home later than usual. It was nearing midnight when I got back and rang the bell. No answer. Maybe he'd gone to bed, I thought, so I rang again and waited. No answer. This went on for about twenty minutes before I went round to the Inghilterra, to find no key there and no message left. I went into the bar and ordered a coffee. After about half an hour Carl looked in and seemed very surprised to see me there. I told him I was locked out, what could I do? We had a drink together, he assuring me Con would be there soon.

'He probably got sick of writing and went out for a nightcap. But I've a big double room upstairs – why don't we go up and sit comfortably? We can telephone from time to time.'

It was a large room with two beds. I noticed on the central bedside table a copy of *The Iron Hoop* Con had lent him. We discussed it, also a book of Kersh's he had borrowed.

'I know,' he said. 'Before it gets too late I'll go along to Kersh's room, ask him to share it with me, and you can sleep here.'

Alas Kersh wasn't there. It was getting very late; we were both tired. The ring of the phone broke the drowsy silence. Carl went to answer it; quickly I said:

'Don't say I'm here. Say you saw me and you'll leave a message with the night porter for when I come back.'

When he put down the phone I asked how Con sounded.

'Rather high and very annoyed.'

I decided to leave the room and either go back to the bar if it was still open, or maybe walk round to the piazza. The phone rang again, and I could hear Con being abusive to Carl. He was coming round.

'I'll go along to the bathroom and wait,' I said. 'Then you let me know when he's gone and I'll go back. I rather dread it if he's drunk.'

It seemed like an hour, sitting on the hard bathroom chair in the dim light. I had started to shake when Carl knocked on the door.

'He's gone. I said you'd be back soon, you'd gone to buy some cigarettes. For God's sake come and have a quick slug before you go, I've got a bottle in the room. You're shaking.'

We were just sipping a brandy when the door was flung open and Constantine stalked in, eyes blazing.

'If you want to have an affair with this, this specimen, I can't think why you don't say so, instead of pretending you're going to the cinema.'

We were both speechless; I was frightened for I knew Con in these moods. He would lash out. I felt trapped and sorry I had got Carl to lie about where I was; but would the truth have been any better? He strode about the room, pulling down the beds which we had only sat on, flung Carl's toilet articles about, then pounced on *The Iron Hoop* I had left open on the bed.

'Ah!' he said. 'Reading aloud to each other no doubt. I *hope* you

enjoyed it.' Whereupon he turned to the dedication page and read
aloud:

This book is dedicated to my wife
Theodora
With love and gratitude

He ripped the page out, tearing it into little pieces, saying:
'This is all the thanks I get for dedicating my book to you.
Gratitude, love: from now on it doesn't exist.'
'You're making a scene about nothing,' I remonstrated. 'You
locked me out and Carl was kind enough to give me shelter and
friendship.'
I moved forward between him and Carl.
'You know quite well you are making all this up because you
feel guilty yourself,' I said. 'For heaven's sake, try to be
reasonable.'
He flung the book at me so that it glanced my temple. Carl
moved protectively, which only inflamed Constantine further.
I turned to look at Con and realized I wasn't brave enough or
masochistic enough to go back with him that night.
'I'll go and get a room here,' I told him. 'Maybe in the morning
you will be more amenable.'
Carl said immediately: 'No, you stay here; I'll get another
room.'
He went out. Constantine stayed glaring at me, saying nothing.
I tried to be as gentle as I could for I could see he was going
through an agony. It was as though another vile person coexisted
in the same body.
'Couldn't we please talk about this, if there's anything to say, in
the morning?' I pleaded. 'I'm deadly tired.'
He left abruptly without a word. I lay on the bed for a few
minutes, then got up and pushed the small bolt on the door. Lying
on the bed I realized sleep was not going to come easily. My mind
raced like a piece of eccentric clockwork. What on earth had
provoked all this? When I left to go to the cinema he had appeared
quite normal, looking forward to an evening's work. There was
wine left over from dinner and some beer in the kitchen. I closed
my eyes, wanting to shut out thoughts of seeing him in the
morning. I must rest at least, for if I was edgy and lost my temper
I feared for the consequences. He could be very violent
sometimes. I turned out the bedside light and went into a light
troubled sleep. I was woken by a splintering crash, and the main
lights were switched on. Constantine had kicked in the door and

was standing over me, a look of fury on his face.

'What have you done with your lover?' he screamed, then went round opening the cupboard doors as though he expected Carl to be hiding in one of them. It gave me a chance to get up and pull on my dress, for I hadn't undressed completely.

'Constantine, please, oh please stop. There's nobody here but me. What on earth's the matter with you? Sit down and be reasonable.'

I went over and pushed the broken door to, not wanting to awaken the whole hotel.

'Have a drink or something, but for God's sake stop all this. We've had enough for one night.'

I think he would have done this but the night manager and the night porter had arrived and were surveying the broken door. Quite politely but firmly he was requested to leave. Whereupon he went over, took the manager, who was a small man, by the shoulders and shook him very hard, shouting at him all the time. The porter came to the manager's assistance and between them they got Con out and downstairs. I hadn't the energy to follow; it was four in the morning and I couldn't see what good I could do. The sight of me seemed to inflame him.

I left about eight o'clock, found the *portiere* up and the door open, so with heavy heart I went up the flights of stairs. On the way up I realized I hadn't got the apartment key either, but fortunately Con hadn't locked the door, only shut it. He was sleeping peacefully on the divan at the far end of the L-shape. Flotow greeted me effusively. I went into the kitchen, made some strong coffee and took it out to the terrace by the other door. About ten o'clock he got up, came out to the terrace and said quite normally:

'Is there any coffee? I'll just have a shower and join you.'

To a stranger it would have seemed like any ordinary household enjoying breakfast on the terrace, but I knew better. His ultra-quiet manner betrayed remorse, but apart from saying he felt like hell and he hoped he hadn't been a nuisance, nothing else was mentioned. It was as though he had managed to erase any of the night's actions from his mind, like rubbing a damp sponge over a blackboard. I saw no point in bringing up the sordid business to be argued back and forth, with no sensible agreement ever reached. It was as if he had had a brainstorm which had left him with no memory of his actions. I said I was going to see my agent, then get some food, and I would be back by lunchtime. What were his plans? He replied he was going to see someone about his film script and would telephone me later. I didn't believe it, for he knew only my friends, and he would surely have mentioned it earlier. However, I was glad he wasn't going to be hanging about the apartment.

Carl accepted my apologies with a laconic smile.

'Is he often like that?' he asked. 'He seemed so friendly and easy the other times we've met. Why, I've never even made a pass at you, have I?'

'It wouldn't make any difference if you'd made dozens of passes, Carl. When Con's been drinking and he gets an idea, that's that. What worries me is, why did he suddenly go out and deliberately get so drunk when everything's been comparatively tranquil? I left him looking forward to an evening's work – I wonder did somebody telephone?'

Carl asked me to lunch, but I refused saying I was going to have a quiet day if possible. In fact I had several quiet days. Constanatine was a model husband; nothing more was ever said about the night. However, we were reminded of it when we were meeting friends for drinks in the Inghilterra Hotel. The manager called Constantine out and requested he didn't use the hotel any more. This he accepted with a shrug of the shoulders. About a week later (having before that insisted on being with me the entire day, even when I had business appointments), he started going out for long periods at odd hours, once staying out all night, arriving home in various moods and having drunk quite a lot. Sometimes he would be extremely amorous, at other times treat me with hostility. There was no pattern to it, which was very unsettling.

Then I got flu quite badly, which made him absent himself as much as possible. This was not unusual; he hated any illness. It took me longer than it would normally to recover from this flu and I had horrible depression afterwards. I'd had to forgo a job because I simply didn't feel strong enough. My money was running out again; Constantine seemed to spend an awful lot. At the beginning of November he came in late one night, looking very thoughtful, and for once quite sober, but he seemed restless, walking up and down the room incessantly. At last he said:

'I can't work here. I think I'll go back to Capri; it'll be quiet there in the winter.'

'But you hate Capri, you've said so over and over. You came up here because you couldn't work there.'

'No, I came up here because I love you and wanted to be with you. Anyway it's Anacapri I hated, especially that horrid little house. Since Riette (Gerald Osborne's wife) left him with the baby, he wants me to go too. He's willing to pay the rent of a villa, and I've got my GI Bill money as well. I must get that book finished.'

'I've got practically nothing left and I don't feel well enough to work at the moment,' I answered. 'Can't I come too?'

'He's only asked me, he obviously can't support both of us. You'll be all right. I'll ask him for some money before we go and let you have some to tide you over.'

I could hardly believe what I was hearing. He was prepared to be bought by Gerry Osborne to live a comfortable life on Capri whilst I half-starved in Rome. Was this a sign of love? Surely not. I honestly didn't feel I had any strength left to argue with him: I just felt utterly depressed. In any case I knew that whatever I said would make little difference, if he had made up his mind to go. He, on the other hand, became remarkably cheerful, saying it would be wonderful to be in a quiet place again, good air, a nice large comfortable villa and so on. I wished he would go at once although my heart was breaking. It had all been an utter failure my coming to Rome. Instead of mending the rift between us, it seemed to have widened it. Now we were to be separated yet again and there seemed no chance of our living together for some time. My friendship with Gerry Osborne, too, had been strained since I had heard from Constantine some very untrue gossip he had passed on about me, well knowing Constantine's violently jealous nature.

Thankfully Con spent a large part of the day away from the apartment, presumably making arrangements with Gerry. Every day dragged interminably and I dragged with it, feeling heavy, sleepy and unlike myself. Constantine by contrast was lively, drinking fairly moderately, quite pleasant to me, although I felt boring and I'm sure I was. It hurt me rather, until I remembered how much he loved change, having almost a child's expectation of a journey. Several days later he came home and, sitting at the table, started to count what seemed to me like a lot of money. He gave me the equivalent of about twenty pounds, shovelling the rest into his pocket.

'That should keep you going until you get some work,' he said. 'We're leaving the day after tomorrow. Can I take your big suitcase? I'll send it back by someone who's coming to Rome.'

The day he left I told him I didn't care to see him leave, so I took Flotow for a long walk in the Pincio Gardens. It was far colder than when we had arrived that day half a world ago, full of hope and love. When I got home I walked out on the terrace; even

Rome seemed silent, as silent as the beats of my heart. I shivered, turned and went indoors, shutting the doors, then lighting a fire. I was cold even so and restless. Pictures of the rumpled bed and the torn-open air-mail letters flashed through my mind. Quickly I drank the half-bottle of wine on the table – a *fiasco*, wasn't that what I was drinking to? I found an almost empty bottle of strega, the herby, strong, sweet liqueur of the north, reputedly an aphrodisiac. Then still restless I went round to the café in the via Frattina; thankfully, nobody I knew was there. I don't know how much brandy I drank, the strong vanilla-tasting Italian brandy with the horse's head on the bottle. My mind was almost a blank. I felt nothing except a vague feeling of warmth and confusion. I suppose I was drunk, but it wasn't like any sort of drunkenness I had had before. The night air made me feel dizzy when I walked home. I went into my once much-loved apartment, which looked strangely unlived-in. I was violently sick; Flotow seemed worried about me and tried to amuse me by bringing a shoe. Later he came up on the divan and curled down the long curve of my back. Thus we slept dreamlessly for ten hours or more.

Surprisingly I felt much better in the morning and I went to shop in the via della Croce. On the way I met Ann Allward, who said she was on her way round to me as Kersh had asked us to lunch; he was leaving in two days' time. As she accompanied me I told her Constantine had left for Capri and I didn't know if I'd be able to keep the apartment on. Immediately she asked if she could share it with me. Her mother was in America, Kersh was going to London and she wanted to stay in Rome. She had an allowance, so could easily pay her way. I said I must think about it, and she must get Kersh's approval. Kersh was in fact against the idea, fearing Constantine might suddenly turn up and make scenes, but I assured him I wouldn't let it happen. It was fortunate for both of us as it turned out, for we got on extremely well together. We both had things to learn from each other.

Sometime later when she woke me up in the middle of the night complaining of violent pains and sickness, I was able to get her to hospital for an appendix operation. When I went to see her the next day she looked very well, but said she was extremely hungry. In the same ward other visitors were giving their relatives hampers of food, which made us both hungry.

'Maybe you're not supposed to have anything yet,' I ventured. 'I'll find a nun and see if I can get you something.'

The nun said yes, she could have food, and went to move on.

'Will you bring her something, then?'

'Oh no, signora, we don't provide food here. You must get it from the café opposite!'

I got her a sandwich consisting of a loaf split in half with ham and cheese, some fruit and milk. It wasn't exactly invalid fare but was better than nothing. Later that day I told Peter and Jerree, Peter saying at once it was a charity hospital and she must be got out of there and put in the Anglo-American Clinic; Kersh would send some money. A young American there said if Peter lent him the jeep he would get her out the next day. Chuck, the American, and I went in the jeep to fetch her. Nobody said anything as I put a coat around her, took a wheelchair from the hall and wheeled her down to the jeep. If they wondered where their patient was they certainly never contacted me to ask. Chuck drove his strange cargo across Rome, leaving me in the hall of the clinic while he went on with Ann, saying he would pick me up later. She was bubbling with laughter when I visited her in the comfortable clinic the next day.

'Did you hear what happened to me?' she burst out immediately. 'Chuck handed me over, and I was put on a table for some time,' she went on, 'then a young doctor came in and examined me. Are you sure you should be here, he asked, and I said of course I only left the hospital today. I can't make it out, he replied.' She started to laugh again before continuing. 'Chuck had asked for the delivery room, so there I was in the maternity section. The doctor and I started to giggle so much I broke open my stitches. But I'm OK now.'

Pibe Packard was just along the corridor in the same hospital, so when Ann was walking I used to find her in Pibe's room sometimes. We spent several very pleasant weeks together, her fresh outlook and straightforward personality being just what I needed to face up to everything again. Together we looked for work and made plans.

Constantine wrote affectionate letters mainly about himself and Capri. To begin with he stayed at the Quisisana, Capri's most expensive hotel, and had 'a total rest'. He had seen Paolo Langheim, who had asked after me 'rather warmly'. He wasn't going to indulge in any two-day drinking and was longing to get to work again. It was much better this way, he was sure. Then an astonishing letter came saying they had all moved into the Casa Solatia, could I lend them some linen and blankets? It was very annoying, he also wrote, of Concetta to keep asking after me every twenty minutes. Somehow, to me, it seemed like betrayal going back to our house, which we had shared with so much hope and love despite all the worries.

There was another problem ahead I was reluctant to face. It was

no use pretending to myself day after day that it wasn't so, and as
another month passed, I knew for a certainty I was pregnant. Ann
was the first person I told when the *malaise* and sickness began to
get worse, and she was concerned for me. I must tell Constantine,
she insisted. This I was hesitant to do. However, when I found
some days I was too sick to work, I did write. He replied very
coolly that I must go to an American doctor, this was stressed, and
get him 'to inform me by letter of the state of your health'. Also
why didn't I go to Positano? He could come over for a bit. He had
a continual headache after flu; he had been drinking with Graham
Greene and Rex Warner; Peggy Guggenheim was expected for the
winter, the mayor and the entire *municipio* had been sacked owing
to a matter of 130,000,000 lire being missing from municipal
funds. It was an oddly impersonal letter, as if written to a distant
friend. There was no word of comfort or concern.

Ann was extremely kind, always helpful. I loved her fresh,
young approach to everything. It made me remember myself ten
year back, determinedly facing up to reality, not knowing or even
caring about the future. Ten years back I had been even younger
than Ann, living in Paris on the small amount of money I had
saved, contemplating, as I sat in the Café Flore, that Paris was
where I wanted to be. There was so much I wanted to learn about
that wonderful city, and I was confident that I could become a
good actress if I worked hard enough, really studied actresses like
Edwige Feuillière or Françoise Rosay and absorbed the timing of
their words and actions. Night after night I sat in cheap seats in the
theatre, watching Madeleine Ozeray in Cocteau's *Ondine* until I
could have played the part, so word perfect was I. Whereas now I
was apprehensive, wondering how I was going to manage, and
pondering much of the time what Constantine's reaction would
be.

Ann urged me to write to Mimi and to go down to Positano for
a rest. She could easily pay the rent, I mustn't worry. Then when I
had sorted something out I could come back, for she would
always welcome me. She even gave me the fare, so I would have a
bit extra to spend there.

Mimi wrote a welcoming letter back saying there was hardly
anyone there and it would be 'fun to see me'. It was beastly cold so
I should bring warm clothes. She was off with Con and expressed
her feelings about him vividly and somewhat coarsely. Once more
I packed up a few clothes and possessions, and one raw November
day Flotow and I took the bus to Positano. I was not looking
forward to it as I left the snug room at the Piazza di Spagna.

CHAPTER THIRTEEN

The old bus had no heating, the only warmth emanating from the *esprit de corps* of the other passengers. As they left, the temperature dropped considerably, but when we made a convenience stop, and I walked Flotow for a minute in the chill air, I was glad to get back to the bus, empty save for the driver. Dim lights glowed feebly and I thought for a minute I was going to be the only passenger. Then a light, quick step sounded; I looked up and saw a man talking to the driver. He turned and came towards me.

'Aren't you . . .? Didn't we . . .?' We both said together.

Then he said: 'I'm Mario Prodan. Didn't we meet visiting Pibe Packard once?' He smiled, an attractive smile, white teeth shining in the dim light. 'May I sit next to you? It's cold, isn't it?' He folded his lapels over and pulled down his hat.

'Wait a minute. I must get Flotow out first. You might tread on him.' Flotow's brown curly head loomed up from under the seat; he looked pleased to be out.

'What a well-behaved dog. I didn't dream he was even on the bus. Here boy, come right out.' Mario sat beside me, Flotow awkwardly in the aisle.

'Why don't we have him on our laps?' he said. 'He'd keep us beautifully warm.'

So that is how we travelled on to Positano, Flotow spread across us like a excellent fur rug, his dear head resting on my arm.

A stranger on a bus driving into the dark encourages confiden-ces. You learn more about a person in an hour than you would over many weeks of meeting in company. I had had similar experiences on long-distance trains; somehow the movement made you feel it was important to say things before you parted. I learned he was a sinologist, had lived in China for many years, spoke good Chinese, had studied Chinese art, at which he was an expert, and while there had married a girl of Scottish ancestry whose name was Cissie. They had two daughters and now lived in Rome, but he made many Far Eastern trips, on one of which he had met the Packards, both journalists for *Time* magazine. He was like many in Italy in those days, film crazy. His ambition was to write and make his own film, which is why he was coming to Positano to a quiet house, up in the hills, to write his script.

'And you?' he enquired.

I mentioned acting, which interested him. I said Constantine was a writer with two accepted novels and other books commissioned, which interested him even more. I found myself describing Constantine as he once was: amusing, clever, full of ideas, altogether charming – all of which he could be still when he chose. It must have sounded an ideal marriage in many ways. The curious thing is, that while I was saying it I thought of Con just like that. I had almost forgotten the humiliations and scenes, so much so I almost looked forward to seeing him when we arrived.

However, there was nobody to meet me when we stopped at the piazza in front of the church. Inwardly I began to quake; supposing he was in the Buca with—? Could I trust myself to behave properly? Mario stamped his feet, turned to me and said:

'Where are you going, then?'

I replied I would walk down to the Buca to look for Mimi.

He said graciously that he would accompany me. The Buca seemed very gay, lively and, most of all, warm. There were quite a few people there I knew: Pinky Hartman, Alex, Isabella, Mimi and a tall arresting-looking woman dressed in a very beautiful velvet trouser suit, with dark hair, large expressive brown eyes and a deep Italian voice, whom I had seen before. She was introduced as Fiore de Henriques, a sculptor. Even while I was admiring her *tenue*, I couldn't help noting to myself that 'flower' was a remarkably unsuitable name. There was no sign of Constantine. Mimi looked up from her seat by the bar, seemingly delighted at a new injection of life into the party. She took charge of Mario and ordered drinks. Everyone ordered drinks in fact, and on an empty stomach they worked faster than usual.

'Is Constantine here, or where?'

'Don't talk to me about that shit of a brother of mine,' she said. 'I suppose he's still in Capri enjoying Gerry's hospitality. There are quite a few people there now, all lapping it up.'

I gathered from subsequent remarks that the main cause for the resentment was because she had been left out. I went over to speak to Luca, the waiter who had been Mimi's lover for some time. I was feeling quite muzzy.

'Can you get me a room somewhere, Luca? I don't want to stay in Mimi's spare room.'

'She's not in Pack's apartment any more. Come, I'll show you where she is now.'

He carried my case as we walked along the narrow street of crumbling houses, all now either restaurants or boutiques, and led me upstairs.

'You can have this room, there's nobody staying here. Mimi's downstairs. I must get back. *Ciao.*'

I sat on the bed and looked around. No, it wasn't the same room, but it was very cold and cheerless without even one of the little brass charcoal braziers going, over which we huddled in the winter. I did the old trick I had been taught during my early theatrical touring days, of putting the electric lamp with shade inside the bed to produce a bit of heat. I remembered an old pro saying to me, 'The real ones like this are called a "priest". Funny name, isn't it?' I giggled to myself at the thought. I didn't remember anything of the last half-hour at the Buca, but consoled myself with the thought that probably no one else did either. Piling my coat and Flotow on the bed, I put on a sweater and went to bed after taking the lamp out. It had produced a faint warmth.

In the morning I was woken up by Mimi coming in waving a brandy bottle.

'If you feel anything like me you'll need a shot,' she said.

'But I haven't had coffee yet. What's the time? No, Mimi, I couldn't face it. I'd be sick.'

She glugged away, making a face each time she swallowed. As the days went by, the same pattern was followed. I had somehow to get her to cut it down. Luca agreed, but how to do it was what we both wanted to know. There was a very charming Hungarian woman living quietly in Positano who was writing a book about her experiences during the war, then her escape. She needed typing done, and general help. Although a slow two-finger typist, I offered to help and roped Mimi in. She didn't do very much but it gave her an interest and kept her off the bottle until the evenings. Then I asked people to meals, anything to prevent her getting bored again. She loved thinking up recipes, 'a change from that bloody pasta all the time', and became both inventive and active. They were simple meals because we hadn't much money, but Luca would get us chickens and meat cheaply, which we transformed into many different dishes.

'How d'you make a curry?' she asked one day. 'I'm dying for a curry.'

Carefully I made out a list of spices for the next person who was going to Naples to bring back. It was very exciting the day they came; just the aroma of them took me back to Paris and the meal Peter Rose Pulham and I had made the day after some money arrived, and we had been living for a week on bread rubbed with garlic. The day came; a few friends had been asked; we chopped and ground spices all morning. We peeled and sliced, had to send out for more charcoal to feed the ugly old stove, but then it was nearing completion, the rich juices tasted endlessly, the warm strong wild smell wafting out on to the street.

'I don't think I can wait until they all come,' said Mimi. 'I hope they're not late.'

Then we looked at each other when the table was laid. No chutney.

'We can't have a curry without chutney.'

'They do in India sometimes, it's a British idea really. You know Major Gray's Mango Chutney.'

'Well, I want chutney. What on earth can we do?'

Eventually we did have a chutney of a very superior and unusual kind. We soaked sultanas, raisins, chopped glacé fruits, chopped lemons and oranges in Marsala wine, then after a few hours when the fruit was fat and plump we added brandy. It was a wonderful chutney which everybody ate lavishly. I shudder to think what orthodox non-drinking Indians would have thought of it.

I heard nothing from Constantine and in a way it was a relief. Mimi and I were getting on very well. I was earning a little money, and the drink bill was considerably less. I felt much healthier and had stopped being sick. In fact I had got used to the idea of pregnancy, somehow 'God would provide', as they always said in Ireland. Luca always kept me leftover pasta and scraps for Flotow, which I would collect daily. Pinky rushed in one day when I was there, crying:

'There's some gorgeous men coming to Positano in a few days' time. They're in Sorrento at the moment.'

Luca and I looked at each other. The Italian grapevine was very strong and he had heard nothing.

'I'll ask at some of the hotels,' he said thoughtfully.

Meanwhile, quite unexpectedly, Constantine arrived, 'for a few days', he said, to see how I was. He seemed quieter than usual and, when I asked how the book was going, all I got was a casual 'all right'.

Then the 'gorgeous men' arrived. Pinki dashed in to ask if he could borrow my black lace blouse for the evening at the Buca, to which I readily agreed. Curiously that evening the Buca was strangely deserted when the four men entered. Just us, a few locals with some Swedish girls and an elderly Italian painter. They were dressed in pale khaki drill trousers with smart shirts and cravats, almost as though it was summer, not the end of November. They seemed to us to have a strange way of talking, addressing each other very formally. Each sentence started *Sar* . . . or *Su* . . . then they would correct themselves and heartily slap one another on the back saying something like:

'What'll you have Bill (or Jack)?'

The locals eyed them suspiciously, as did Luca. I saw him disappear to the telephone in the back and when he returned he was smiling. Mimi had put on some records, which cheered the place up. One of them came over to Mimi to ask her to dance, but she said promptly:

'Why don't you ask Pinky? He's a much better dancer!' He eyed Pinky disconsolately, standing nearby, fetching in my lace blouse.

Luca beckoned me and I followed him. He was longing to tell someone his news.

'They're all policemen,' he said. 'They're here to find out where the English are getting the money from to live here. That's why Alex and the others have driven off.' We laughed quietly, conspiratorially.

'I'll tell Mimi and Con. We'll have some fun with them.'

And fun it was too, quite lucrative fun as it turned out. Con and Mimi had played cards together since childhood, and were both extremely good at bridge and poker. They seemed to know just by looking at each other what cards the other one had. For several days they played cards with the policemen and won quite a lot of money. Then, when a cunning question was aimed at them as to money, Con said in his most English voice:

'Oh, it's no use asking us anything, we're Americans. I was born in Lenox, Mass. That's my sister.' Which of course was true.

Shortly afterwards the policemen moved on, sadder and no wiser. I often wondered how they accounted for the losings on their expense sheets. It certainly cheered us up during the long winter evenings.

Constantine stayed much longer than he had intended, mainly I think because he enjoyed Mario Prodan's company. Together they thought of a film for the Holy Year which was to be in 1950 and many days he would walk up to Mario's house in the hills to work with him on it. They both talked about it incessantly, and because he was working after a fashion, Constantine's behaviour towards me was reasonable. It was easy to work here, he said, Casa Solatia had too many people in it now. I resisted asking who was there. Then one morning he asked if I had the big suitcase he had borrowed. Gerry had taken it back to Rome and Riette was supposed to bring it round to me.

No, she didn't; but I could pick it up when I went back.

'You wouldn't like to go up and get it, would you? I think I'll leave Solatia; everything's getting too complicated.'

No, I wouldn't like to go and get it. What was the hurry anyway?

'Well I'll go, then. I want to see the GI people about transferring my grant. I think I'll go to Paris, then maybe on to England. Pity you're pregnant. It's come at a very bad time.'

He said this as though the pregnancy was parthenogenetic.

'I'm not staying in Italy if you're going back to England. You might have talked to me about it.'

He kicked at a hole in the carpet, walked to the window, and said:

'It's only just occurred to me, actually. I think I'd do better there with my book coming out next year. I might be able to sell my new novel, which is all but finished. I do love you, darling, but we seem to be getting deeper into a morass of drink and debt.'

'I don't owe anything, and I only occasionally get drunk when everything seems too much. It's a funny way of loving someone, to rush off and leave them when they're carrying your child.'

'From all I've heard I'm not even certain it is mine,' he said. This really incensed me. I almost shouted:

'From whom? From Gerry, I suppose, who ever since I refused to go to bed with him has hissed untrue gossip at you? For heaven's sake, be reasonable; check the dates if you like, but don't ever say such a thing to me again. If you do, everything is finished between us, damn you.'

He left abruptly and I heard later from Luca he had taken the bus to somewhere. I should have known; he always had to have a plausible excuse if he wanted to do something of which I would disapprove, to stop him feeling too guilty.

Mimi was very loyal, urging me to stay with her. She would write to her mother, who would send some money, she was sure. She became quite protective towards me, very kind and thoughtful, almost too much so, stopping me having more than two or three glasses of wine at a time, also restricting herself. She also decided that where she lived was not suitable for me, not warm or comfortable enough. Cleverly she negotiated winter rates for us both at an hotel near the top of Positano. The hundred steps were too much for me! I was very touched, finding myself very close to her. In the closed circle of one's emotions, one tends to discount other people's. She, too, had had to leave the husband she loved. I grew to love her. Luca, her lover, was very kind too; he was very fond of Flotow, unusually so for a young Italian man. His strong sturdy body, with the age-old face betraying its Greek origins, and the puckered smile, all appealed to me. His determination to have his own restaurant was realized within five years.

Some weeks later, in December, Constantine arrived back to Positano with my suitcase, intending I think to return to Capri and possibly pack up, but I insisted he stayed a little to discuss any plans. I had begun to realize the foolishness of staying on alone, possibly unable to work, certainly to act, no proper medical attention, or indeed any sort of attention, However, there was Flotow. I wouldn't leave him with Mimi lest she start drinking again when I had gone; we could never have afforded quarantine fees and I hated the thought of having him put down. We were discussing it one day when Mario called. He stroked his beard, looked thoughtful, then said:

'I'll take him; he's a most lovable animal. Cissie will love him, we've just lost our old dog. Come on, boy, walkies.'

When Constantine was leaving for Rome, I went as far as Sorrento with him. From the bus in Positano we saw Mario standing with a contented-looking Flotow on the lead. He bent down to pat him, then gave us the thumbs-up sign. It was my last glimpse of my companion of many years, but he was to have a happy life until the end of his days.

It had been arranged that Con would spend some days in Rome before going on to Paris, where he would wait for me at the old Hotel Montana. If he wasn't there at the time he would also leave a letter at the Café Flore. Would I go to Anacapri and collect a few things of his he had left with Tony Paanaker? I had left most of my possessions in Rome, and these I had to pack up too. He would leave me half his GI money at the American Express for the journey. It seemed comparatively simple. Mimi was sad at the idea of my going, toying with the idea of coming too, but I pointed out I didn't know where I would end up, as I couldn't stay indefinitely at my mother's tiny flat in Chelsea. The thought of going back to Anacapri hung over me and depressed me utterly.

It was a cold and windy day in January when I took the ferry from Sorrento to Capri. The seas were high; the boat looked very small as I looked out of the window of the Excelsior Vittoria Hotel where I was having some coffee. Soon I would go down in the old hotel lift to the harbour, but I felt apprehensive and unwell. This I put down to going back to the place where we had been so unhappy, from where I had left with Mouche that horrible morning which seemed so long ago when she had had to be put down. As I picked up the empty canvas bag I had brought, knife-like pains shot through my stomach; my head and legs ached. Was this what was called psychosomatic? I wondered. Pulling myself together, I went downstairs, on to the boat; it smelt horribly of oil which made me feel queasy, so I had a brandy in the bar. There were a few Italians there and a young American man who smiled at me.

As we got away from land I began to feel very sick. I had never felt seasick in my life, going to and from India, to America in the winter on a small steamer, even during a typhoon in the Indian Ocean. Nevertheless I was horribly sick then. The pains in my stomach increased.

'You look very pale. Are you all right?' asked the young American. 'Can I get you something?'

He ministered to me during that short journey; I learned he was going to say goodbye to his girlfriend, one of Edwin Cerio's daughters, before going back to America. He was very much in love and very sad. When we arrived he insisted on seeing me to the bus, even saying where he would be later on if I felt ill again. The Cerio girl was fortunate, I thought, as I took leave of him.

Tony Paanaker, in contrast, seemed even more repulsive than I remembered. He rolled his frog-spawn eyes at me, putting forward propositions 'if I stayed on'. The lunch was interminable. Poor Ilda the maid, whom he had taken over from Con, looked quite cowed and nervous. I took what I could carry, for the books weighed heavily, saying I would come back sometime for the rest. I searched and searched for the slim volume of Merimée's stories I had taken from Peter in Paris, but I never found it, which distressed me further. The walk to the bus tired me immensely; the twirl of Paanaker's stick and the rhythm as he kept putting it down jarred my head. The journey back seemed interminable and in between trying to rest in the bus I was only thankful I hadn't got to get down all those steps to the old room at the Buca.

Mimi took one look at me and put me to bed. I was racked with pain and had a fever, but the nearest doctor was in Sorrento, an hour away at least, even if he came at once. Mimi went off to get Assunta – that kind, large, motherly woman – who bathed my forehead and gave me some sweet-smelling herb tea to drink, muttering comforting phrases I didn't understand. Later that night I lost the baby which had caused such contention. Assunta said prayers over it, wrapped it up carefully and departed, leaving me clean and comfortable. She would be along in the morning after the *bambini* had gone to school. I slept.

For several days I rested, feeling drained. I ate but little, thinking I would give several years of my life for a cup of Irish tea. I could almost smell the turf burning under the blackened kettle in the kitchen, the warm aroma of soda bread taken from the range, spread when hot with golden country butter. As I gazed out over the sea, I came to hate it, wishing it was the green, so-green pastures of my home, horses nibbling peacefully, the mist-enshrouded hills in the distance. That's what I would do – go back to Ireland for a while. One extra person in that house never mattered: I could look after the soft-nosed, nuzzling horses, help on the land. But, as I thought, I knew it was a fantasy. I would never be able to lift and carry heavy bales of straw and hay, lift milk churns or any of the most essential things. They would give me love, wonder how long I was going to stay, and ask, where was my husband? Had I met any 'fillum' stars or made my fortune in the lands beyond the avenue gates?

Mimi interrupted my reverie, sounding just like her mother, saying:

'It's just like Con, going off just when we want him; *and* we don't know where he is. I wonder if he's still in Rome. Shall we try and ring up someone?'

On very bad, indistinct lines we rang Ann, who had seen him once, but knew nothing more. Then we rang the Tompkins, and Peter said he'd rescued him from the contessa who owned the Anacapri house. Apparently she wanted some money, and as her lover was chief of police in Naples, well . . . you know. He thought he'd left, but couldn't be sure. Mimi said she'd send a telegram to Paris but I scoffed at the idea, knowing how the ones from Capri to Rome got scrambled. However, send one she did, announcing it proudly.

'What on earth did you say?' I asked.

'I said the calf had slipped and you couldn't travel for a few days. I sent it to the Flore.'

I burst out laughing:

'Oh, Mimi, in the unlikely event of his ever getting it he won't understand it.'

Then we both laughed until the tears rolled down our cheeks, but afterwards I felt much better.

In Rome, Ann welcomed me at the apartment when I arrived from the train. It looked so cosy and charming that I felt many pangs of regret at having to leave it. She had made some enquiries and thought Con had stayed much longer than a few days, more like a week, but she had no idea where he'd been living. She remarked how thin I was, so I had to tell her what had happened.

'Are you sure you can make the journey?' she enquired. 'Stay a little longer until you feel stronger.'

'If I do I'll probably never go back, Ann. I think I'd better go; I can always come back if things turn out better. I'll go and see what there is at the American Express across the road tomorrow.'

My agent had been telephoning every day; apparently I had missed all sorts of offers, which I wouldn't have been able to take in any case.

I looked at the electric sewing machine which Dylan Thomas had once tried ineffectively to pawn, realizing I couldn't carry it. So finally I sold it to a contessa's English nanny, the name 'Singer' working magic.

My money stretched to a second-class ticket, but not a couchette, with a little over; so I borrowed something from Peter to have enough to stay over in Paris if our meeting went awry. Packing up was difficult, for I didn't want to take things Ann was using; it consisted mainly of personal items I wouldn't like to be without and a few clothes, anything which would fit into the old secondhand Revelation case I had bought in New York. On my last night, Reinhard and Bendi came to dinner. Bendi was very excited about a job he had got in, of all places, Tahiti, so the mood was festive. The thought of England with no friends was depressing, but I turned it aside. Peter drove me to the station, efficiently dealing with everything. It was a sad leave-taking, especially so without Flotow. I was determined to come back.

As I settled in my corner seat, I hoped some of the other passengers would leave before we crossed the frontier, otherwise we would have very little room to stretch out and sleep during the night. I started to read the Thurber book I had brought from Bermuda, conjuring up my meetings with him; the laughter, warmth, anticipation and love Constantine and I had shared there. Unaccountably John Donne's lines came into my head:

> I long to talk with some old lover's ghost,
> Who died before the god of love was born.

Did I still love Constantine? If I didn't, why was I leaving this beautiful country I felt at home in and going back to England? Would we be able to live peacefully – I dared not think of the word 'happily' – again? I still had a battered kind of love left, I decided, but I was hurt and bruised, both physically and mentally. Maybe a few days in Paris with Con would bring us closer together, for his fondness for that city equalled mine. My thoughts whirled round incessantly, punctuated with maybe's and ifs.

If only Con could write again, I knew other things would fall into place. I looked out at the harsh February light which made the fruit trees of Tuscany stand out like regiments of well-trained soldiers; every scrap of ground was diligently cultivated, here and there a farmhouse with its vineyard, the vines twisted and bare, waiting for the sun of spring to clothe them in pale green leaves. Florence, the city of gold, containing enough beauty to last several lifetimes. The noise of the engine seemed to hammer out: 'why leave, why leave, come back, come back . . .' – through the Emilia Romagna with its fertile land tucked under the mountains; Parma, its cheese, pale gold honeycombs of pleasure, the whey-fed pigs making the pale rose ham, paper-thin slices of sweet tenderness. It was making me very hungry, and realizing I had had no lunch I gathered up my things and made my way along the crowded train to the restaurant car. That too was very full, and in hurrying to get one of the two vacant seats I was thrown by a jolt in the train almost on to a man's lap; my book went flying across the table. The man picked it up and closed it, looking at the title before handing it back to me.

'Thurber,' he said almost to himself. 'I haven't read him since I was in America just before the war. He's a very amusing writer, isn't he? Are you American?'

I took the book and sat down.

'No, I'm not. If anything, I'm Irish.'

This was said a little ungraciously, for I was annoyed at stumbling, the contents of my travelling bag were strewn about on the floor, my purse had rolled out of sight and I felt panicky.

'Here you are,' he said. 'I think that's everything. It's amazing how far things will roll, isn't it?'

As he sat down, I looked at him, smiled and thanked him very much. He was an Englishman, about fifty years old, fair thinning hair over a kindly but undistinguished face. He was easy to talk to and we talked of Thurber, my meeting him in Bermuda and many things, as we lingered over our coffee. I was turning over in my mind whether I had enough Italian money for a sandwich (the last taste of Parma ham) and some fruit as well as to last me until we reached Paris, when he asked me to join him at dinner.

After dinner I felt exhausted. Realizing I would have to sit up all night, I mentioned I must get back to my seat, otherwise people would be spread over it.

'Don't you have a couchette?' he enquired. 'You can't possibly sit in a compartment full of people. You look very tired and pale. Wait a minute.' It was comfortable in the restaurant car and I was almost asleep when he came back.

'It's all fixed, come along.'

'But no, what about you?'

'Don't worry, please. I'd be most happy if you would take the compartment the steward is preparing for you. See you in Paris in the morning.'

I don't know where he slept, but after a comfortable night I didn't see him in Paris in the morning. I took a taxi to the Montana; Monsieur had left two days ago, no there was no letter. It was then about nine-thirty in the morning so I left my luggage, then walked to the Café Flore, where I would have breakfast and think what to do.

Although the Flore looked very much the same, they were all alien faces there. Pascal had retired and there was no message for me.

'*Deux oeufs sur le plat, s'il vous plait, avec du pain et café.*'

When it was served, the taste took me back ten years. When Peter and I had any money, that is what we had for breakfast at the Flore. We could boil or fry eggs at home, but we didn't have any of those lovely little stainless-steel dishes to cook them this way. How grandly Pascal would serve them, beaming with pleasure, sometimes a curl of sweet, crisp bacon added. Automatically I broke the still warm fresh *baton* of bread and dipped it first in the orange yolks as we always did. Why did they taste so much better in France? Was it the good Normandy butter they were cooked in? I wondered if he and Mary were living in Paris, and thought how perfect it would be if that enormous hunched-up figure walked through the door. Cautiously I counted my money to see if I had enough to spend a night in Paris, with perhaps a bowl of soup tonight, and to telephone my mother. After all it was almost ten years since I had seen the armoured cars full of German soldiers rattling down the streets, and before I started on the long bicycle ride to St Jean de Luz for England. Almost without thinking when I left the Flore I found myself turning into the rue du Bac, then on through to the rue de Bellechasse which crossed it. I stood outside the building where Donald McLean's apartment had been, the apartment Peter and I had shared and left Paris from, albeit at different times. The brass plate containing the bells had very different names; the window I used to look from had an unfriendly face which seemed to tell me to go away and not waste

my time there. I turned into the Boulevard St Germain until I came
to the rue des Saints Pères. On the corner of the turning I bought a
bag of hot chestnuts, asking the seller if the Hôtel des Saints Pères
was still there.

'*Mais oui, mademoiselle.*' He said it as though I had asked if
Notre-Dame was still there.

As I went on walking, I thought: if they have room number
seven, I'll stay there overnight. The hall was as I remembered it, the
brass clock with the loud tick, heavy curtains and large, old
furniture. Yes, number seven was free and I could afford it. The
huge, downy brass bed still dominated the room. I moved to touch
the left-hand knob at the top of the bed. It still wiggled and came off
easily when I lifted it. I heard myself saying:

'If we get separated during the war I'll leave a message for you
under that knob.'

I had forgotten, though, and there was no message, except the
welcome of the silent over-furnished room. That was all a grief
ago.

How very different the French bourgeois atmosphere was, even
from some English hotels, where those of a similar class were often
still imbued with a rakish Regency air; or sometimes a slightly
erotic Edwardian muskiness hung about the embossed walls and
the tasselled curtains. Illicit love and memories of *Fanny by Gaslight*
were not too far away. On the fringe of memory was Dostoevsky's
account of a summer month in London, from which he fled in
horror at the licentiousness on and off those gracious streets, some
with rural-sounding names like Haymarket.

The hotels of Europe filled my mind. Was the first one clear? Yes.
I was a five-year-old child recovering from measles in the darkened
room, a screen around the bed, endless dishes of bread-and-butter
pudding; so that for many years it was impossible to taste it without
thinking of that room and the half-light. Then the pleasure when
the screen was removed, the blinds raised, several people standing
around the bed asking the question:

'Will she be all right to travel so far?'

Being warmly dressed despite the July sun, scarf wrapped round
the face so that only the eyes showed, and seated on cushions with a
rug, in the 'dicky' at the back outside part of the open tourer, which
had a seat, usually reserved for children 'because the air is good for
her'. On to the boat at Dover, standing on the quay and watching
the car swung high in the air, on a crane, to be put on board.

Whisked away to a cabin, the tickly scarf and coat taken off, then

some biscuits and a glass of milk. Watching the glasses and de-
canter on the wall swinging in a brass holder; the sleep-inducing
effect. Excitement of the arrival at Calais, fright lest the car be
swung into the sea, then snug in the small seat in the 'dicky', not
even missing the little King Charles spaniel, Yetty, who usually
sat alongside. The funny pointed houses with turrets, but not as
big as in the fairytale book. Driving on the other side of the road.

The pointed-roof hotel seemed very large, as did the bedroom
up the stairs. Biggest of all was the bed, and so high, a little stool
was there to stand on, to help you reach the top. The fairytale
book, which had been taken away when the measles were bad,
was beside the little girl, me, and I was happy.

Later a large bowl of creamy soup with chunks of all the
vegetables I liked, melting butter trickling over the top forming
the shape of a dog's head. Stirring it about so that other shapes
formed, and then drinking it from the large spoon. That was my
first, never-to-be-forgotten memory of an hotel, for as I got better
the others on that journey to the south were obliterated by the fun
of travelling.

There were the rabbit-warren hotels with endless corridors
where the White Knight or the Red Queen might be expected to
appear, and sometimes did, especially if it was Rosa Lewis's
extraordinary Cavendish Hotel in Jermyn Street, with its unorthodox owner.

Clearest of all in the glass of memory is the sweet ecstasy of first
love in the old, shabby Paris hotel: the sagging bed, peeling
wallpaper, the view of the higgledy piggledy Paris rooftops from
the spattered, never-cleaned windows; the brightly coloured print
of Napoleon, a pretty watercolour of someone's dream garden.

Even now it all seemed very real to me as I sat, alone, apprehensive as to what would happen in the future after I reached London.

The next day, as the train rattled through the French countryside
on its way to Calais, I thought of the kind Englishman who had
bought me a sleeper then disappeared. Catch a Frenchman or an
Italian behaving like that! Maybe England wouldn't be so bad after
all.

Surprisingly I met him again on the boat, which made my
journey to Victoria Station very pleasant. As we were leaving the
barrier in the dimly lit station, the slender, graceful figure of my
mother emerged from the shadows.

'Where's Constantine? Isn't he with you?' she asked.

'I've no idea. I thought you might know. Didn't he phone?'

My new friend insisted we had a drink before parting, during which we arranged to meet him at lunchtime the next day. However, the next day I wasn't able to meet anyone; the doctor was called and said I had a serious infection and must go to hospital as soon as possible. He would call an ambulance. We had been waiting for several hours when the telephone rang. It was my grandmother, who said quickly:

'You're wanted by the *News of the World*. Take this down.'

My immediate thought was that Constantine was in some sort of trouble, and at that moment I didn't feel able to cope. I said I would ring back, and put the phone down. It rang again almost immediately, simultaneously with the arrival of the ambulance.

'You must listen. You're wanted in the unclaimed money column. You're to ring this number.'

The ambulance men were in the room. Quickly I asked my mother to ring the number, then to come to the hospital to tell me about it. As I came out of the anaesthetic haze I saw my mother's face; she was talking:

'. . . said it's a will that was made in 1872 and you're one of the last descendants. It's several thousands, but he wouldn't tell me exactly. Isn't it exciting? Do hurry up and get well.'

ENGLAND AND IRELAND

CHAPTER FOURTEEN

England in 1950 seemed a very different place when I left the Chelsea hospital. There were new words to be learnt, such as 'cosh boy', the cosh being a home-made heavy stick like a super-truncheon; other accoutrements such as bicycle chains, broken milk bottles, 'flick' knives and knuckledusters were displayed in photographs of the 'cosh boy's' armoury. 'Spiv' was another word new to me which my fellow patients assured me meant 'diddler'. For instance, I was told the time-honoured coster-monger often held a matchbox concealed in his hand, with a Cox's pippin apple, when crying: 'Lovely ripe Cox's: hear the pips rattle!' My mother had mentioned a nice fat chicken she had bought in Soho, only to find smoke pouring from the oven when cooking it. It had been tightly stuffed with newspapers to give the illusion of plumpness. Crime, which had dropped considerably during the war, owing I suppose to most men being drafted into some service, had risen dramatically. This was blamed by a large number of the population on the wireless (as the radio was called) serial *Dick Barton, Special Agent*, which had been running unin-terrupted since 1946, the year I had left England.

The Archbishop of York enlarged on the 'moral chaos', and the Bishop of Exeter said chastity had never been held in lower esteem since the reign of Charles II. Again, large numbers of the popula-tion laid this at the door of the American Dr Kinsey, with his *Report on the Sexual Behaviour of the Human Male*, an instant bestseller, a strange bedfellow of the numerous war books. Indeed a friend told me that after her charwoman had glanced through the book, she remarked:

'Men is beasts, Mrs Watkins!'

Norman Mailer's war book *The Naked and the Dead*, commonly known as 'the effing book' was severely slammed for its obscenity by the *Sunday Times*, who called for its withdrawal.

The BBC now employed an 'expert' psychiatrist to answer everyday problems; psychiatry was popularly accepted. T. S. Eliot's play *The Cocktail Party* had as the central figure Sir Henry Harcourt-Reilly, a cross between a psychiatrist and a priest, per-haps a symbol of the era. There should be nothing to hide, or maybe no place to hide it.

So much I had learned or read during my stay in hospital. However, later, certain things were as I remembered them in England. Petrol was still rationed. The meat ration for instance was one shilling's worth per week. Milk came off the ration while I was in hospital, but cream was impossible to find in the city. The five shilling limit for restaurant meals was still in force.

The beauty of Chelsea Embankment still bewitched me; the atmosphere in the small shops and pubs was as friendly and inviting as I remembered them. The Crossed Keys pub in Lawrence Street, where I had spent many pleasant hours in wartime, now served excellent food, as did some other pubs. In fact, for good unpretentious English food it was hard to beat them. Although for the first time for some years I had no dog, I walked my mother's in Battersea Park; it was not in the least like the sun-filled Pincio Gardens, but had its own melancholy, austere English charm and beauty. This beauty was enhanced by the open-air exhibition of modern sculpture which galvanized me into excitement when I came upon it set in a green grove in the park. For the first time I saw Henry Moore's sculptures, having previously known only his fantastic drawings of London tube or basement shelterers from the bombs. They opened my mind to a new world of form and dimension. I loved walking about Chelsea on my own, even though I was trying not to think of the immediate problem of 'where was Constantine?'

Con had telephoned several times while I was in hospital, but hadn't visited me. I gathered he had been staying with Patrick O'Donovan, the writer, but had left saying he was going down to Harold Scott's cottage for a while. Harold was an old and valued friend, an extremely good actor, very much in demand for certain parts, but I had no idea where he lived now, or indeed where the cottage was. Meanwhile we went down to see the country solicitor in Chelmsford to find out about my inheritance. This proved very simple once my passport had been examined; and subsequently when the bonds, stocks and shares were forwarded to my old bank beside the Chelsea Town Hall, I had the brief yet glorious moment of saying: 'Sell them.' It was a comforting and miraculous feeling to have money in my pocket and a cheque book for the first time for nearly five years. I enjoyed my largesse immensely: a present for my grandmother's char who had seen the notice, and for favoured members of the family. Some days I felt like Caitlin Thomas who, when Augustus John (well known for his meanness) gave her ten pounds, tucked a fiver in the pocket of a sleeping tramp she passed in a Soho doorway. I found a few friends' telephone numbers in an old address book, all of whom warned me against extravagance. Now, they said, was the time to strike out on my own, go back to acting, make a new life for myself. But the newly found game of spending money was most attractive. Their clichés fell on unheeding ears. I discussed the problems with my mother, who flatly refused to give any advice, helpful or otherwise.

'I haven't made much success of my marriage,' she said. 'I'm the last person to ask.'

An old friend, who had loved me for many years, pressed his case even more strongly. He had written several very successful books and painted a future life together which sounded almost too idyllic. My thoughts about Constantine were ambivalent. Some days I missed him so as to feel only half a person; other days a hard knot of resentment rose up in my body like a malignant tumour. There was still no word from him.

Every day I thought about him and discussed with myself what it was about him that produced such turmoil in me. It was not so much a sexual attraction, for many times I found his sexual drive too fierce, with never a sign of tenderness to heighten by contrast the moments of pure passion. After seven years of marriage it was still like Mrs Patrick Campbell's 'hurly burly of the chaise-longue', not the 'peace and quiet of the double bed'. Sexual understanding had not come with the years; his sexual powers were as violent as during the first months of our love. It was not so much sexual dissatisfaction for me, but that the friendship and camaraderie we still shared at other times simply disappeared in bed. I loved him as much for his power of using words, for his writing, the lucidity of his prose: that is where his sexual under-standing lay, not in his physical actions. I was as hungry for his genius to emerge as another woman might be for her to make a lot of money. Any woman connected with a creative person will tell you the same thing. The work and the man are inseparable, and the woman plays the secondary role no matter how much love there is. When the creative person is unable to work, life is nigh impossible on both sides. The dreadful void for the artist is often filled with deadening drink, or the quest for other women who do not see, or even want to see, what lies behind the curtain which is drawn down over that void.

These thoughts ran haphazardly through my mind; they were there the day I casually met Harold Scott in the King's Road, Chelsea. His cottage was on Romney Marsh, he was going down for the day next week, would I like to come too?

The primitive cottage was set in the flat, secretive Marsh country, cold winter winds sweeping in from the sea, the skies brooding over past scenes of murky death and smugglers' tales. As we walked on the long, narrow, squelchy path to Jackson's Cottage, as it was called, I noticed some hardy, long-coated sheep huddled along one side of the house, seeking shelter, their breath coming out almost like smoke. From time to time they stamped their feet and coughed hoarsely.

Constantine looked very young, a cherubic smile on his face, as he opened the door.

'How wonderful to see you, darling. You too, Harold. I'm getting weary of these consumptive sheep coughing outside the window.'

There was a large fire of wood in the small shepherd's room, making it warm and giving out the smell of apples burning. A wooden table was covered with typing paper and it was obvious Constantine had been writing.

'Only sausages and baked beans, I'm afraid, and a few bottles of beer. How long are you staying?'

When I said I was going back with Harold his face darkened. I could sense his disappointment, but I didn't see how I could stay there with no change of clothes or indeed anything else.

During the afternoon Harold said he wanted to call on some people in the village, so when we were alone I asked Con if he had got Mimi's telegram in Paris. He hadn't asked why I was in hospital – so as far as he knew I was still pregnant.

'Telegram? No, I didn't get any telegram. What was it about? I had practically no money by the time I got to Paris so I thought I'd better get to England as soon as possible.'

I told him what it had conveyed; he looked thoughtful, then asked:

'Why are you going back with Harold? Don't you want to live with me any more? Admittedly I haven't much to offer, but I'm writing again and *The Iron Hoop* is due out with Cassell anytime now. I can probably get some money from Desmond Flower on this book, which is almost finished.'

I realized he didn't know about the money I had inherited, so, minimizing it, I recounted the strange and unexpected story. If anything he looked a bit annoyed, and his mood changed from one of coaxing to aggression. In minutes we were into a hellish scene in which accusations were shouted from both sides, some true and some untrue. When Harold came back and said we must be starting for the train, I was torn between reconciliation and a desire to leave at once. In my heart I knew there wouldn't be a reconciliation for many murderous hours.

A few days later a letter arrived from him: not at all apologetic, but saying he wanted us to 'build a new and sensible life' together; that everything he wrote, he wrote for me, because he loved me; 'we were the same person'. He could never again live through the chaos and misery of last year, and without me his work would count for nothing. Would I please come down again? I went down for about a week and we lived the life of the nineteenth-century peasantry – collecting wood, trimming oil lamps, filling stone hot-water bottles, rising and going to bed very early. Meanwhile Constantine wrote all day while I busied myself with the never-ending process of keeping warm, cooking simple soups or stews, and reading. I took long walks garbed in a duffle coat I found behind a door, wellingtons and woollies, and I thought and thought. We were careful with each other, stifling unkind thoughts or resentment, trying desperately to achieve even a gloss of the harmony we had once known. It was impossible for me to go on staying in my mother's small house, so it was agreed I would go back to London and look for a flat in Chelsea which we could both share and then see how things worked out.

I found a flat on the top floor of a pleasant house on Cheyne Walk, overlooking the river, just past Whistler's house. It was bright, and that part of Chelsea concealed no ghosts for either of us. It was near enough to stroll along the embankment to pubs we knew like the Crossed Keys, the King's Head and Eight Bells, and the Pier. Acquaintances would nod greetings which made us feel as if we had come home. One evening just before we moved in we went to the Crossed Keys to eat and a large brown poodle came over and nuzzled my arm. He was a proud, handsome dog who seemed unattached to anyone except us.

'He reminds me of Flotow,' I said. 'Isn't it strange that as soon as we arrive a brown poodle so like him should come over to me?'

The dog continued to sit by my side, nudging my arm from time to time. We got up to leave. Turning round, I saw a few tables away Barney and Sue Fawkes, whom we had last seen in Bermuda before they were married. Sue's sister, Natalie, had bought one of Mouche's puppies when we were at Cheriton, Sue and Barney having taken him over. No wonder I thought the dog, called Beau, was like Flotow; he was his brother! The Fawkeses had that day moved into another flat in Cheyne Walk, and we all marvelled that Beau had remembered his foster-mother over the years. For he had left me when he was three months old and seen

me only a few times in New York. The Fawkeses were delighted
to have Constantine to stay for the short time before we moved. It
was good for our relationship to be able to meet in the atmosphere
of love and warmth which Barney and Sue exuded.

Once into Cheyne Walk we began to look for old friends such
as Diana Graves, who was acting again. One lunchtime Constantine brought Peter Ustinov back for a meal. They had first
met when Constantine was seventeen and was at the Barn Summer Theatre in Shere. Estelle, his girl then, was acting Clytem-
nestra in Racine's play and Constantine was translating *Britannicus*
for her to play Agrippina in later on. The theatre, as the name
implied, was a converted barn. The semi-professional actors lived
in an old farm building. Constantine had enjoyed being treated as
a coming prodigy, then felt very deflated, he told me, by the
arrival of Peter Ustinov, who at the age of sixteen had produced,
written and acted in his own play there.

'And as long as I live,' Constantine would remark, 'Peter will
always be one year younger than I am.'

Peter was fantastically good company that morning. He kept us
enthralled by detailing the plot of his play *Love of the Four Colonels*,
acting almost all the parts. Although I later saw it staged, it is that
day's performance I remember with the greatest pleasure.

The Six Bells pub in the King's Road looked remarkably
unchanged when I looked in one morning, the mahogany
gleaming, the brilliant green of the billiard table showing through
the hatch behind the bar just as it had always done. Only Curly
was missing, the Irish barman who had been killed in 1941 when
the pub was bombed. It had a strange effect on me, even more so
when I saw, sitting in the corner where we had both sat so often in
the past, Peter Rose Pulham. As usual he was making notes on a
sketching block, so he did not see me sit down opposite him. I
knew he would look up in annoyance at having a stranger at his
table, and he did. Then his face softened into a broad smile as he
said:

'Pussy, how clever of you to appear just now.'

'I thought you lived in France. What on earth are you doing
here? Is Mary here too?'

'Yes, I do, but I'm over to arrange my exhibition at the Redfern
Gallery in a few months' time. I've had a lot of exhibitions in
London since you left, Pussy, and some in Paris. Pity you've just
missed one at the London Gallery. Mary's still in France. But let's
talk about you. Let's spend the day together, there's so much to
say, isn't there?'

Constantine didn't seem at all pleased when I rang, but agreed rather grudgingly. Peter was in one of his few exuberant moods when I got back and had ordered Pimms to drink. 'A sort of celebration,' he said. We had a glorious day, first to the back bar of the Café Royal, where we found Dylan Thomas who seemed surprised to see us together. He asked after Constantine and told me Caitlin had had a baby boy they called Colm the previous July. He had great hopes of an extensive American tour to read his poetry in a few weeks' time. He was extremely excited about it. Then we had an excellent lunch at L'Etoile which went on for some time while we reminisced, explored each other's ideas and felt very happy. It was like ten years ago when we were in love, as if for a day we had been transported back in time. We both knew it would end at midnight and there was no magic except what we were making ourselves.

Then we had to go to the Colony Rooms, an afternoon drinking club, as Peter wanted to see Francis Bacon. What about Constantine? I thought, and said so. He waved his hand.

'Nonsense, he can let you go out for a day. After all, he snitched you from me all those years ago, he can't possibly complain.'

Desmond Flower of Cassell was a kind and friendly man, who entertained us several times. He suggested that a lot of our worry in the past could have been lessened if Constantine had had an agent. When told of the disastrous effect of the original agent's letter, in Bermuda, he told Constantine to get in touch with Pearn, Pollinger & Higham (now David Higham Associates), whom he was sure would be helpful. They were, too, and remained his agents all his life.

The Chelsea flat was fine for a short stay but not for permanent living. I suggested finding a house in the country, not too far from London.

'Not that stockbroker belt,' said Constantine immediately. 'I know, let's try Hertfordshire. Estelle and I had a little cottage there once.'

So we looked and looked, but found nothing we felt was right. We asked in pubs and country hotels; somebody suggested that nearer the Essex border was better. So we went to Bishops Stortford to an agent who sent us to look at houses in Much Hadham. A good rural name, we thought. A friendly publican sent us to call on the Levy Teasdales who lived in a pleasant house there, and so we found what we were looking for. Stephen Thomas, who had been Sir Nigel Playfair's stage manager at the Lyric Theatre, Hammersmith, held it in trust for his son Billy. It was called Sacomb's Ash and we were to live there for nearly ten years.

CHAPTER FIFTEEN

The name Sacomb, we were told, was a corruption of 'Saxon combe', which might have been true. It was in a hamlet called Allen's Green, consisting of a score of dwellings, mostly farm-workers' cottages, a small school, a wooden church and a pub which sold only beer. None of these had electric light although London was only twenty-eight miles away. There was no shop, no bus and no telephone kiosk, so it was truly rural, and apart from the modern house of the farmer Mr Knight, who also cultivated mushrooms, it was as it had been for many years. The nearest shops were three and a half miles away at Sawbridgeworth, but the larger town, Bishop's Stortford, was over six miles. We had no car so it meant bicycling, which I enjoyed.

The house was a quarter of a mile from the hamlet at the end of a twisting no-through road, set in its seventeen acres, ten of which were rented to the farmer. To the back and side were very large flat fields of corn. Along one side of the house was an oblong pond surrounded by willow trees. There were nine rooms, one an addition the opposite side to the pond. The outside of the house was half-pargeted, that is plastered, with traditional designs incised on to it. A small lawn in front was bounded by a beech hedge, with a beautifully shaped walnut tree in the middle with a bench round it. The rest of the land available to us was a half-acre paddock, a large orchard with lofty and well-built barns, loose boxes and an exercise yard; then a huge lawn which we subsequently made into a croquet pitch. Overgrown flower borders enclosed it, beyond which was a walk between a long hazel hedge with an eighty-year-old mulberry tree to the right and a lot of rough land. This was encircled by a hedge layered intricately by two of the villagers. Also, unusual for that time, a big boiler centrally heated the house. It was remote, pleasant of aspect and peaceful. I paid the rent for a year to ensure that peace.

The indigenous villagers were a strange folk; old grudges were harboured and many of them had never ventured far from Allen's Green. One family, in which the mother had died some years before, hated their father, even going so far as when his cat was run over to string it up in the bicycle shed so that 'when the old bugger puts his bike away tonight he'll walk into it!' They thought this a great joke. I urged some of the almost grown-up sons of that family to go to London, even for the day; they went to the zoo, told me the wild animals frightened them, so they came home. They seemed quite content to go to the pub and play darts endlessly. I never saw them with any girls.

There were, of course, exceptions – notably Len and Minnie Rix who ran the pub, Rixie, as he was called, also having a job elsewhere. Old Bob, a relative of Minnie's, lived with them and he went as far as to make the sign of the index and little finger extended against the evil eye when certain people came in. Then there was Old Lil and Old Herb who lived together next to the school of which Old Lil was caretaker. Apparently the job went to the senior widow, which might have accounted for their unmarried state. Herb must have been fine looking as a young man, for even at seventy he was tall and upright, with very good manners. Lil was small and dark with very merry twinkling eyes which must have fluttered a few rural hearts in days gone by. Next to the church lived Mrs Howe and her husband George, a happy little man whom I never saw without a smile. He and Herb worked for the farmer and Mrs Howe was a loyal and good helper in the house all the time we were there. The others were in general small, dark, round-headed people, whom the local doctor swore were true ancient Britons, the Romans having gone up the river Stort without stopping to colonize the small hamlets on the way. It's a theory I like to believe. Halfway down the lane was a small thatched cottage in which lived Bert and Jane Wellstead with their small son. The husband was a small, sad-looking man, born a Rothschild, but who changed his name to his mother's maiden name, for as he said:

'Who wants to know a poor Rothschild?'

He lived a curiously introverted and almost secret life, which largely excluded his wife and son. Jane was to become a steadfast friend of mine over the years. She lived the life of a country woman, growing flowers, vegetables and tending animals such as goats and Chinese geese with which Bert, from time to time, arrived home. Opposite the Queen's Head pub were two thatched cottages made into one, where Andrew and Elizabeth Foster-Melliar lived, Elizabeth being Irish born. They, too, were to figure in our lives in many ways. There was also Kathleen Fraser who was to become Constantine's typist; she lived with an enormous number of dogs and cats.

Although there was a little furniture in Sacomb's Ash, it was far from furnished, so we bicycled to auctions all over the place, and my grandmother produced many things, as she had during the war when we were married. Georgette, Constantine's mother, had left some of her pretty furniture in store in London when she returned to America, and that was also given to us. So gradually we were able to make an attractive home with some of our own things for the first time. We explored the nearby villages, mostly by walking across the fields behind the house. Green Tye was the nearest, about two miles away, boasting a pub and a few houses, but nothing else. However, it was a pleasant walk; the pub was bright and clean, frequented by the villagers.

The village further on was Perry Green, which was bigger, with some larger houses, no shops but a pub called the Hoops. It was here one Sunday morning that we met Michael O'Connell, who had built himself a story-book house nearby in a little copse which he had cleared himself. Attached to it was his long, low work-room, for he was an expert tie-dyer of cloth, having gone as far afield as New Guinea and West Africa to learn his craft. He also perfected resist-dyeing, where the pattern is painted on the cloth with a thickened paste, preventing the dye from penetrating where the paste protects it. Some of his designs were spectacular and adorned offices such as the Time-Life Building in London. He was a kind and interesting man. In this small colony of interesting people there was also a painter and his wife, a fashion designer, who lived on the outskirts of Perry Green. Outside the pub there was a wooden table and benches where we sat when the weather was fine. It was on such a day that we saw coming towards us a man of about fifty, of medium height, with a very jaunty, quick walk. He was talking volubly to a tall white-haired man who had difficulty keeping up with him. Behind them was a small dark woman with Slavic features talking to a pretty English-looking girl. As he approached he smiled a greeting and entered the small pub. It was the first time we met the sculptor Henry Moore and his wife, Irina, who lived almost opposite, with Carl Sandberg the director of the Stedelijk Museum in Amsterdam, and Susan, a girl who helped to look after Mary Moore, their small daughter.

We became good friends with the Moores, spending some time in each other's houses. Irina intrigued me; she seemed so very self-contained, although it was obvious she thought deeply. Her slightly Asiatic cast of feature added to the strangeness. She was small, with slanting brown eyes and close-cropped grey-black hair. Apart from Henry and their Mary, her only other visible interest was in collecting cacti, which were housed in a separate greenhouse. She often talked to me of their early years, having met Henry when she was a student at the art college; their extreme poverty to begin with, sometimes living on cheap oranges bought from a stall late on Saturday nights. She had been determined not to have any children while Henry was struggling for recognition, deciding to wait until she was forty years old. This she did, in the perfect way Irina managed her life; they both adored Mary. Irina couldn't remember her parents in Russia, as during the Revolution she had walked many miles with other children until they had found sanctuary in Switzerland. Then she was either adopted or looked after by an English family. This was only said briefly, never elaborated, and Irina was not the kind of person you asked questions.

Henry seemed the opposite type of person – smiling, outgoing and full of fun, with a delightful giggle.

'Irina's quite right about those early years,' he said once. 'My first big sale was when Selfridges had an exhibition on their roof garden, and somebody accidentally knocked my scupture over!'

He told me he thought his feeling for form came from the time he was a child in Yorkshire, the youngest of seven children.

'My mother worked so hard for us, father was a miner, and she had awful rheumatism in her shoulder.' He paused for a moment as if reflecting, then went on: 'She used to say, "Come on, Henry boy, give my old shoulder a rub." Yes, I can remember the feel of the rounded bone.'

Going round his large studio was always interesting and I noticed on shelves a collection of odd-shaped stones, some piled one on top of another. They almost looked like small Moore sculptures, they were so rounded and beautiful. It was a great part of the country for odd-shaped stones, so I started collecting them too. Behind the house was the 'engine path', so called for a huge steam traction engine which went up to do the ploughing of the two huge fields on either side. This path was a good hunting ground for these odd stones. Often I would find one to give to Henry, some for myself. I still have one which resembles a minute Moore standing figure.

To begin with, our life together was like a convalescence; we both wanted to avoid any of the horrors of the previous years, and we took pains to study each other's sensitivity. However, we knew that to ensure this, Constantine must finish his novel and then decide what else he wanted to do. I was more than willing to make everything as easy as possible. *The Iron Hoop* was published in England and had excellent notices. He did finish the next novel *Cousin Emily*, and Desmond Flower accepted it happily; but there was a paper shortage at the time, so no date was yet given for its publication. Before he had time to worry about what he would do next, Con's agent telephoned asking if he would, or could, translate a book from German into English. The publisher was Allan Wingate and the book, *The Burned Bramble*, was by Manès Sperber.

Manès Sperber was a remarkable man born in Zablotow, a small town in the Ukraine. He had studied under Alfred Adler, the Viennese psychologist, and became a professor of psychology at the University of Berlin. Pre-Hitler he held high posts in the German Communist Party, then after 1933 he went underground and finally left Germany. In 1937 after the Moscow Purge trials he left the Communist Party and became a fugitive from both the Gestapo and the NKVD. Manès now lived in Paris with his wife Jenka and their son, Dan. His book (the first of a trilogy) was about the Communist movement in Western Europe and the betrayals of its heroes. It was a fascinating book, and although Constantine hadn't spoken much German since the war, he was convinced he could do it.

'After all,' he said, 'one needs to be able to write well in one's own language. I can always look up words in a dictionary.'

Our house was furnished in all but our books, which we had left in Italy, and we missed them as much as anything.

'I would like my dictionaries now,' remarked Constantine, 'and so many other things, my manuscripts and notebooks particularly. You remember what Norman always said: "Never throw any work away; you never know when it will come in useful." I might even be able to finish the Douglas book in the sanity of the English countryside.'

It was decided that I would go back to Italy to collect our things, as well as to repay all the kind people who had lent me money during those last months.

My thoughts were very confused as the train rumbled across Europe to Rome. I felt at home in Italy and I loved certain people who had given me warmth, and indeed their love, which had sustained me through days of bleakness, endless dark tunnels of misery. Despite the years of unhappiness and pain I had experienced in Italy, I looked forward to being in La Bella again. I pushed away the soul-clinging mire and thought instead of those sunny mornings when I set out for work, the murmur of '*bella bionda*' from the first good-looking man I encountered, and the automatic clutching of the genitals as he passed me, to avert any impotency from the blue-eyed girl who *could* possess the evil eye. This superb blend of paganism and Christianity was what attracted me about Italy, and particularly Rome, not only in the layers of earth but also in the people. I thought of Samuel Rogers's remark, penned in 1820:

The memory in Rome sees more than the eye.

Probably the only other place I felt like that about was Ireland.

The Tompkins had moved from the via Gregoriana to a beautiful apartment on the top floor of an old house in the via Margutta, for years the street where painters and writers lived. It had a glorious view, high enough up to muffle the street noises. A young man was sitting on the terrace typing, and he was introduced as Pabst's son who was staying with them. Instantly my thoughts went back to the time I had met his father, the hopes and fears I experienced then, but I said nothing for I knew that if such opportunity should occur again, I would not return to England. When I visited my apartment in the Piazza di Spagna it was to find Ann had left; some said she had married an Italian and gone to Canada, but nobody really knew. Sybille Bedford now lived there. She looked so happy and comfortable that unfairly I almost resented her being there. The signora had taken my things, she told me, but I was welcome to any books I saw of mine. I picked out a few favourites which she would keep for me until I was leaving.

After a few days I went down to Positano before going to Capri for the books Paanaker still had. Mimi was drinking very heavily again, delighted to see me, but somehow vague when I suggested to her that she come back to England with me and stay for a while at Sacomb's Ash. Not now, she might come next year, maybe . . . Luca found me some large sacks to put the books in when I collected them from Capri. What few possessions we'd had apart from books seemed to have disappeared.

Back in Rome, Peter had said I couldn't possibly take books in the sacks, some would get cut open or stolen; so he got packing cases from somewhere, these were filled, then nailed down and labelled. He was to bring me to the station to deal with the officials, who apparently could be capricious about non-personal luggage. Somehow the nailed-down cases made my decision to go back irrevocable. I had spent the last evening, way into the early hours, with Reinhard, and we both knew we were unlikely ever to meet again. That part of my life was over, sealed into its own secret compartment.

On the journey homewards I realized that Constantine and I
were going through an uneasy peace; we were not really behaving
quite spontaneously to each other. What was it Georgette had said
in Bermuda?

'I know everything will be all right between you both because
you laugh so much together.'

There had been precious little laughter over the past year and I
knew it was as much my fault as Constantine's. If your relationship with yourself is honest and understood, then, no matter
what, your relationship with other people falls into place. I had
mistrusted myself many times and been full of suspicion and near
hatred. There was one way to sort out my thoughts and that was
to go soon to my family in Ireland for a while. The rain like soft
mist, the smell of wet earth, even the pace and attitude to life
would calm the many turbulent feelings that coursed through me.

CHAPTER SIXTEEN

It was some months later that I stood leaning over the old bridge at Killaloe, looking up the Shannon River to Lough Derg. As I looked at the Lake Hotel where my father had been living before he died I wondered if there was any more beautiful place in the world: a serene, peaceful beauty now, the watery sunlight casting pale shadows, the puffy clouds fast moving, giving rapidly changing colours to the hills and the lake. No wonder Ireland was difficult to paint, the colours changed so frequently. The Dalcassian Kings knew what they were about when they sited the royal seat here. I had just left the twelfth-century cathedral, attributed to King Donal Mór O'Brien, now Church of Ireland, marvelling again at the rich romanesque doorway. Was it really the entrance to King Murtagh O'Brien's tomb, nearby the shaft of a cross with runic and ogham inscriptions? So much had taken place here, it was impossible to sort out fact from legend, but the magic remained.

It was the same kind of magic as I had found in India, yet the countries were vastly different to live in – two countries which had cast a never-to-be-forgotten spell over me with their mysticism, fatalism and religious strength, whether one had belief or not. The sages of Ireland and India, the guru and the priest, both gave consolation to those in need. There were the cruelties and the kindnesses, the superstitions and the fears, the catastrophes of famine and wars. Now they both had their independence from the British Empire. Was it because of all these similarities that the colours of the Indian flag were the same as those of Ireland?

I remembered the first time I came to Ireland at the age of about seven. My aunt Roberta, known as Bobby, who lived but ten miles from this spot, had remembered that my father had another daughter whom she wanted to see. I was sent for from my convent during the school holidays; not that I was a neglected child, merely that I had insisted on staying for some weeks after term had finished. For I felt far happier with the ebullient South American girls and the Italians who never went home than I did as an only child with my grandmother. I worshipped a girl named Cordelia de Freitas, the eldest of about four sisters, who was much

older than I was. She had promised we would put on a costume
play, written by her, and we would have very colourful clothes,
made by the younger nuns. It was wonderfully exciting; we
seemed to have the run of the school and spacious grounds, for the
nuns, too, adored Cordelia and let her do many things forbidden
to us. She had enormous flashing eyes which rolled as she told us
of the carnivals which went on for some days and nights in her
native town. However, I think some of it must have been hearsay
for I cannot imagine a strictly brought-up South American girl
being allowed to wander the streets day and night.

It was fortunate that my aunt's request came just after the play
had been performed, otherwise I might have refused to go.
County Clare in Ireland seemed a long way away and none of my
immediate family was able to accompany me. So a courier was
found from the best travel bureau to take me to Dublin. When we
got on the boat the courier must have thought it a cushy job, for
he spent most of the time in the bar, telling me his 'tummy was
upset'. At night I was handed over to a kind stewardess, who
tucked me up in what I thought was a queer bed, then brought me
hot cocoa. The following morning the courier's tummy seemed
even more upset for he could hardly stand, clutching on to the
walls to help himself along.

'You'd better hold on to me,' I said, but when he did I too
nearly fell down – he was a very heavy burden for a seven-year-
old to carry. Going down the gangplank was the worst, for he
lurched from side to side until I was frightened I might fall
through the ropes. His face was very red and he kept coughing.
Passengers behind were saying:

'Imagine that poor little child with that drunken man. Someone
ought to do something.' But nobody did.

My new uncle and aunt met me. They were smiling, then my
uncle Terry laughed and said:

'You're a great little girl to have handled that so well,' and he
patted my head. 'Do you want to stay in Dublin tonight with us,
or be getting down to your cousins? They're about the same age as
you. You'd best stay with us, I think, and go down on the
morning train. I'll ring your uncle Jack to meet you.'

Uncle Terry put me on the train in care of the guard, a common
occurence in the 1920s and 1930s and very thrilling it was. There
were often dogs and other animals such as chickens or pigeons to
be talked to. I sat on a small tip-up seat in the guard's
compartment, and when the train stopped at stations I was
allowed out on the platform with the guard until he blew his

whistle, then waved his flag for the train to move on.

The train stopped at Limerick Junction which, in true Irish fashion, is in fact in Tipperary. It was just a junction and there was no one to meet me. The stationmaster was fond of children and pressed a cup of hot strong sweet tea into my hand. I'd never had tea before; the nuns brewed their own kind of weak beer which we were given at mealtime, with milk for breakfast and supper. I didn't like the tea at all, so I just sipped it.

'Too hot, is it?' he asked. 'Have some more milk.'

Luckily another train was coming through so we ran and took back the gates.

After what seemed a very long time to me the old AC car drove up.

'Have you been here long?' Uncle Jack asked. 'There was a man looking at a horse so I couldn't get away.'

I couldn't think what he meant; why was he looking at a horse? Why not ride it? I thought how my grandmother would have disapproved – 'It's just as easy to be punctual as late' – but it never was and never has been for my Irish relations.

Never could I have imagined how wonderful it would be as a child in Ireland. Cordelia and her play were soon forgotten as I learnt to ride, a special pony being designated just for me, played wild games with my boy cousins, climbed huge trees often without shoes and went to race meetings. I reflected how much life had improved since those early days, for an unforgettable memory is of us children sitting on one of the farm carts they used to have at country race meetings, eating oranges and throwing the peel on the ground. A group of ragged children appeared from nowhere, gathered up the peel and ate it avidly. To a well-fed child like myself it made a lasting impression. A job I loved was naming the foals: when I was about twelve years old I was handed the stud-books and told to make a list of names for the horses appropriate to their breeding. I became quite good at this and even today I find myself doing it if I glance through a race card.

But my familiarity with horses and race meetings was to cause me trouble when I was about eleven. We were allowed to make small bets of about a shilling when our own or friends' horses were running, so when I went back to school I continued it, putting on bets with the gardener. For some time I was very careful, never exceeding my pocket money, but the day came when I won the fantastic sum of thirteen pounds, four shillings and sixpence. There was chocolate fudge all round and a healthy balance left. However, a few weeks later my luck plunged and I lost nearly fifteen pounds. The gardener kept coming to me, saying I must pay. But how? It was an astronomical amount for a child in those days. Finally I asked him for the name and address of the bookmaker, and in my childish hand I wrote saying my daughter was at present abroad but would settle the debt on her return, a form of letter I had glimpsed written by several of my uncles.

Alas, the next thing I knew, I was in the Mother Superior's office together with the gardener and my mother. The letter was on the Mother Superior's desk. There was no denying it and I didn't attempt to. Sadly, I was asked to leave 'because I had a bad influence on the other girls'. In Ireland, where I was sent until another suitable school could be found, I was treated like a heroine.

We were allowed to do almost anything; there were few restrictions that might stifle our initiative and imagination. One of my young cousins in Ballybunion on holiday, while we were paddling and swimming, bought and sold donkeys on the beach making himself a handsome profit. He is now a rich man – and no wonder.

Whenever we felt ill, or had the slightest thing wrong with us, it was referred to as 'growing pains', which made sense to me as daily I grew taller. The cure was always the same: bowls of hot, creamy-white onion soup and afterwards, before going to sleep, hot whiskey with lemon and funny little black things with a spicy taste when you bit them, which we were told were cloves. I was even given this 'cure' when I cracked some ribs after a fall when riding. To a certain extent I was treated by the boys as a foreigner, therefore with a mixture of awe and good-natured disdain. There were so many things I didn't know about Ireland which my cousins were quick to capitalize on. Sometimes their plans didn't come off, but at other times I fell straight into the trap.

One day in the early 1930s after my father had taken us to see his sister at Ballymackey, we were returning home by O'Brien's Bridge. As often in Ireland we could see a group of young men standing and talking on the bridge as we approached. We were sitting in the back with a good view. My cousin Desmond grabbed my arm and hurriedly whispered:

'When we go past the men, put your head out and shout "Up the Blueshirts!" '

This I did and the car was immediately pelted with large stones, one cracking the celluloid of the side window. My father stopped the car, getting out in a fury.

'What the hell . . .?'

Straight away I told him what I had called out, not however mentioning who had prompted the act. Staring at my cousins, he said:

'Of course you couldn't know, but O'Duffy had his head-quarters at Killaloe during the civil war a few years ago, so he isn't popular here now he's head of the Blueshirts. I wonder what put the idea in your head anyway.'

(General O'Duffy led the Blueshirts, a mildly Fascist party in Ireland, which is said to have gone to fight in the Spanish Civil War six-hundred-strong and to have returned six hundred and one!)

We were expected, or rather the boys were, to help with the haymaking, so all the farm machines were at our disposal to drive about the place, which is why no doubt I was attracted to an Austin Seven open tourer when I was about sixteen. It cost five pounds, so I bought it, to find out later that this very cheap price was because the brakes hardly worked at all. This didn't deter us one bit, for we stopped by driving into either a soft hedge or a haystack, and slowing down was done by all the passengers put-ting their feet out and dragging along the road. We had cousins in Clarina the other side of Limerick, and to get there I had to drive along the quay which was flat, just in case we ran into too much traffic in the main street. It was always great fun at Clarina, the home of the Craigs, one of the twin boys being Harry Craig, later known as H. A. L. Craig. He wrote poetry and was to become a well-known film scriptwriter and author of many BBC docu-mentaries.

We were very late getting back one day and my aunt was standing wringing her hands at the open avenue gates. We had got up a good speed down the hill on the approach, so there was no possibility of stopping quickly. She saw what was happening and nimbly jumped on to the verge, astonishment on her face, as we made for the safety of the hay barn.

When I had arrived a week before it was as if I had left only recently. The atmosphere and love were the same, the Virginian creeper sprawling all over the house, almost obscuring the win-dows. I was taken up to the room that had been mine, looking out over the park and Slieve Kimalta, the 'Hill of the Sorrows', in the distance. Old Trixie, the grey mare, was to be seen munching placidly with the other mares and young horses. I looked around the room.

'What beautiful murals!' I exclaimed.

My aunt Bobby looked puzzled; then I realized the 'murals' were young, lacy strands of Virginia creeper which had grown up over the roof, down the chimney and fanned out over the walls like the espaliered fruit trees in the walled garden of pre-war years. It looked lovely and my aunt said:

'I hadn't the heart to cut it down.'

She turned and looked searchingly at me, critically I thought.

'What's happened to your skin?' she asked.

I ran my fingers over my face. 'Is it dirty from the journey?'

'No, it's the colour, a sort of biscuit-brown.'

'I have lived in hot places for four years, you know, auntie. It's suntan. Don't you think it's rather nice?' I pulled up my sleeve to show my brown arms, but she looked doubtful.

'I don't know, I'm sure. You used to have such beautiful white skin.'

Later, during my stay I was to lunch with a local historian in Limerick who was a family friend. My aunt came into my room as I was getting ready and said:

'I've arranged that lunch should be early, it's nearly ready now.'

'But I'm going out to lunch, I told you. Have you forgotten?'

Again she looked sad, hesitated, then said: 'You'd better have a little something, dear. It wouldn't do to go out with a man alone and eat too much!'

My father's words came back to me: 'Every time I go back to Ireland, it's still fifty years behind the times.' This was the first time I had been back to Ireland since I had married in 1944, as it was almost impossible to get over during the war. My historian friend, Michael, was also an amateur genealogist and seemed to know a lot about the FitzGibbon family.

'The FitzGibbon house is not far from here, you know. It's called Mountshannon, a ruin now like so many others. There's an old man who is alive in Limerick who was a boy when Lady Louisa FitzGibbon had the duns in and was sold up. You ought to call on him. His father was head groom there. He loves to talk about it. I've got an idea Lady Louisa's farm bailiff's daughter lives out Ballyneety way; Greene Barry, I think the name is.'

Like many Irish people he was fascinated with the past, filling me with such enthusiasm that I, too, began to think of them as people recently gone, not shadowy figures from long ago.

'You ought to go to Castleconnell too, it's only a few miles from your uncle's house. The church there is full of memorials to members of the FitzGibbon family. One of the family had a house there by the Donass Falls. I think cousins of your family had one adjoining, so you see you might still have met your husband over a hundred years ago.

'Coolbawn House there is going to be a hotel. Kitty and Adza should do well with it, during the salmon fishing season. Adza's a fine looking girl, and capable too.'

I looked at him with astonishment. 'Adza, did you say?'

'Yes, Adza.' After a moment he looked equally astonished. 'Of course, she must be a relation.'

Never in my life have I heard of anyone else being called Adza; it had to be my sister, whom I hadn't seen for years.

We weren't brought up together, but during our childhood Adza's mother, Kitty, who had been a singer, often took us – the 'two little girls' – away for holidays. She was an expansive, passionate woman with a deep love of the theatre. The holidays were always unusual and exciting. Heredity must count for something, for as we grew up we shared the same enthusiasms and ambitions: a love of the theatre, a love of good food, and travel. With such common interests it was always easy when we did meet to take up almost where we had left off, even though our childhoods had been so very different. We also shared the same sort of ingenuity and sense of humour.

Some years later, when Adza decided to sell the hotel, it was an inclement time of year; guests were scarce, but this didn't daunt her. She was great friends with the cast of a touring company which was playing at the Limerick Theatre. They were all engaged to play their part in the sale, for she invited them to be her guests when the prospective hotel buyer came. The bar was full, drinks and lunch being on the house.

'What'll you have, Charles? Same again?'

'Thanks, Aidan. Maybe we should get the menu and the wine list to make sure the wine's the right temperature.'

'Two gin-and-limes, please,' said the two young ladies next to them. Other orders came thick and fast. The lunch was long, lingering and delicious. The buyer looked impressed.

'You've a good clientele, haven't you? Is it regular, or just casual trade? Will they be here long?'

The sale went through; the evening's performance of the play had an additional sparkle; everyone was content.

Once I start thinking about Ireland it is not only of people but of places: the bicycle ride from Ballylickey up the long winding hill to the Pass of Keimaneigh (the deer's pass), the glacier-washed rock enclosing it; the merry tinkle of the stream, the mountain sheep and, incredibly, a raven uttering its sad cry; then on to Gouganebarra, a still, shining mountain-hemmed lake with its tiny island and the shrine to St Finbarr, the first bishop of Cork in the sixth century; Dinny Cronin's simple, bare pub (the scene of some of Sean O'Faolain's stories), draughts of Guinness, bacon, eggs and potato cakes, then waking up in the cold, crystal clear air, feeling more sparkling than after champagne; the field of gentians near Inchigeela, so impossibly blue they dazzled the eyes.

Dublin: the crowded pubs where the sound of people talking was like several hives of contented bees. The late-night sessions which went on in the back rooms of small hotels, talking, talking all the time, the glasses filled regularly. Sean O'Faolain, the biographer and brilliant short-story writer, delightful, witty and malicious, his alert blue eyes moving quickly as he went from subject to subject. Old Joe Hone (biographer of Yeats) and his wife Vera, Joe so absent-minded I remember a lunch at their house where he ate the string tied round the asparagus as well as the vegetable, without noticing. Then Arland Ussher, whose tall, spare mien decried his nature, for underneath that shy, hesitant exterior was the most agile of brains and the most passionate of hearts. He wrote exquisite prose, and was also a Gaelic scholar, having translated *The Midnight Court* in the 1920s, and other Irish books. When I first met him, his book *The Face and Mind of Ireland* had been published to great critical acclaim. John Betjeman wrote of it: 'It is penetrating, as entertaining as a thriller, witty, but not chatty, catty but not unbalanced . . .'

In the early 1950s when I was there, he had just finished a book about the Jews, to be called *The Magic People*, which became one of my favourites. He was fundamentally a philosopher, hence his *Journey Through Dread*, a study of Sartre, Heidegger and Kierkegaard. But then he was working on studies of Bernard Shaw ('Emperor and Clown'), W. B. Yeats ('Man into Bird') and James Joyce ('Doubting Thomist and Joking Jesuit'). It was called *Three Great Irishmen*.

In company Arland hardly spoke at all and many found him dull, but with one or two loved friends he was not only very talkative, but very entertaining. His almost ascetic appearance and introverted manner did nothing to prepare you for either his thoughts or his behaviour, both of which were extremely unconventional. He was a little over fifty when I first met him and hardly resembled the red-haired, sensual young man Augustus John had painted. We both found pleasure in each other's company, for he talked very openly to me, often late at night in a dim room, the only other sound perhaps the crackling of a fire and the constant hiss of a match as he lit yet another cigarette. Our meetings were rare, but in between there were many letters. It was almost a love affair by letter, for there were times over the thirty years that we shared a great affection. Arland admired George Moore very much, having known him in the 1920s, and he once said he felt about me the way George Moore had about Lady Cunard.

There were other journeys, each one memorable, and some with Constantine who, after my recounting stories of the FitzGibbon family, wanted to find out more, to write a book about them. This was to be *Miss Finnigan's Fault*★. We met the old Limerick man who as a young boy had held the horses outside Mountshannon. He vividly described the last ball Lady Louisa, Constantine's great-grandmother, gave while the duns were in the house playing cards.

'Millions!' he mumbled through toothless gums. 'Every window was flaming with great gas bowls. She spent more money in twenty years than Queen Victoria in her whole lifetime!'

I visited Miss Greene Barry, who had inherited a few of the FitzGibbon paintings from her father. She was a charming sensitive woman, who hinted that we might like some of the paintings, but alas she was unable to make us a gift of them. Through her solicitor I bought a pleasant portrait of the Second Lord Clare, Lord Byron's close friend at Harrow of whom he wrote in his poem 'Childhood Recollections'.

> Friend of my heart, and foremost of the list
> Of those with whom I lived supremely blest . . .

Some three weeks before Byron died he wrote a letter from Missolonghi to Clare, saying: '*I hope you do not forget that I always regard you as my dearest friend and love you as when we were Harrow boys together.*'

In the basement of the Limerick library I discovered the bronze panels depicting scenes from the disastrous battle of Balaclava in the Crimea, which had decorated the sides of Macdowall's statue of the young Hussar, Viscount FitzGibbon, the statue having been tipped from its place on Sarsfield Bridge, Limerick, into the Shannon, during the Civil War. I photographed them.

Now I reflected how very curious it was that, although Ireland and her people had known but little peace, or indeed prosperity, yet the atmosphere could calm and bring such hope to troubled hearts; not only to the inhabitants, but also to others from across the seas.

★ Cassell 1953.

CHAPTER SEVENTEEN

The peace and hope I had experienced in Ireland were still alive when I got back one early summer's day to Sacomb's Ash. The catkins on the hazel hedge, dusted with yellow powder, tossed a welcome in the zephyr-like breeze. Constantine greeted me with delight, saying what a lot of work he had done on the translation of Manès Sperber's book. He was looking foward to finishing it as he had an idea for another novel. The only thing missing to me in that shining, charming house was my dog. The parting with Flotow was still very vivid in my thoughts.

Our life assumed an order it had seldom had before: Constantine worked all morning, when he broke off to walk down to the pub, or across the fields; then again in the late afternoon until dinner time. Since petrol coupons were no longer needed after May 1950, the first time for eleven years, friends usually drove down for the weekend. We had a pin or firkin of beer at weekends from the pub and a little wine, but no spirits unless somebody brought a bottle. The five-shilling meal limit in restaurants had been lifted in May too, also the points system for canned meats, but fresh meat was still very scarce; there were, however, good country chickens, rabbits and fish to be bought. Even so, many foods were impossible to get in the country, and I would go up to London to Soho and buy some of the things I had been used to in Italy. I spent days experimenting cooking dishes so that the huge larder was full of food for the long weekends. There was goat's milk and cream to be got from Mrs Pugsley in the village and I made goat's cheese, at that time little known in England except by well-travelled gourmets.

Most Sunday evenings we would have a large cold buffet of pâté, quiches, poultry or tongue, with a tureen of hot soup and baked potatoes. It was then regularly open house for local friends like the Foster-Melliars, Henry and Irina Moore, together with our guests.

The flat countryside produced exceptional sunsets; in summer we would sip our drinks on the large lawn, watching the changing colours, while the scent of stocks, tobacco plants, roses and lilacs pervaded the air, an added delight. The rapture of the early days in Bermuda or Italy was gone, it was a more sedate pleasure now for we had changed. There was so much to be done; the large garden had to be planted, then kept under control. Constantine made the back lawn his special duty, by rolling it constantly, weeding and scattering grass seed, so that in some months it looked very fine, making a splendid almost full-size croquet lawn. Neither of us had ever gardened before, but our flowers and vegetables seemed wonderful. Most of my knowledge came from my nearest neighbour Jane Wellstead who could make a dry stick grow, or so it appeared to me. The large orchards bore great crops of apples, pears, plums and the rarer greengage.

Some of the hard fruits I stored on fruit-racks in the huge black barn, and it was there one evening when going out to collect some fruit that I saw some rats performing an extraordinary feat. One rat was lying on its back holding a large apple on its stomach with its four legs, while another rat pulled him along by the tail to their nest. I stood fascinated for some minutes, neither animal taking the slightest notice of me. We decided a cat might be a good idea to prevent the rats coming into the house, and luckily Kathleen Fraser, Constantine's typist, had a litter of half-Persian kittens, from which we chose a pretty little female we called Jocasta. Also looking through the advertisements in *The Times* one morning I saw a standard poodle puppy for sale, in Cornwall. I went up to London to fetch her and somehow felt I knew her at first sight. She reminded me so strongly of that brown puppy with us in Bermuda. It was extraordinary to find, on looking at the pedigree, that she was in fact Mouche's granddaughter.

There was always something new going on in London, only an hour away by train. Peter Rose Pulham held a successful exhibition at the Redfern Gallery; one of his paintings, 'La Salle des Pas Perdues', is still so alive in my memory. Those that weren't sold were bought by the French surrealist painter André Masson. Ealing Film Studios were well on the way to making extremely good popular English films – *Passport to Pimlico* with Margaret Rutherford and *Kind Hearts and Coronets* with Alec Guinness playing six or seven parts were assured successes. Alec Guinness was now becoming established as a fine actor in films such as *The Lavender Hill Mob* and *The Man in the White Suit*, which portrayed characteristically British types instead of the Hollywood model. The drabness of wartime and post-war food was much altered with the launching of some small owner-run restaurants and country pubs. There was the bistro-like Ox on the Roof in the King's Road, Chelsea, which amongst good French bourgeois dishes also served snails steaming hot with garlic butter. The first

Good Food Guide was started by Raymond Postgate, a fine out-spoken man, who earlier had written an article for the *Leader* magazine called 'Society for the Prevention of Cruelty to Food'. I would often lunch at one of these new places, perhaps with my friend Diana Graves, who always had her flat full of interesting people. Constantine, too, refound friends he had known at Oxford, some of whom came for weekends. It was a full life.

When the translation was finished, Constantine was going to Paris to see Manès Sperber, who worked in a publishing company and couldn't get away to come to England. Con insisted I go with him, an invitation I naturally didn't refuse.

The Sperbers lived at that time in a flat near the Porte de Versailles. Manès was a small man, grey-haired, with rather thoughtful stern brown eyes and a most determined mouth. He spoke good but accented English, quickly but forcefully. He gave the impression that he would not change his mind easily but would be a loyal friend. Jenka, his wife, was Estonian, large in build with an attractive, kind face and an easy manner. She too spoke English well, with less of an accent than her husband. Manès was very pleased with the translation and, after giving us some wine, he started to talk about the book and other matters of interest. They were stimulating to be with, Jenka a good cook, Manès an excellent host; they became good friends, even lending us their apartment when they went on holiday. They both drank very little – Manès had always been afraid of the comrades with him who drank, for he said they were the first to crack. I think Constantine's consumption of Pernod, wine and sometimes cognac after dinner rather alarmed him. He loved the cinema and we saw many French films. Constantine couldn't enjoy *M. Hulot's Holiday* with Jacques Tati, so he got up and walked out. After-wards Manès was astonished:

'But where can he be? Why did he leave the cinema?'

I assured him I thought Constantine would be at the nearest café and I was right. However, there were times when I too was worried by Con's behaviour after consuming too much alcohol. Although he held his drink well, it always had much more effect on him (although strangers would not perhaps have noticed any-thing) because for a big man he ate very little, only small amounts of everything, not minding if he missed a meal. I never once heard him say he was hungry, especially if he was drinking.

Together we wandered about Paris, the city we both loved and had spent so much time in years before. We explored each other's childhoods in a way which hadn't been possible earlier. The Place des Vosges, colonnaded and exquisite, the Place Royale with the King's Pavilion on the south side; an imaginative nun had told me as a child about the duellists in the gardens in former times, and had shown me where Camille Desmoulins had plotted with his friends during the French Revolution. Another day we went to Passy to see if Constantine could find any trace of the old Russian lady who had looked after him for a while when he was a child.

'She must be dead by now, for she seemed old to me when I was about eight. But children are notoriously bad about adults' ages, aren't they? It's like houses you thought were enormous, but when you go back they are quite small. I adored her; she wore a bright red wig, saying her hair had fallen out with fright during the Russian Revolution, and she used to tip it over one eye to make me laugh.'

Alas there was no trace at all, nobody remembered her, though she was alive in Constantine's heart. As we walked through the streets past the Musée Clemençeau, we saw the Musée du Vin which Con said made him feel thirsty, so we stopped for a drink.

'Are we near that extraordinary school you went to, darling?'

The taste of Rome had been heady for my father on that journey back from India, so when he suggested we visit other European capitals before returning home, Manny and I were delighted. We were at last in Paris, but a day's journey from England, when unpredictably my father announced to me:

'I think you'd better go to a finishing school for a bit.'

Furiously, I answered: 'Really, after racketing around Europe with two middle-aged roués, to be sent back to school is a bit much.'

Manny joined in with my father against me as I protested vociferously: 'Manny, you've soon forgotten I stood up for you over the papal audience, it's a funny way of thanking me.'

He looked a bit sheepish as my father continued: 'You've still a few rough corners to be rounded up.'

So off I went, after saying I would only stay for a term, to an exclusive school for young ladies. I have to admit it was far better than any other establishment I had been to; there was more freedom. Still it was school, a word that had become anathema to me. As at my convent, the girls came from many parts of the world and, as before, it was the foreign girls I felt most at home with. We were taught many things I had learnt in India such as placement at table, etiquette, deportment and flower-arranging. Once a week we were brought out to Passy to a middle-European ex-queen of a country which had disappeared after the First World War, who gave classes in 'behaviour'. I think we were all expected to marry into minor royalty or the nobility, an ambassador at least, for the classes were very stringent.

The ex-queen lived in a detached house of quite humble proportions. We were received in a room of moderate size – in no way could it called a *salon* – with a small dais at one end on which was a carved chair, called the 'throne'. She was a forceful elderly lady, grey-haired, with very large, dark flashing eyes and a domineering manner. Several young, thin girls lived there too; these were referred to as 'ladies in waiting'; they looked frightened of her. It seemed to me that whatever language one spoke, she would answer in a different and usually alien one, which encouraged quick thinking. She would have parties just for us students at which all the food tasted horrible, for we must be taught to cope with any situation all over the world. If, when eating, very fragile pastry crumbs were dropped, we lost points in our tests. To this day I seldom ever make crumbs when eating, also I can still walk backwards beautifully, without bumping into anything, so rigorous was our training. Alas it was never completed, for true to my word I left after a term; but often those curious lessons come back to me, given by the sad old lady who was waiting for the 'old days' to return.

Now, when Con and I went to look, the discreet brass plate that had adorned the column by the gate was gone. The house looked different; the curtains hanging up at the windows would never have been approved by the ex-queen. I was pleased to think that perhaps she had not lived to see the aftermath of the war, when the map of the world had changed yet again.

As we had a weekend to spare we went down to stay with Peter and Mary Rose Pulham. They lived about an hour's journey from the Gare du Nord but quite in the country. Valmondois was a large house of nearly thirty rooms very sparsely furnished but beautifully situated. How Mary entertained large numbers of people with the primitive cooking arrangements is a mystery, but she was an excellent hostess, and had become a very good cook.

Peter was painting well, telling me of a series of paintings he had in mind, large canvases of the four seasons. The horse's skull I had gone to such pains to find for him during the war was still there; the secondhand easel my mother had given him about the same time was in daily use. It was a pleasant, relaxing few days with old friends, in a region of France neither of us knew. Peter and Mary looked well and happy – a perfect ending to our visit to France.

CHAPTER EIGHTEEN

One of the things I liked most about Sacomb's Ash was its wild life. There were some very beautiful birds, not all approved of by the farmer, but I enjoyed them: brightly coloured woodpeckers, called 'yaffles' by the locals, both the red and green variety and the spotted woodpecker; pink jays with pale blue eyes talked loudly in the trees; bullfinches, green finches, yellowhammers, flocks of noisy field fares in the winter; all flew about in numbers and fed on the lawn. My mother, who was very fond of birds, caught a young raven with a damaged wing which I nursed back to health in the stables. It was the time of Lorenz's book, about birds, *King Solomon's Ring*, and I read that corvines should be called by the first sound they made. So the raven was called Ark; when I freed him after about nine months, I would call his name in the garden and for some time afterwards he would circle round my head waiting for a piece of meat. The farm labourers looked up in surprise the first time they witnessed this.

There was a young hare who used to come and sit with me as I hung out clothes; at first I took it to be a little brown dog. There was a badger set in the spinney and one night we went down at dusk to watch the young badger cubs playing, an enchanting sight. At that time there were plenty of rabbits too, including black ones breeding in the wild. The land around us was rich with pheasants and red-legged partridge, and many of the small American owls hooted through the night. They were not much more than six inches high. There were nightingales too, and bats fluttered through the air on warm summer evenings. A beautiful vixen and her mate wandered nonchalantly along the engine path, and once, when I was walking along it with Minka, who was in season, I saw the brush of the dog fox in the corn field as he waited for us to return. I looked after a deserted cub for some time before releasing it; he too visited us for a little while. A solitary water-hen made her nest every year at the bottom of one of the willow trees around the pond, but her eggs were always unfertile. One morning, looking out of the bedroom window I saw something dart quickly at the top of the walnut tree – some red squirrels, delightedly taking the top nuts for their store. I wonder how many of these animals remain today.

My small inheritance didn't last very long, but it gave us nearly eighteen months of security and pleasure. Constantine, too, was making a certain amount of money from his translations and books. My grandmother died of pneumonia one cold January day, in her ninetieth year, refusing to let me come and see her as she lay ill, saying she wanted me to 'remember her, as she had been'. Could I ever forget the taste for adventure and originality she had given me as a child? She had got me out of the convent in Bruges I hated; 'an unhealthy place for a child, with all those smelly canals.' My first aeroplane flight with Alan Cobham's circus; her beach pyjamas at over seventy in the French resort; the party in the bedroom when a guest leaned on the hot-water basin and it came away from the wall, cascading water everywhere:

'Let me handle this,' she had said. 'You all go back to your rooms.' She had handled it so well, we got better rooms and preferential treatment.

She bought me my first sailor suit with a sailor's cap, HMS *Tiger* on the ribbon around it; I sat so proudly with it on, next to Deare the chauffeur in the Ford V8. Impossible to forget. The small amount of money she left me in the will 'to enjoy' (underlined); the small pieces of furniture, her mother's little sewing basket ('*you* will appreciate it'), are with me to this day.

Over the years many people came to Sacomb's Ash, as they had in Bermuda. One of the first to appear unexpectedly was Derek Verschoyle, who had left the Diplomatic Service and was starting a publishing firm. I was delighted to be able to return some of his hospitality of Rome days. We met Nigel Dennis the writer, who was a tall, dark man with a craggy face, deep-set brown eyes and a slightly hooked nose. Every Sunday he would come to dinner bringing with him his meat ration, usually giving it to me, with the words:

'If it's no good to you, give it to Minka.'

But during the time meat was rationed, it was very useful. At that time he lived in a pleasant cottage with some land where he grew vegetables and soft fruits – these he also shared with us. It was in a wood at Broxbourne, a very secluded and rural situation, with a magnificent selection of trees including the beautiful hornbeam. One day Nigel took me for a walk in the wood and as we came into a clearing and looked over the top of some high bushes we saw a group of about twelve people in green cloaks, dancing in a circle. We watched for about a minute, then he said:

'I think we'd better leave them to it. I did hear something about a witch's coven roundabout here. Maybe that's what it is.'

Nigel never drank alcohol, yet such was his personality that it was never noticed. He was an interesting person to talk to, having been at a progressive school in Germany, and after a variety of jobs became assistant editor of the *New Republic* magazine; later he joined the staff of *Time* magazine as contributing editor and reviewer of English and Continental books. He was planning to write his famous satirical book *Cards of Identity* when we first met him, so each week we would get a bubbling account of its progress. When it was produced as a play at the Royal Court Theatre with the young Joan Plowright playing a leading role, it received a good response.

Harold Scott frequently came down, often with his daughter, or with a young actor or actress. Harold bought six terraced cottages in the village, all occupied at a nominal rent, except one which he let to friends. This became known in the village as Scott's Lot. The Wakemans, who were living in Florida, were coming to Europe for a few years, and they rented the Foster-Melliars' cottage one summer whilst they were on holiday. It was a good summer with them. Surprisingly, too, Peter Rose Pulham arrived one day saying he and Mary had separated; could he stay? Of course. For me it was a gentle memory of once-upon-a-time. He stayed with us for some months, once looking after the house while we were away researching Constantine's Irish book.

One weekend at a large luncheon party Derek Verschoyle said:

'You're always giving us such delicious meals, Theo, why don't you write a cookery book?'

'But who would publish it?' I asked.

'I would. I'm just starting up as a publisher.'

No more was said at that time, so I quickly forgot about it, but a few weeks later he rang me, saying:

'How are you getting on with the cookery book?'

We discussed what form it should take and I suggested I write recipes from all the countries I had lived in, adapted to what was available in England then. It should be mentioned that in the early 1950s in England there were very few cookery books being written by women; the only names I can remember are Elizabeth Craig, Margeurite Patten, Fanny Craddock and Elizabeth David, who had published *Mediterranean Food* and *French Provincial Cooking*, although there were several books by well-known chefs. I enjoyed researching and writing for I had found that too much domesticity did not give me enough mental stimulation. With the money I got for the advance I bought a beautiful gouache by

Henry Moore which I treasured. That first book, *Cosmopolitan Cookery in an English Kitchen*★, went into several editions and was to start me on a new, absorbing career.

Alas, Derek's publishing firm didn't last all that long; he commissioned a book from Peter Rose Pulham about his life in the Indre district of France; Denis Johnston's *Nine Rivers from Jordan*, my own and others. By the time my second book was ready he was in bad straits; the writers on the list were transferred to André Deutsch, for whom I wrote five books in all. Deutsch became the most prolific publisher of cookery books and it was due to his publicity and good reviews that I was asked to do freelance articles for the *Daily Telegraph* and *Harper's Bazaar* and broadcasts on the BBC. As I got a little more money I bought a small bronze from Henry, who generously allowed me to take several home to make my choice.

Although at first Constantine was pleased with my moderate success, as time went on he seemed to resent anything that gave me even a slight independence. When I went to London to see a publisher or editor he was always very bad-tempered when I got home, and if I missed the six o'clock train and took the fast later one, there were often violent scenes, with accusations of infidelity. My denials only seemed to inflame him, so I learned to say nothing. I was never allowed to spend the night in London alone, even with my mother, who Con said harboured and encouraged my lovers. It was extremely unpleasant to live with; the remoteness of our house didn't help for there was nowhere to escape to except the garden, not an attractive proposition on a winter's night. However, I was determined not to give up my days in London – even the hated dentist got more visits than ever before! For the first time in my life I became secretive and introverted. I devoted more and more time to writing; short stories, ghost stories mostly, a play which was produced by the BBC, more cookery books and a novel, later published by Dent and made into a television play. I converted a small room off the drawing room into a writing room and library for myself, although my hours of work were restricted to after dinner when Constantine was reading or listening to the radio.

I was always delighted when the BBC wanted to see me, for afterwards I would go to the George pub nearby to have drinks with the exceptional people who were writing for the features programme: Louis MacNiece, the Irish poet, tall and commanding, with a satirical wit which amused me; he once described Dylan

★ Derek Verschoyle, 1952.

Thomas's visits to London as like 'a sort of Welsh night-bomber'; Bertie Rodgers, another Irish poet, so quietly spoken that the beautiful prose he used when talking was like soft, exquisite music. He was probably the first person to present a well-known character through the memories of people who had known him or her. When Norman Douglas died I was asked to contribute my memories to a similar programme. My cousin Harry Craig, whom I had last seen as a boy in Ireland, was often there; Dylan too sometimes. Afterwards we might go to a nearby Italian restaurant, then inevitably to the afternoon drinking club, the ML. It was very difficult to conceal my exuberance when I arrived home.

Fortunately I am a resilient person, for there was another reason for unhappiness. I had several distressing miscarriages, one resulting in peritonitis which required a long operation. I thought how much pleasanter, and in a way easier, to have had a healthy, bouncing baby. It took me some time to recover both physically and mentally, for I could not help remembering the never-to-be baby that lay forgotten in Italian earth. Constantine had a pathological hatred of sickness, so he always went away at the worst time of my illness, getting my aunt or someone down to look after me, and returning as soon as I was getting better.

He translated not only the other two books of Manès Sperber's trilogy, but many more from German and French. He also wrote a book of his own every year, so it was not entirely lack of work which made him restless, but the knowledge that he was not writing the kind of books he had set out to do. He produced one short novel about a disastrous holiday in Italy which led to tragedy, a readable book but lacking the beauty of the earlier novels. Carl Forman did take an option on it for a film, and for a week or so we lived in a cloud of thousands of dollars; then silence, for ever.

Several ideas were explored, sometimes started but never finished; he was drinking more and I feared a recurrence of what had happened in Italy. He ate even less than usual and seemed discontented in the country, making frequent trips to London, hiring the local taxi to drive him there, waiting, then returning sometimes late at night. He justified this by saying the taxis to and from the stations were expensive, the trains all the wrong times, and really it didn't cost all that much more to go up in comfort. So it was perhaps fortunate that about this time he met Giles Playfair again, son of Sir Nigel Playfair of the old Lyric Theatre, Hammersmith.

Giles was a good friend of Diana Graves, who no doubt

brought them together once more. Giles had been a barrister but had given it up as he hated prosecuting people, he told me, and had written four books by now – one about his father (*My Father's Son*), a biography of Kean the actor, his experiences in Singapore at the radio station there and lastly a theatrical novel (*The Heart of Fame*). Apparently years before when Constantine was about nineteen they had talked of a book Giles thought of writing about the little countries of Europe, the really little countries like Andorra, Monaco and Liechtenstein, where Giles had been with his father, and San Marino. He hadn't ever written it as unfortunately 'the war got in the way'. He and Constantine decided then it would be good for them to collaborate on such a book, but as they both lacked even an elemental knowledge of cameras, I was to come too, as official photographer. Cassell agreed to publish the book and accordingly lent me a Rolliflex camera, which was fortunate as it was like the camera Peter Rose Pulham had shown me how to use during the war. It was to be a momentous journey.

On a late April day in 1953, we set sail in a wine-boat, the MV *Grebe*, from Southampton for Bordeaux. The days before Constantine and I had spent with Sue and Barney Fawkes, he now Rear-Admiral, Flag-Officer Submarines, at their pretty Queen Anne house nearby. As we had had a late night we decided to have a siesta before looking around the little ship. We were both lying naked on our bunks when the first officer knocked briefly, then looked in. Unperturbed, he said:

'Oh, turned in, have you? The captain thought you might like to see the radar.'

When I remarked to Con that it was an unorthodox introduction, he replied:

'Oh, don't be silly. They're used to people resting at odd times with all those watches they have to keep.'

Steaming up the Gironde River in the early morning was a pleasant ending to the first stage of a delightful trip. However, at Toulouse we found the road to Andorra was still closed by snow. So we went down by train to L'Hospitalet near the Andorran border, spent a few noisy nights, uncomfortably, as Constantine said, 'like a wood-louse inside a banjo' amongst what we were told later on were probably smugglers. From there we took a car for about four miles, and with just rucksacks walked another two or three miles to the frontier.

Andorra, past the control post, seemed just a simple street with shacks, a café, then huge mountains in the background. We had been told a bus would take us on from here, but alas there was no bus on the blocked road, no way of getting there except to walk around the mountains. The snow was waist-high and there were times during those three hours when I was certain I wouldn't make it; our rucksacks were like millstones, the camera round my neck like lead. Then, miraculously, a guardian appeared, astonishment on his face. No one, he said, except those on skis or snowshoes had ever come over the pass before when the snow was like this. At least we gained some pleasure from being pioneers. We still had a perilous drive, with Constantine and Giles on kitchen chairs sliding about in the back of a van to Les Escaldes. I had frostbite in my toes, but after a sulphur bath from the natural sulphur spa waters which made me smell of bad eggs for days, we explored the primitive charms of Andorra. Getting out was as difficult as getting in. There was no question of going back the same way except through Spain, for which I had no visa. I was given a pass by the Episcopal Viguier of Andorra (both Spain and France have joint claims), which was torn up without being examined. After endless bureaucracy and a lecture for daring to enter Spain without a visa, I was allowed to enter Urgel. We had to go back by a long route to L'Hospitalet to collect our luggage before going on to Monaco. There we would stay with the Wakemans, who were now living at Antibes.

It should have been a most pleasant reunion, and to begin with it was, but somehow Margaret Wakeman and Constantine were antipathetic. Everything was argued about, and their four-year-old son's constant habit of lifting out Con's ice from his Pernod, sucking it, then putting it back brought about a monumental row between them. We left for Monte Carlo to continue the research for the book.

Gambling has always attracted me; it has taken great willpower sometimes to say 'no more' to myself. The ornate, legendary casino at Monte Carlo was too tempting. Giles and I bought a small amount of chips while Constantine looked on disdainfully before striding off to the *salles privées* to play baccarat. Giles soon lost his money and went off to buy some more chips, whilst I put mine first on 3, which came up, so I moved it all to number 7; that came up too. In a brave gesture I put the whole lot on number 21, when I saw Giles was beside me again. When that won, too, I was all set to go on, but he clutched my arm and said:

'Stop now, Theodora, please. I'm Scottish and you're Irish. Believe me, you'll lose it all. Let's go and cash it in, then go to the bar.'

I had won what was to me then a considerable amount of money – about three hundred pounds. But I still wonder, should I have banked more on my winning streak that night? Constantine had lost quite a bit when he joined us and suggested I take us all to a nightclub which of course I did.

Liechtenstein was even more expensive than Monte Carlo, beautiful to look at in the mountains, but truth to tell rather boring. San Marino was the most lovable of them all, making up to a large extent for the rigours we had encountered on the way. In fact Giles decided to stay on there for a few weeks. As we had let our house to friends for a specified time, we didn't know quite where to go, finally deciding, as we were travelling by train, to go to stay with Peter Rose Pulham at Conives in the Indre for a while. He had gone to live there after his final separation from Mary. Although he seemed quite content and extremely pleased to see us, I was quite shocked by the primitive conditions he was living in, above the stables in the old groom's quarters. All right for June, perhaps, but not for the winter. Until we came he had been eating nothing but bread and garlic, with a little cheese, washed down with a lot of wine. He had almost no money, but was writing the book for Derek Verschoyle, part of which I brought back with me. I left feeling very concerned for him.

Giles came to stay with us while they were writing *The Little Tour*★. I was pleased, for he acted as a sort of buffer between Constantine and myself. Also he was an amusing person and very kind. I don't think the book – although I found it very enjoyable – was really what the publisher had envisaged; it wasn't a travel book as such, for instead of telling people where to go, if anything it told then where not to go.

When it was finished and Giles left to live in London, the house seemed empty without him. The problem arose once more of what Constantine wanted to write next.

He had done nothing much with the Norman Douglas material, except after Norman died in 1952, he put together a little book of photographs of Norman from his early years to the end, with a long essay about him. I suggested he turn the whole thing into a novel, incorporating his own experiences with Norman's life. I still think it would have made an excellent book, written from the heart, but it was never attempted. When Nancy Cunard was writing her book about Norman Douglas she would come down to stay so that she could hear about him from Constantine.

★ Cassell, 1954.

Never having met her, but knowing of the legends surrounding her, I was apprehensive before our first meeting with Nancy. That tall, emaciated figure, with incredibly bright blue eyes, hair swathed in a chiffon scarf, countless necklaces and bangles, jangling on stick-like arms and a long, thin neck. 'Cunard covered in ectoplasm', she once remarked to me; her clothes, of an earlier fashion, enveloped her thin body, flowing out behind her, and concealed the most enchanting warm-hearted woman. Not for nothing had she been the mistress of the best minds of her generation and characterized by Aldous Huxley in *Chrome Yellow*. The high, light, slightly gabbling voice would talk until three or four in the morning, changing from English to French to Spanish as the night wore on and the subjects changed so rapidly it was sometimes difficult to follow. When I brought up her breakfast in the morning, the cat would be on one side, Minka on the other, something they never attempted with other guests. 'I love these *animalitos*,' she would say. How she hated her mother, whom she always referred to as 'her ladyship'. Naturally we talked of George Moore, who had loved her mother for so many years. She told me he had once said to her:

'You're my daughter, I hope!'

Nancy said the story going about that he had once asked to see her in the nude was quite garbled. What he had asked her was if he could see her *back* without clothes.

I would sit in the bedroom chatting with her. She seemed to wear the same kind of clothes in bed as out; the chiffon scarf was always in place. We discussed many intimate details of her life, and I grew to love Nancy. She was kind and helpful to me in many ways, especially with one of my books, for she got her cousin Sir Victor Cunard to lend me precious papers from his library. We had long, lovely lunches at the Café Royal together. Although the Café was not the same as I remembered it, I had the feeling Nancy always would be.

She arrived, late, one bleak November Sunday evening. Some guests we had in the house had stayed on, as they were anxious to meet her. In her breathless voice she told us that Dylan Thomas was seriously ill in New York, news which stunned Constantine and myself; only a month ago I had seen Dylan in the George, where he had told me excitedly that Stravinsky had asked him to be his librettist for the new opera he was writing in America. We listened to the late news on the radio, which gave little hope. About two o'clock in the morning we were still talking quietly when there was a loud, persistent tapping at the window. It was a windy night so I thought one of the long branches of the climbing rose outside had come adrift. I pulled back the curtains, to see that it was a robin pecking hard at the glass. When I opened the window he flew on to the sill, looked at us and flew out again. In Ireland a bird in the house means a death. I turned to face the others in the room.

'Dylan's dead,' I said flatly.

Everyone said I was being melodramatic, but the next morning's newspaper, November 10th, 1953, announced his death.

Later his wife, Caitlin was to write to me from Laugharne: 'You and Constantine are two of the few people who have any conception of what we meant to each other: it was all, and now it is nothing!'

CHAPTER NINETEEN

Living with a temperamental writer for some years is very different from a life with a man who spends most of his day away from home. For one thing, he is there all the time, except perhaps for a few weeks a year. There is no business partner or secretary to vent displeasure on; every nuance of feeling is directed at the one person who is present. With an emotional man this can be very exacting. You try to understand the rapidly changing moods but it's not always possible; you interject your own, invariably a mistake. After over twelve years you may fall into the trap of complacency. But marriage is far from being a race where you eventually come into the straight: there is no finishing post and it is at the point when you think you know someone that you become lazy and fall. Neither person is really to blame, for the gap opens slowly and you do not realize what has happened. It is only noticeable during a period barren of creativity.

After Constantine had finished his book about the July Plot to kill Hitler*, he was emotionally exhausted. He had researched for over a year and we had been in Germany several times for him to talk to the widows of those few brave men, but the grimness and irony of the story only added to his exhaustion. At the time I thought his bitterness was directed at me, whereas in reality it was against inhumanity and I was the sole recipient for his anger. The witticisms I thought of fell very flat; my ability to make him laugh had gone.

You forget that the day once started with laughter, as now you sit silently waiting perhaps for the postman to bring the magic letter which would put back the smiles again. It is a very gradual process, like an unsuspected disease which one unhappy day manifests itself. The physician is yourself until you realize your knowledge doesn't go far enough; you are no longer on the register. You look up at the once-cherubic face, now stern, trying to think of some untrivial thing to say; you stare at the china bee on top of the honeypot wishing it would come to life to make a diversion. Instead you take the dirty crockery to the kitchen and look out of the window at the countryside as desolate as your heart. The

* *The Shirt of Nessus*, Cassell, 1956.

smiles are reserved for strangers, and they no longer come from that heart.

It was an unhappy time in other ways. Dear Peter had died suddenly at Conives in May at the age of forty-five. I had received many sad letters from him over the years about his continued lack of money, and had sent what little I could spare to buy him food, as by now I had almost nothing of my own left. He could not sustain himself. The warning signs had been there, for his vision had been badly impaired during the winter, but I knew little of what those symptoms meant. The cold, too, must have been frightful in that dilapidated outbuilding with just a tiny wood-stove in the kitchen. Towards the end, unable to afford canvas or wood, he painted on fallen roof slates, charming, sad and evocative little pictures, one of which Mary gave me later on. Despite his great talent and innovation, both as a photographer and a painter, like so many before him he had to wait for recognition until after his death. Now he lives on through his work in many museums and private houses. He was a brave man, an exceptionally good friend, one to whom I owe a lot.

Mimi had been to England a few years back and was drinking very heavily again. In June 1956, the American Hospital in Paris telephoned to say she was a patient there suffering from alcoholic poisoning. Constantine went over to bring her back to England. He put her into a nursing home in London in the charge of a doctor who specialized in an alcohol-revulsion cure, which in short meant she was given alcohol all the time from early morning on, together with pills which made the taste repulsive and brought on sickness. Afterwards she came down to stay with us, a frail-looking ghost of what she had once been. I loved having her there; we worked in the garden together and cooked meals as we had done in Italy. Whether Constantine thought I was spending too much time on her I don't know, but after a week or so he said he couldn't work properly with her there, wondering if she would be nipping out to the pub. In fact, she showed no inclination to go down to the bare pub and drink beer.

However, my aunt in Chelsea was very fond of Mimi and she said she would take her in there, she had plenty of room. In the basement of her house lived the young unknown Sean Connery, then with little money, playing small parts on the stage and in films. Sean and Mimi got on well together, sharing meals of spaghetti Mimi had cooked. He knew about her drinking, and one night when she came in and he thought she had started again he was very angry with her. He made her give him the doctor's name and telephoned him.

It must have been a lonely time for her as she had been out of England for so many years – most of her friends had dispersed. We would meet when I came up to London, and although she was looking much better I could see she was getting restless. She had had a disastrous affair which had worried all of us, leaving her sadder than she had ever been.

'I must get it out of my system,' she said. 'I'm writing a novel all about it. If only I could find a cottage in the country. There are too many ghosts in London.'

She went down to stay with her sister Fanny in Kent, finally finding a cottage in the same county. She finished her novel, which was full of imagery, strange but confused. It didn't seem publishable then, but I think with a little editing it would have been. She telephoned Constantine frequently asking him to lend her money 'until her allowance arrived', which he always refused to do. Then early in February 1957 she telephoned again saying she was ill, he must help her. He rang her doctor in the country, who said she had a bad liver complaint and was under treatment. At last she rang in desperation, first to my aunt, who wasn't in, then to Constantine, asking him to send a car to bring her to London as she felt ghastly. The scene is etched in my memory:

'Mimi's always "crying wolf"; I just haven't the money to indulge her whim to come to London.'

He refused to send the car.

On February 20th, 1957, a hospital telephoned to say she was dead. She was a little over forty years old. The love and tenderness she had shown to me in Positano, the naughty days and nights we had spent together, the charm, beauty and gaiety were gone for ever.

My mother and I went down to collect her clothes and the finished novel. Constantine refused to have any of them in the house; the novel he burnt, saying 'it was too personal'. I tried to snatch it from the flames, succeeding in rescuing only a few pages, which are today more evocative of Mimi than her photograph is.

Constantine had loved Mimi. They were the nearest of the four children, not only in age but also in personality. Late at night he would tell me he felt guilty about turning her away; but what use is remorse? Instead of being warned by her death, he too began to drink more – spirits, which up till then we hadn't kept in the house, were bought lavishly, and as they were consumed, the aggression increased. I tried to dissuade him, saying that drink only increased the mood he was in; if he was miserable it made him maudlin or aggressive, and if he was bubbling, his mood developed into euphoria. He always agreed, then poured himself another large whisky, and so it went on.

Money was getting short again. Unless Con wrote another book we would be perilously broke. Perhaps it is because of all this that I was not aware of what was happening; I was so relieved when his mood changed, I encouraged him to go on the long walks he was taking, also his increasing visits to London. For about two months he was as he had been when we first came to Sacomb's Ash. I was quite unprepared one Sunday evening when the Tompkins, who'd stayed the weekend, were to drive home to London and he suddenly announced he would go with them. He wrote me a cheque for ten pounds, saying he didn't know when he would be back; to which I bitterly replied that ten pounds wouldn't last very long. Then he left, hardly saying a word to me. I walked down with Minka to the pub, crowded with locals swilling beer, and I felt out of place as everyone enquired where he was. Some friends drove over, which helped, but it was a melancholy night. I had no idea where Con had gone, why, or for how long. All night I wondered, but I was not in doubt for long. The following afternoon he telephoned saying he was coming home that evening, would I order a taxi? His voice had the stern inflection of some months earlier.

He came into the drawing room, walked up and down saying nothing for some minutes, then took up his customary position leaning his arm on the bookshelf.

'I went to London to meet C.' Here he mentioned the name of a woman friend of mine. 'We were going away together. However, she didn't turn up.'

Before I could even register my astonishment, he went on:

'But if in the future she would change her mind, I shall go.'

'Meanwhile you will stay here?' I asked.

'Of course. Where else would I go?'

The words didn't register with me. My brain seemed to stop taking in signals. I went out to the kitchen to prepare the dinner. Why did he have to tell me? I asked myself. Never would I have thought of it; and if I had I would equally quickly have dismissed it as being absurd. Why inflict unnecessary pain? He followed me out, drew some beer from the barrel, then looked at me.

'I've had other affairs,' he started, 'but I still loved you. Maybe I do now, I simply don't know.'

He seemed to be using me as a sounding board, not realizing the wounds he was inflicting. Then with all the insouciance he could muster, he said:

'What's for dinner? I'm hungry.'

It was the first time I had ever known him express such a thought. After dinner he went to play the gramophone.

'Oh, damn, I'd forgotten it was in London being mended. I could have picked it up.'

Quickly I said:

'I'm going to London tomorrow for a few days, I'll get it.' This was one time when I felt he was unable to stop me going.

My mother was a very calming influence. 'Of course it's a shock, but I suppose it's bound to happen in any marriage, and it's usually one's best friend. I can't see why he had to tell you, though. He must be quite insensitive to your feelings. Anyway it's lovely to have you for a while, I never see you these days. Let's have a drink.'

It might seem as if I was making a lot of fuss about something which happened all the time, but ours had never been a marriage of convenience. The only point to living the way we had was to be held together by affection and trust. My mother was quite right about infidelity in marriage, but there are many different kinds. Sexual relationships outside marriage, should remain the concern of the two involved people. To flaunt an affair is an expression of sadistic behaviour, which I think is wrong. If it is a question of loving another very deeply, then one ought to leave, allowing the wife or husband to make another life. It is very different if one is separated through force of circumstances, as happened so frequently during the war. I had not been blameless in that respect, but it has remained my own secret. Constant infidelity which isn't felt to be satisfying unless it is boasted about expresses frustration, hostility and resentment.

It was difficult to know quite what to do in my present situation. I had almost no money, so I couldn't go to Ireland, which would have been one solution. London was difficult too, for I kept meeting friends who knew us both. My mother sensibly pointed out that I couldn't just walk out leaving everything, including my dog, Minka.

'You'd have to go back sometime. Better to do it soon and make up your mind when you see how things are,' she said wisely.

Constantine had telephoned every day to know when I was returning, as he missed me. After about a week I decided to go

back and see what the situation was between us. I collected the
repaired gramophone and telephoned Peter and Jerree Tompkins
to tell them of my decision, for they had been wonderfully
helpful. Peter's last words to me were:

'He'll be pleased you're back, but be warned, he'll find something to lose his temper about before the evening's through.'

He was quite right; luckily it wasn't with me, but with the
gramophone, which although better now needed a new sapphire
stylus. Constantine was very euphoric that evening, saying he had
been asked to rewrite a film script for Orson Welles, which he
could do easily while doing a book of his own. It could lead to
getting his own film option taken up again.

'We can look for a new house too, if you like,' he told me
excitedly later. 'Aunt Olive's giving us all five thousand pounds. I
had a letter from her this morning. What do you think?'

I thought how Mimi would have enjoyed that money, how she
might have had better treatment a few months before and not now
be lying in a Kent churchyard, but I didn't voice these thoughts.
Somehow his words didn't penetrate my consciousness. Occasionally a phrase would be clear and loud, then an excited
mumble. I felt hollow and empty, fixing my eyes on the calm
ethereal beauty of my Henry Moore painting.

'. . . don't you think so?' I heard his voice questioning me.
'When you've finished your book?'

Yes, that is what I would do, finish the book that was two-
thirds written, then I would have a little money and maybe a new
commission.

It was getting late on this warm summer's night. Even with the
windows open there was no wind.

'I'll take the dog round the garden before I go to bed,' I said,
then: 'Shall I sleep in the blue room?'

He laughed. 'Good heavens, whatever for? I'll come round the
garden with you, wait a minute.'

The little owls hooted from the paddock, the scent of the
tobacco plants was almost overwhelming as we strolled around
the back lawn, yet I felt like a stranger walking with another
stranger. And I wished that it was so, for I no longer knew what
to expect from this man who looked like Constantine, yet
behaved very differently. I tried to recollect what he had been like
when I had first met him in 1943, but that man, too, was a
stranger from the one who walked beside me. Would he make
love to me tonight? I hoped not for I felt so cold inwardly, as
though my skin was filled with sawdust, dry and useless. In the

dark of the garden in a confused way I tried to put my thoughts into words, but they sounded so banal I stopped mid-sentence. I tried once more, but he stopped me, saying:

'Come on, darling, Minka's been out long enough. Let's go to bed.'

Constantine's ability to change his moods with unpredictable rapidity was a contributing factor to being able to go on living with him. For they were genuine changes, not assumed for effect; he believed in them himself and transmitted that belief to me. Now he was determined to find another house, to settle down and start afresh. We went all over the immediate countryside looking at houses, but there was always something wrong with them: too small, too ugly or wrongly situated to please him. At last we found a perfect house at Letcombe Bassett in Berkshire. Admittedly it was very large, but the rooms were beautifully proportioned, the gardens delightful. There was even a very fine old mulberry tree under which, it was reputed, Dean Swift used to sit to write. Alas, when at the behest of my aunt we had it surveyed, it proved to have wet rot, dry rot and the death-watch beetle amongst other things. Constantine said he couldn't possibly live in a house that 'ticked' all the time. In any event, he bought Sacomb's Ash, but by the time the sale was complete he was saying it was too 'cottagey' and alternating between planning to rebuild or take a flat in London and use it as a weekend refuge. He did neither.

During this time he was writing short stories and also translating, for the first time into English, the beautiful long poem *The Cornet* by Rainer Maria Rilke. This he dedicated to his aunt, Olive Antrobus, as a gesture to thank her for the handsome gift. Vernon Watkins the great Welsh poet, friend of Dylan's and of ours, read the manuscript, making several suggestions some of which Constantine accepted. The film script for Orson Welles was finished and approved. Eventually when it was made it seemed quite different from what I had read and it had another title, so no doubt it was rewritten yet again. Con's book *The Blitz*★ and a translation of La Rochefoucauld's *Maxims* had been published, to critical acclaim. Once more friends came for the weekend, the Sunday evening buffet was brought back, and to my knowledge he never deliberately saw the non-eloping lady again.

Henry Moore enjoyed being with Constantine and liked talking to him. When Henry was asked to be chairman of a committee for

★ Allen Wingate, 1957.

a sculpture personifying the horrors of Auschwitz, it was Constantine who went with him on that grim journey. Therefore it was not entirely a surprise, when a large sculpture of Henry's was being exhibited in Paris, that Henry suggested we both accompany him and Irina.

The Moores always travelled separately as long as Mary was a child, lest there be an accident. We all met up in Paris. They were delightful to be with – Henry full of energy, determined to see as much as he could; Irina, always calm, compliant and serene. Going round museums with Henry was an unforgettable experience, his quick sculptor's eye pointing out things I had never before realized. Striding through the Louvre behind him, down the long hallway where Henri III used to ride up and down on a camel, through the Rubens room, we went quickly, but not too quickly, for from time to time he would stop to look at something he wanted to see again. Then upstairs to the Egyptian room, where the pace slackened considerably until he stopped beside a wooden carving a little over three feet high of a tall man with his arm around a woman's shoulder.

'Look,' he said. 'Look at the movement in it. You feel the sadness, they are going from somewhere they do not want to leave.' He walked slowly round to the back of the carving. 'Look at how the man has his arm about the woman's shoulder. In that arm is love and tenderness which has lasted over five thousand years.'

We went to Rodin's house, and walking round Henry would show you why Rodin was such a good sculptor. We all forgot we were in a museum and looking at a portrait head; he said:

'I wonder how much that one weighs.' Immediately he started to lift it up. Burglar alarms rang, custodians gathered, while Henry stood shamefaced, like a little boy scrumping apples, as Constantine explained who he was: handshakes and smiles instead of stern faces. Then on to the Musée de l'Homme, Henry stopping in front of a primitive drawing:

'Oh, Picasso's been here. You can see the influence.' Then as we went further, he would stop from time to time, again saying:

'They've *all* been here, look at that!'

We discovered the Musée Guimet, where upstairs we found the most exquisite small pieces of pre-Grecian sculpture from some part of Afghanistan, mostly heads, but of such vitality, gaiety and life that we stood amazed. The day when we went to see Henry's sculpture was also memorable, for as we walked around it, he put out his hand and stroked the long, rounded thigh. At once the custodian approached, telling him he mustn't touch the exhibits. He put his hands behind his back immediately, standing with chastened expression, not saying a word.

However, it was not all culture. There were delicious meals at Drouant's restaurant in the Place Gaillon, where the Academie Goncourt always met; La Laperouse and La Closerie des Lilas in Montparnasse, where Verlaine usually drank, or maybe a small café if Henry was in a hurry to get to another place. He also wanted to go to the Moulin Rouge which he had heard so much about, but that proved a little disappointing to him, so we went on to a small *boîte*, where we ate. It was amusing when a chic, pretty woman came on to do her turn, for Henry at once loudly said in his slightly Yorkshire voice:

'That's not a woman; the shoulders are all wrong!' As it turned out, he was quite right.

We also accompanied Henry to Dublin. A piece of his sculpture had been bought by subscriptions from admirers of his work in Ireland, and he wanted to choose a suitable site in St Stephen's Green. He showed as much interest in the early Celtic gold work in the National Museum as he had in museums in Paris. The Horse Show seen from the presidential box entranced him, and I thought how well he fitted into the many parties that inevitably followed. 'Surely,' I said, 'with a name like Moore, you must have some Irish blood?' But he didn't know of any.

I never remember any time we spent with Henry and Irina Moore that didn't create an atmosphere of happiness and understanding.

CHAPTER TWENTY

Writing is a solitary occupation. Not only does it entail sitting alone and putting your thoughts on paper, but a large part of every day and some nights is spent in sifting, analysing and ordering those thoughts. There are some fortunate people who have the facility to do this quickly, even able to dictate into a machine, but for most writers this is not possible. So I understood the desire Constantine had to see friends at the weekend, for he was a very gregarious person, and I encouraged it.

It was probably due to this solitary life with me in the country that offers to write more film scripts attracted him. Also the money was extremely good, paid on completion of work and not months later in arrears, as book royalties are. After the preliminary script was written, there were script conferences, which brought him in enjoyable contact with people who had lively minds. To begin with, some of these conferences were held at Sacomb's Ash, but as time went on and the finished script became more pressing, they were held in London. At first he would stay with friends, often arriving late Friday evening with several people not always known to me. Then on Monday he would return with them for another working week. During this time his own work, a novel he was outlining, was pushed aside.

Several of my books had gone into second impressions, one into paperback, and I was working on another, so I was quite pleased to be able to devote this much time to writing. I read omnivorously in the evenings, went for walks with Minka, and planned food for the weekend. A novel was forming in the back of my mind, for which I made notes. The peace and quiet of the countryside were very comforting. This way of life continued for some months, until Constantine would telephone and say he couldn't get back for the weekend; I should expect him perhaps the weekend after. After I'd finished my book, the days seemed very long, for often I was entirely on my own after Mrs Howe left at lunchtime until she came the next morning. Occasionally I would make a brief visit to the Foster-Melliars or to Jane Wellstead, otherwise I saw nobody.

I took the opportunity to go over to Ireland, as I had a little money from the book I had just delivered. Emotionally I was still insecure, so I wanted to see friends, to be on neutral ground in a pub or a restaurant, rather than be in the close-knit cocoon of my family. I was afraid of questions that I couldn't answer, of telling half-lies to those I loved. Arland Ussher had been staying with us on his way back from China some months previously, and had asked me to stay with him and his wife when I came over. Arland's wife, Emily, was looking after their grandchild, so Arland entertained me.

Together we wandered about Dublin, Arland showing me places I had never seen, like the Brazen Head Tavern in Bridge Street, the oldest in Ireland I think, where the United Irishmen met and Robert Emmett the patriot used to go; out to Marino to see the exquisite eighteenth-century casino built by Vierpyl in 1762 for the Earl of Charlemont, looking almost like a surrealist picture surrounded by a housing estate; to St Michan's Church, near the Four Courts, on the site of the first church of Norse Dublin in 1096 – the vaults have contained bodies for centuries without showing signs of decomposition, owing to the walls' construction of magnesium limestone, which absorbs moisture; the 'Lucky Stone' of St Audoen's Church in High Street, founded by the Normans and dedicated to St Ouen of Rouen in France. All of this was taken at a leisurely pace, Arland being a charming and erudite companion. It reminded me a little of my walks with Norman Douglas, a man Arland admired very much. So as we were strolling along I would recount some of my meetings with him.

There would be pleasant stops for a drink or food: the back bar of Jammet's; the Dolphin with its delicious grills; the Red Bank restaurant, which for years as a child I had thought was a bank, when my father used to leave me in the car and nip in; Neary's pub with the bowls of gas along the counter; Davy Byrne's, the pub James Joyce writes about in *Ulysses*; and others. We met friends of Arland's including Brendan Behan, who seemed very fond of him. They joked and talked together, often in Irish.

Usually we had dinner at the house, but on my last evening Arland mentioned a bistro-type restaurant called La Taverne which had newly opened. It was owned and run by a friend I had last seen in Paris, Leona Ryan. It had good cheap food and wine, a pleasant atmosphere rather like a Continental café. We were finishing dinner when Arland looked round the room and said:

'Oh! There's George over there. I must bring him over to meet you.'

He came back accompanied by a fairly tall, slender man of about thirty-five, with fine features.

'This is George Morrison. I've known him since he was about six years old,' said Arland. 'You'll have a lot in common, for he's making a film.'

They sat down and I looked at the young man opposite me. The sensitive, thin face with a broad forehead was dominated by the large blue-grey eyes, one moment with a sad, thoughtful expression, contradicted by deeply etched laugh-lines at the corners. When I asked him about his work, the eyes grew even larger, soft and deeply expressive. He had long fingers on his well-shaped hands, hands he used in a very graceful way when talking.

After a little while Arland said he must be getting back, he had promised Emily he wouldn't be late. Maybe he saw a slight disappointment in my face, for he went on:

'You stay for a while with George. He'll look after you and find you a taxi later on.'

I asked George more about the film, which I gathered was an epic feature about Ireland from the turn of the century until just before the Civil War in 1922, using old newsreels.

'But surely, there weren't many such films?' I asked. 'How is it possible to find enough to make a feature-length film?'

He looked at me, the large eyes smiling:

'My cutting room is only a little way off. Why don't you come and see some of it on the moviola?'

Looking through the small viewing aperture and seeing scenes of real events in Dublin at the time of the 1916 Easter Rising, I couldn't believe I was actually looking at what had always been, to me, stories told by my father, uncles and aunts. I felt very excited.

'They are all running or walking at a normal pace,' I said. Other old films I've seen show people scurrying about. Why are these different?'

In his soft voice he explained to me the elaborate process he was using for the first time in a long film, and how since his twenties he had been to many places in Europe, cataloguing film of Irish interest. It was from this catalogue that his idea for the film had developed. Again his face changed completely as he talked with dedication about his art. We arranged to meet for lunch the next day with Arland, before I left later to catch the plane home. It was a cold, damp November day, which made me dread leaving the friendliness of Dublin to go back to an empty Sacomb's Ash. They both accompanied me to the airport, waiting as I left for the plane. However, the plane did not leave that night owing to fog in England, so we were returned to the departure lounge to await further news. George was still there, and sat with me until they announced there would be no more flights that night; I'd have to return in the morning.

I booked a room at the Gresham Hotel, which was almost next door to the check-in office. George and I had drinks and a sand-wich in a pub before I went back to the hotel. I thought I had better telephone Constantine, who had rented a flat in Bloomsbury from Sonia Orwell, George Orwell's widow. There was no reply. In the morning I spoke to someone I took to be a cleaning woman, leaving a detailed message with her.

The fog had closed London Airport so we flew to Manchester, then on by a crowded slow train to Euston. To my surprise Constantine was there to meet me, but as I quickly realized, he was very drunk. We went back to Sonia's flat in Percy Street which was very untidy, the bathroom and bedroom littered with make-up and women's clothes which I took to be Sonia's. It was far from a happy homecoming, for he was quarrelsome and aggressive, so much so that I slept in a small spare room, deter-mining to go back to Sacomb's Ash the next day. Before doing so I went to buy some food to take back home, and coming back to the top-floor flat I passed an elderly woman opening the door to her flat on the lower floor. She smiled at me, hesitated a little, then said:

'Do you know when Mrs FitzGibbon is coming back? I want to ask them down for drinks; you too, if you'd like to come.'

I packed quickly and left a note saying where I was going, and that the woman in the flat below wanted him to call.

Seldom, if ever, have I spent a more solitary time than I did then. The weather was damp and harsh, with frequent fogs which muffled sounds outside but seemed to intensify them in the house. Boards creaked, doors groaned as they opened, winds whipped the isolated house making the lath and plaster tremble; the cat's large eyes opened even wider and her tail twitched as she sat in front of the fire. Minka seemed constantly on the alert, staring at me, going frequently to the front door and sniffing underneath it.

Behind the house was a very overgrown lane, once a carriage-way to Green Tye, so Mrs Howe told me. One terrifying night, standing in the kitchen I heard loud moaning coming from that direction. The dog growled, then the noise stopped and I con-tinued preparing my dinner. It started again, softer than before, but working up to a crescendo. It sounded like a large animal such as a cow in pain. I decided that's what it was and I wondered if I should telephone the farmer. Then I realized there were no cows nor cattle anywhere near the house – only the vast ploughed fields waiting to be sown with corn. The melancholy noise continued as I waited, knowing I must go out with the lamp to see if I could help. The sounds were intermittent as I pulled on trousers and a sweater, then lit the lamp. Minka and I stumbled through briars, fallen branches and stones for some time but found nothing. However, that night I took the two animals up to my bedroom and pulled a chest across the door.

Sometimes the fog was so dense I lost my way going down to the pub, ending up in a ditch, so that I would put the lead on Minka and let her take me. There were nights when I would wake up cold with fear. I worked for most of the day on my novel, not knowing whether what I was writing was good or bad, but I felt compelled to keep on. The characters became my friends. When they were happy, I shared it with them. When Constantine occasionally came home, they were kept out of sight.

Just as suddenly as he had left to live in London, Con returned, a little before Christmas 1958. His moods were still very changeable: during the daytime he was usually a pleasant companion, but as the evening came he often became aggressive for no apparent reason. He sometimes questioned me about events of long ago.

Once he said: 'I'm a trained interrogator, you know.' And as he stood over me, looking down from his great height, his eyes full of hostility, I was frightened. This constant interrogation became an obsession with him. Then the next morning he would behave as if nothing had happened. To say it was confusing is to understate how I felt. I wondered if I had imagined these scenes, perhaps misunderstood them, or had I dreamt them?

At this time he was working with the ex-Ealing film director Charles Crichton who had made *Hue and Cry* and many other successful films. He had a charming, amusing personality, very easy to work with, and I enjoyed the days and nights he spent with us. They were working on a film called *Graziella*, a 'vehicle' as it was called for the one-time Parisienne cabaret singer Juliette Greco. There were trips to Paris to see Daryl Zanuck the producer, with whom she was living, which Constantine enjoyed. There were never any rows between us when they were in the house. I began to feel there was something lacking in my behaviour which made me increasingly awkward and nervous when we were alone together. I longed always to be in company with other people, but as time went on even that didn't prevent the most shattering scenes of violence and humiliation. I found it hard to disentangle the reality from the enveloping fog of emotional insecurity which surrounded us both. Sometimes the sound of voices was as clear as that of a blackbird on the lawn. At other times words that were said became unnaturally loud and distorted, or seemed to merge into each other, as though we were both being moved very rapidly on a revolving stage. There were occasions when I felt like the onlooker and not a participator. My health became affected. I would pray that there would be a miraculous end to this torment.

In June 1959 there was some respite. Constantine was beginning to work on a new novel, concerned with England under Fascist rule. I didn't like what he outlined to me, but said nothing. I don't think he was very enamoured with it, for later he changed it to being under Communist rule and it became *When the Kissing had to Stop*★. I hoped desperately he would work off some of his aggression in the book, which he did to a certain extent.

Earlier in the month I had bought a small secondhand car, which made me feel much freer. News came from Ireland that my aunt was ill, asking to see me. I went over for a week, spending some time with her until she seemed to be getting better, then a few days in Dublin where I gave a dinner party for some of my friends, including George. My mother had been staying at Sacomb's Ash to look after Constantine, and was still there when I got home. We sat together in the June sun under the walnut tree; I felt refreshed and wished for this contentment to continue. The little car was a help, for if I saw signs of boredom I would suggest driving out to visit friends. There were still quarrels but not the destructive scenes of earlier months. If only, I thought, there was some way of knowing exactly what triggered them off.

A little over two weeks after I returned from Ireland, three people whom neither of us knew very well came down to lunch. Proud of my new acquisition, after lunch I drove them all around the country; after a swim at a friend's pool we stopped frequently at pubs or hotels for drinks. However, I was very careful and all day I only had two beers. It was a pleasant, easy day which we all enjoyed. I drove two of them to the station, the other woman preferring to stay with us. Once home, I remember the relish with which I said:

'Now I'm going to have a real drink, my first today.'

It was then about ten-thirty at night. The three of us talked for about an hour. Constantine left the room and after a little while I went out to look for him. As I opened the kitchen door he shouted something at me, but it was too late, I was in the room. He was

★ Cassell, 1961.

standing naked by the central heating boiler, burning his clothes. He had done this several times before and I knew he would be in a fury afterwards. When he came back, fully dressed in other clothes, he started a menacing attack on me. The other woman protested, saying I had been very good to them all that day. I knew it wouldn't stop that night, so I excused myself to go to bed. He followed me to the dressing room where I intended to sleep, still haranguing and pushing me so that I banged my head against the washbasin. Then he left. My heart was beating very fast; I felt helpless, wondering when it would all cease.

Quietly I slipped out the back door with Minka to the car, but it wouldn't start. Over and over I tried. I would go somewhere, anywhere, away from that accusing voice. Then I saw his figure looming up out of the darkness.

'Just as well it won't start,' he said. 'You'd only crash and be more of a nuisance.'

I went back to the house, upstairs into a spare room. Eventually I must have fallen asleep from exhaustion. It was very quiet when I woke in the morning, sunlight coming through the window, although I had no idea of the time. I tiptoed along the corridor to get my toothbrush from the dressing room on the far side of our bedroom. Quietly I opened the door to go through, but stopped at once as I saw two heads on the pillow in our large bed. Downstairs the kitchen clock said nine-fifteen; the tick sounded unnaturally loud in the large kitchen as I put on the coffee pot. Despite the warmth I was trembling. All I wanted to do was to get away. Once more I tried to start the car in the garage – it was as dead as I felt. I walked round the garden with Minka, praying:

'Please, God, let me get away before they wake up.'

When I got back to the house, Constantine was having his breakfast as I went to telephone the local taxi driver to take me to a nearby hotel. We did not speak to each other. Upstairs I packed a few things in the empty bedroom. A voice from the spare bedroom called:

'Is there any coffee?'

I replied there was some downstairs.

Constantine looked up as I came down the stairs. Before he could say anything I said:

'I'm going to Gilston Park for a few days. I want to think everything over. There's plenty of cooked food in the larder. Please don't forget to feed Jocasta. I'll take Minka with me.'

Gilston Park was a sham-Gothic hotel set in very beautiful grounds; I wandered down to the lake with Minka and the hotel dog, the wild thoughts tumbling about in my head like autumn leaves swept hither and thither by a cruel wind. One part of me wanted to say forgive, the other knew there was no end to the hurt and humiliation that could be inflicted. Perhaps a few days alone here, in these peaceful surroundings, would enable me to come to a reasonable answer, would stop me feeling like a puppet in the hands of a mad puppet-master.

Walking back up the gentle green slopes towards the oak-panelled, antlered room used as a bar, I was much calmer. Minka darted ahead of me at the open french windows. I looked up; there at the bar were Constantine, Elizabeth Foster-Melliar and Con's companion of the previous night. They looked like any Sunday-morning drinkers, chatting and laughing together.

'Hullo, darling, we came over to have drinks with you.'

Another stormy scene was the last thing I wanted, so I joined them, talking mostly to Elizabeth. Then I said I must have my lunch as the dining room would soon close.

'The *boeuf à la mode* you left us was delicious, a superb soft jelly,' said the woman.

I smiled briefly, then I left.

That evening I telephoned my mother, who said I could come to her, but she thought London was not the answer. I should get right away for a little. What about Ireland? Wasn't it much cheaper than England?

As I left the phone box, Constantine was in the hall saying he wanted to talk to me. Over drinks I told him I must go away for a month at least. No longer could I stand this life of destruction; we must both think very seriously about any future life together and he must give up drinking spirits if I was to return soon. He left and I was glad, for I was being pulled first one way, then the other, until I no longer knew what I wanted. Over dinner I decided to telephone Arland Ussher in Dublin, to see if he could find me a small flat there.

'Oh, I'm no good at that sort of thing, Theodora. I'd have to ask someone to do it for me. Why don't you get in touch with George about it?'

'But, Arland, I've only met him three times, and I don't even know his phone number. I can't impose myself like that.'

'Nonsense. He's very good at doing that sort of thing. Wait a minute, I'll give you his number. He won't mind, I assure you.'

Arland was quite right. George sounded as if he was finding homes for people all the time. Maybe he was, I knew so little about him. I explained it mustn't cost more than five pounds a week and it must have a small patch of garden for Minka. I spent the next day alone in an agony of indecision. Constantine rang asking if I was determined to go away; when I said I was, he began shouting, accusing me of going to a lover. Then surprisingly he said he had got an old friend down to be his housekeeper, and he was spending the next day in London. It seemed obvious that he expected me to go. I knew that whatever I did must be done at once, it was like severing a gangrenous wound.

The next day I went back to pack a few clothes. I only took my personal belongings, a few books, Peter's painting on the house slate and a small print I had bought when I was sixteen. I looked lovingly and longingly at my Henry Moore painting but decided it might leave a mark on the wall, which would be a constant reminder. Anyway, I'd probably be coming back. It was the only home we'd ever had of our own.

George rang that evening to say he was on the track of a small house. Did I like cooking on gas or electricity?

There were more meetings with Constantine which merge into a haze of sadness in my memory. At the end of the week I left Gilston Park and went to my mother's flat. That night George rang me there, told me he had found a not very nice little house, and would I like him to come over to accompany me to Ireland? As I surveyed the assorted luggage and regarded the now elderly Minka, the thought of transporting them all by train and boat dismayed me. I willingly accepted his offer. I told Diana Graves, my truest friend, what I was doing, mentioning George's kind offer. In her husky voice she said:

'Darling, would you like a second opinion? If so, bring him over!'

On Sunday July 19th, 1959, one week since I had left for Gilston Park, I went back to Ireland, never to return to Sacomb's Ash. This was not entirely my own decision, for someone I had never known had replaced me. I never again had the Henry Moore hanging on my walls, nor indeed could I recline in my *chaise-longue*, or drive my little car. Yet, ultimately, Constantine and I were to be the best of friends, and in future days of crisis and unhappiness it was to me he always turned.

I was frightened, unhappy and unsure of myself when I arrived in Ireland. I did not know what kind of reception my family in County Clare would give me. They seemed so untouched by the banalities and brutalities of the sophisticated life. I need not have worried; the family that was determined enough to coin their own money a century ago had their own original views on everything.

'Why didn't you tell us?' they asked. 'And why did you not come back to us before this?'

My future was very uncertain for some months, but the tenderness, care and love given to me by George gradually restored my emotional security. That we had no money to speak of hardly mattered, for the relationship we built up was bound by common interests as well as by affection. We were able to work together in complete harmony. As only children, we had both known what inner loneliness can be felt, but at last it was shared and understood. I could not have visualized the hours of research and work my life-giving career of writing would take – or the heartbreaking struggles of helping George to make original films without money. Nor could I ever have imagined the years of happiness that were ahead of me.